Second Sea

checkout →

P9-CLC-000

Hellespont

◆ Troy

Mount Ida ▲

Tenedos

Aegean
Sea

Siphnos

Third Sea (Black Sea)

Second Sea

◆ Troy

(Turkey)

Cilicia

(Greece)

Aegean Sea

Cyprus

Sidon ◆

Sparta ◆
Amyklai

Siphnos

Crete

Mediterranean Sea

(Egypt)

Nile R.

DATE DUE

SEP 2 1 2002	JUL 1 1 2003
SEP 2 8 2002	JUN 2 9 2004
JAN 2 6 2003	9/06/06
MAY 2 0 2003	
JUN 2 9 2004	
AUG - 4 2004	

Demco, Inc. 38-293

GODDESS OF YESTERDAY

OTHER BOOKS BY CAROLINE B. COONEY

GODDESS OF YESTERDAY

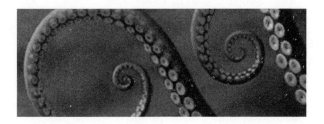

CAROLINE B. COONEY

DELACORTE PRESS

Published by
Delacorte Press
an imprint of
Random House Children's Books
a division of Random House, Inc.
1540 Broadway
New York, New York 10036

Visit us on the Web! www.randomhouse.com/teens
Educators and librarians, for a variety of teaching tools, visit us at
www.randomhouse.com/teachers

Cataloging-in-Publication Data is available from the Library of Congress.
ISBN 0-385-72945-6 (trade)
ISBN 0-385-90051-1 (lib. bdg.)

The text of this book is set in 12.5-point Columbus.

Book design by Melissa J Knight

Manufactured in the United States of America

June 2002

10 9 8 7 6 5 4 3 2 1

BVG

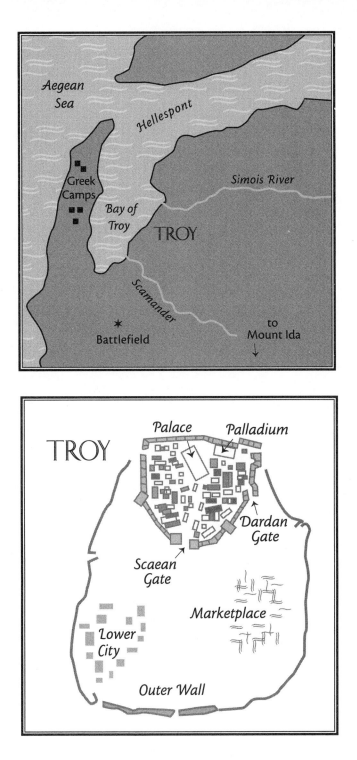

I

I WAS SIX YEARS OLD when King Nicander came to the island of my birth, demanding tribute and a hostage.

I did not know what a hostage was, nor tribute.

The king was taller than Father. His oiled beard jutted from his chin like a spear point. His arms were hard and tanned, his eyes twinkling. I liked him right away. "So you are Alexandra," said Nicander.

I corrected a king. "Not *Alex*andra. *Anax*andra."

His eyes crinkled at the corners when he smiled. "Anaxandra, you are coming for a sail with me. You will be companion to my daughter, Callisto."

A sail? I was so excited I hardly bothered to kiss my parents goodbye. My brothers got to go to sea and have adventure, but I always had to stay home with Mother. And I had never met a princess. Callisto means "the fairest," just the right name for a princess, the way Anaxandra was just the right name for me. Mother packed some clothes and my fleeces and put my doll in a box, which I hugged to my chest. I had never owned a box, and Mother kept jewelry in this one. It was heavy, which meant she had left some jewels in it. I would have a guest-gift for the princess.

An officer sat me on his shoulders and off we went. I

never looked back at my brothers, standing in a row, silent and envious, and I never waved to my parents.

Our village was perched a thousand feet above the sea. The path to the harbor tilted steeply. I clung to the officer's neck so I wouldn't fall off. "What's your name?" I asked.

He peeled my fingers from his throat so he could breathe. "Lykos."

This means "wolf," which made me think of my puppy. I had named her Seaweed, because when she romped in the water, she came out hung with green fronds. I almost told Lykos we had to go back and get Seaweed, but I remembered that I would be home by bedtime to tell Seaweed all about it.

The sailor carrying my clothes and fleece said to Lykos, "Why didn't the king take sons for hostages? A little girl isn't going to make Chrysaor double his tribute."

Chrysaor was my father's name; it had the word for gold in it. My mother's name was Iris, which means "rainbow."

The king caught up to us. He tugged on my long curls and told me I had hair as red as King Menelaus. I had never heard of King Menelaus.

"A girl as hostage?" said Lykos to the king.

"Chrysaor needs his sons to pirate with him," said the king of Siphnos, "but his daughter he loves. He'll obey me for her sake."

The donkey path was slippery with pebbles and sand. The men struggled for balance and swore at my father for not chiseling steps into the stone.

Steps would make it too easy for pirates. Father knew because he was one. He loved to tell about the towns he had sacked and burned. We had many slave women he had brought back. The men he couldn't keep, because they knew how to use weapons and were too dangerous.

2

All around the island the sea sparkled. We wound down the bare bones of cliffs to the harbor, where there were so many ships, I could not assign a finger to all of them.

I used up ten fingers counting ships, tucked my elbow into my side to keep the first ten safe, used my fingers over again, and had to tuck in my *other* elbow. All together there were ten ships, ten ships, and eight more ships, long and slim with black hulls and red sails. Each sail was stitched with a white octopus, its long legs tied in knots.

"You have enough ships to take Troy, don't you?" I said to the king. My father sailed past Troy every year. He admired Troy but hated her more.

"Troy," repeated Nicander, and he and his men looked east, where Troy lies, far far away.

Troy is built on a citadel above a strange rough river that runs uphill into a second sea. Beyond the second sea are endless supplies of slaves and grain, gold and amber. The river is the Hellespont and only with a very strong wind can a ship go up it. If there is no wind, a ship waits in the harbor of Troy. On the return voyage, when the ship's hold is full, Troy takes her share. She is the richest city on earth.

"No," said Nicander. "I could not take Troy."

We waded out to the ships. Seaweed and I played here. The stones were flat and good for skipping. "Is Callisto on the ship," I asked the king, "or is she at your house?"

"Callisto is at my house," said the king, "although my house is called a palace. She isn't very well, Anaxandra. She can't run and jump the way you can. You will sit quietly with her and spin."

What kind of adventure would that be?

A man as hairy as a goat leaned over the edge of the king's ship to lift me on board. He laughed at the idea of a girl hostage when there were boys to take, and he tossed me high into the air. My father threw me around all the time and I loved it. But when the goat-haired man caught me, I saw he had expected me to be afraid. "I am never afraid," I said severely. "I can do anything. I can swim underwater and my brothers can't do that. I can even swim into Father's caves."

The king was still waist-deep in the water, his men cupping hands to give him a leg up. "Can you now?" said the king. "And what caves are those, Anaxandra?"

"Where Father keeps the real treasure," I said.

It took Nicander's men all afternoon to get my father's treasure out of the caves and loaded into the ships. How they laughed, congratulating Nicander on his wisdom—taking a silly girl as hostage instead of an intelligent boy: a girl who had just sold out her own father.

The king's ship was hollow inside, the deck planks removed to reveal the hold. In went piles of spears and bee-waisted shields, ingots of bronze and a silver sword pommel, a gold mask and ivory combs.

I sat on a coil of rope. It was damp and salty, the color and texture of an old woman's hair. Waves lapped against the ship like dogs drinking from a puddle. What would Father say to me when I got back tonight?

At last, Lykos bellowed, "Deck the ships!" The slamming of timber was heard on all sides as the cargo was covered by the deck beams. The masts were lifted and placed in their supports and the anchor stones raised.

Nicander flung wine into the sea. "Earth Shaker!" he shouted to the god. "Give us a safe return home!"

The wooden ships groaned and creaked. Bright banners

slapped in the wind. There was no need for rowing with the wind so fine and the men relaxed on their benches.

I had not known that when you sailed away from your island, it got smaller. I had not known it would vanish. I kept my eyes fastened to the place where my island had been.

The sun was going down. The sea turned molten gold and the sky purple.

"It's bedtime," I said to the king. "I can't play with Callisto after all. We have to sail back home now."

"You're not going home, Anaxandra," said the king. "Not tonight or any night. Siphnos will be your home."

I stared at him. How could anything be home except home?

"Not that you're much of a hostage now," he added. "A hostage is useful only if its father wants it back. I doubt if your father ever wants to see you again."

I? My father's favorite?

"Your name, Anaxandra," said Lykos cheerfully, "will never be spoken in your house again."

I could not go home. My parents and my brothers would not want me. It was so shocking that I could not cry.

A few hours later I learned why I had my fleece—so I could sleep on the sand of an unknown island, having eaten cold hummus from a bowl. I had not known that you could be made to fall asleep without your mother to tuck you in.

On the second day, the wind failed us and the crew rowed. We passed many islands. From a distance, each looked like my own, but as we drew close, the island always turned out to be larger and greener.

When nobody was looking, I opened my box. There lay my best doll on a bed of Mother's gold necklaces, and next to her lay my stone Medusa idol. Medusa is always shown with her scream pouring out of her mouth and the snakes of her hair writhing. Medusa has the power to look upon an enemy and turn him to stone, so she is very powerful to have at your bedside. Of course I had never met an enemy. My father and mother protected me.

And now I had failed them.

On the third day, the king took me on his lap. "I have a great debt to the Lord God Apollo," said the king, "and with your treasure, I will go to Apollo's temple at Delphi and pay what I owe."

Apollo was an immense god, too big for our little island. "I hope the Lord Apollo refuses the treasures," I said to the king. "They aren't yours."

"They are now," said Nicander, grinning. "We have caves on Siphnos, too, Anaxandra, but yours are natural and ours are dug in order to mine gold. Every year, we make an egg of solid gold, as large as a man's fist, and offer it to the gods at Delphi."

My father had been to Delphi. The priestess there was the Mouth of God and could answer all questions. I imagined my father's gift sitting next to the great gold eggs of Siphnos. The egg is very blessed, being a perfect container of future life.

"One year," said the king, "I thought Apollo had enough gold, so I sent him an egg of lead wrapped in gold leaf."

I was shocked. He looked the same as any other man, but he had purposely cheated a god. I said silently to my own goddess, When we land, even though they may not know you on their island, I will honor you. You shall have real gold, not lead. I will keep the doll and the Medusa and you will have Mother's necklaces. I don't want to give Callisto a guest-gift after all.

"Apollo took his revenge," said the king. "First, he sent plague."

I had never seen plague. Mother said it lived best in cities. She had been born in a city and never once went back after she married Father. I thought about never going home.

"Then Apollo sent rust to infect the crops. We were hungry that winter. And then my baby son died—the fourth of my sons to die."

Four dead sons? I held my mind very flat so no thoughts could fly off and be heard by such a god. Plague and dead babies! I prayed to my goddess to keep me safe on an island where such a god ruled.

"Then," said Nicander, "Apollo flooded my gold mine with seawater."

I thought this was rather clever of Apollo. He would just keep the gold to start with and Nicander could never cheat him again.

"The oracle at Delphi said if I brought all the gold on Siphnos, it would end the god's anger. But though I brought all the gold, my fifth son died. Then the oracle told me to bring more gold." He stared out over the waves. The sea was empty. Not a dolphin, not a gull, not a ripple. The name of his island is Siphnos—"empty."

"To raise that, I have been visiting every chieftain who owes me allegiance. Your father, Anaxandra, is a famous sacker of cities. In song, he is compared to the crafty Odysseus and the great Achilles. Yet your lovely mother had only jewels and clothing for herself, and your father's cache of arms was hardly enough for two ships." He grinned at the frothy waves and the rising tips of many oars. "You solved the mystery, little Anaxandra."

On the fourth day we reached Siphnos. It was an island

as bare and bony as my own. We climbed a path so steep it bled stones. A cliff reached over us like rock fingers, hoping for an earthquake and the chance to drop on our heads.

But at the top, the land relaxed. Fields of barley were green and gold, and grapevines grew in rows as even as weaving. There were flocks of sheep so large that Nicander taught me a new number: thousand. We walked for a whole hour to reach the walls of Siphnos town. The people had painted the stones white, so the walls glared in the sun. We went in through a gate twice as tall as the king, and the walls around the gate curved, and I was amazed, for I had thought walls must be straight.

What had looked like an unbroken wall from the outside was houses on the inside, every family's house fastened to the next family's house. These formed an open square bigger than my father's entire town. In the center of the square sat a massive chunk of green marble with a hollow bowl chiseled into its center and a spout at the edge. Around the altar were the treasures wrenched from Nicander's chieftains. I had to admire a king of such force. Strength comes from the gods, and in the end, Apollo desired Nicander to be strong.

Great crowds of people filled the square to embrace their returning men and honor their king. Women pounded the bottoms of copper kettles while old men stood in stiff salute. Girls brought flowers and boys brought lambs. And then the king disappeared through another gate, Lykos went to greet his own family, and I stood alone, too short to be seen, too small to be remembered.

I clung to my box. Finally I followed in the king's footsteps and found myself in another courtyard. All the way around were ground-floor porches and all the way above were porches in the air. Boxes of flowers hung off railings and pots of flowers stood in corners.

In the center of this second courtyard was the most beautiful and horrifying thing I had ever seen. A child had been turned to stone. He stood in water that splashed out of his hands, and around his feet tiny fish swam and lilies bloomed.

I could not breathe.

What had he done, that Medusa turned him to stone?

Was this one of Nicander's dead sons?

The boy was about my age. Even his eyes had been turned to stone—blue agate that glittered in the sun.

O my goddess, I prayed, *have pity on this little boy.*

"God's knees," said the king's voice. "I forgot Chrysaor's daughter." Nicander strode over. The frozen child watched us both. The king was surrounded by rich townsmen whose clothing was embroidered and pleated and whose beards and hair were oiled and braided. "This is the child who gave me the treasure," said Nicander, and they all laughed.

I did not know how they could laugh when the dead son of their king was frozen beside them. "What happened to your little boy?" I asked.

The king looked around, puzzled.

"The boy now stone," I said.

There was a moment of silence and again came men's laughter. The king picked me up and held me straddling his hip. "The boy in the fountain was never a real boy, Anaxandra. He was carved by a mason. He is called a statue."

I did not believe that. The boy had been caught midstep and his bare toes curled. His limbs were smooth and round, as if his mother had just bathed him, and his hair was thick and dense.

And perhaps it was his mother who now joined us, a woman as beautiful as her stone son, with intricately braided black hair and earrings that hung to her shoulders.

"Lady Petra," said the men, turning their faces to the ground to honor her.

She was laughing. "The little girl has never encountered a statue before?"

"Anaxandra comes from a primitive island, my dear," said the king. He set me down and put my hand in the queen's. "She will take considerable instruction. Her value as a hostage is gone, but she will be fit company for Callisto."

The queen and I went up a ladder, which the queen called stairs, to an air porch, which she called a balcony. Their house was indeed a palace. There were six rooms on each floor. We passed through a sleeping room for the queen alone. If five of my babies had died, I would not want to share a room with my husband either.

We entered a bathing room, its smooth cold floor painted with dolphins and blue waves. Slaves stood me in a low tub and scrubbed me, and when I was clean, the queen massaged perfumed oil all over me. "The skin of a peasant is dry and flaky," she told me. "The skin of a young lady should gleam like sunlight on water."

I had not known this rule.

It turned out there were many rules I had not known. When the queen oiled my feet, she was appalled to find my soles as tough as oxhide. I never wore sandals. I could run over hot sand and sharp rocks without flinching. "You will wear slippers or shoes at all times, Anaxandra. A young lady has soft feet."

She toweled my hair so hard I bounced, and as she combed out the snarls I looked up to see a pale thin girl sit-

10

ting on a high stool, staring down at me. "Hello, Anaxandra," she said softly. "I am Callisto. I think you are fortunate to have such tough feet. You can use your feet and I cannot use mine."

"What happened to your feet?"

She drew up her gown. Her legs were sticks and her feet were not flat on the bottom. I did not see how she could put weight on them. Then I realized that she couldn't.

"I almost never go out. Father says you will have a score of stories to tell me about your island," she said eagerly.

"Maybe a thousand," I said, using my new word.

But the queen shook her head. "The feast is beginning. Come. There is much to rejoice in. The king is safely home, he has brought riches, the gods will be pleased, and no man was lost."

I was not safely home. I was not rich. I was afraid of their gods and my family was lost.

Down the stairs, out of the palace and into the town we went, Callisto carried in a chair. I saw that I did have something to rejoice in. I was not frozen like Callisto and the boy of stone.

Through the Curved Gate was brought a creature so massive I could not believe it submitted to men. Its four great legs moved slowly and its wide dark eyes looked ahead without anger. Very large horns curved from the sides of its great white head. I was awestruck. "What is that?" I whispered to Callisto.

"It's an ox. Have you never seen one pulling the plow?"

I had hardly even seen a plow. Our fields are narrow strips of dirt terraced on sharp hills.

Behind the wondrous ox came six horses. I had never seen a real horse, only pictures on vases. Father captured horses now and then, when he took a foreign city, but carrying horses on a ship was difficult and feeding them on a ship was worse. He never brought one home, for we had no place for a horse to run and no grain to spare. Besides, horses had weak backs, Father said, even though they looked strong. Donkeys were better.

Two of the horses pulled a real chariot, and beside the driver stood the king, splendid in purple.

Callisto sang the invocation, her voice high and warm like a wooden flute. *"Listen, daughters of thundering Zeus. Listen, sons of great gods. Dance in honor of golden-haired Apollo."*

The ox was brought to stand over the marble altar and how clearly now I saw the difference between a mere chieftain and a real king. My father made things holy with a little lamb, but a king made things holy with a beast so great and calm.

The priest lifted his double-sided ax while the people lifted their voices. Grasping the ox's horns, the men pulled its head back and with one great plunge the priest slit its throat from side to side. There was so much blood it overran the hollow and spilled out into the basin below, and when that had filled, a second basin was brought.

No wonder their fields were so green. No wonder their sheep were counted with that number thousand. When they diluted this holy blood with water and walked the fields, scattering it drop by drop, how blessed would be the soil.

One by one, we dipped our fingers in the holy blood. I raised my hands high to the goddess of my island, that she might not be omitted from this event. *"O goddess of yesterday,"* I sang.

The crowd fell silent to hear me. I was frightened, but having addressed the goddess, I had to go on. I pitched my voice to carry across the sea. *"Hear my cry. Stay with me. Be also my goddess of tomorrow."*

A pair of swallows swooped above me. Nothing is more holy than the flight of birds, for they cross the divide, equally at home in heaven and earth. It was a good omen.

"You are strong in the magic, Anaxandra," whispered the queen. She marked my forehead with her bloody thumb. "There," she said, kissing each side of the print. "Your goddess who was with you yesterday will be with you tomorrow and every tomorrow to come."

And so I feasted with the people of Siphnos, and danced among them, while the blood print crusted and dried. I wondered just how blessed I was, marked by a woman from whom the gods had taken five babies.

II

THE KING AND QUEEN had buried the babies in the wall between his bedroom and hers. We did not do that on our island, preferring graves far removed from houses. I never quite got used to having their little sets of bones inside the wall, just beneath the plaster. For a whole year, I slept in a ball to keep my feet safe.

Every morning when I rose, I smoothed away the impression of my body from my mattress. Otherwise evil might lie down in my shape and wait for me. I opened the bedroom door carefully to allow Night and Day to trade places without tripping over me. It made Callisto laugh. "Nobody does that anymore," she would tell me. "Not even the peasants in the hills."

In this place called a palace, they took a knife to their bread, slicing their loaves instead of tearing hunks off. A knife is a weapon. A blade should never attack bread, the most important gift of the gods.

The king himself would wade through a creek without first washing his hands. What could the water think, knowing that even the king did not care if he was pure? I thought a family whose only daughter was crippled and whose five sons had died in infancy should take more care.

My hostage father the king loved feasting and celebration. Every time a ship of his came back safe and rich, he roasted a ram for the gods. Every time we had guests, I stayed up late to listen, hoping to hear news of my parents, Chrysaor and Iris, but I never did.

Sometimes I cried myself to sleep, and although I buried the sounds in my fleece, Queen Petra knew and came to rock me. More than one night she slept beside me because I would not let go of her hand. Petra said that my fate had come from the gods and could not have been avoided. "When you are born," she said, "Zeus takes his two jars and shakes them, the joyful and the sorrowful. Your fate is poured out. No one escapes."

Yet not a day went by that I didn't escape in my heart. When I was under the sky instead of the roof, I was closer to home. I explored hollows and hills. I ran along slender beaches and brought back just the right sea stone for Callisto. I followed the sheep and the goats up hillsides too steep for crops.

I was drawn to an empty silent meadow with a single olive tree, old as time.

It was a hideous tree. In some distant decade, farmers had cut the trunk almost to the ground, and out of the great flat stump had grown massive side trunks, now rotting and split around the table of the stump. In each decaying knot and elbow were staring eyes and open mouths that screamed silently, like Medusa.

The shepherds, who were teaching me to use a slingshot, warned me away from this tree. "Beneath that olive, take no rest, Anaxandra. Pan, god of chaos, visits there."

But I thought myself braver than any shepherd or

warrior, for I swam underwater into caves. I poked my bare fingers into a rotted mouth and left my mother's jewels in the olive tree for my goddess.

I explored every tiny lane in Siphnos town, with its alleys as tangled as fishermen's knots. The town huddled nervously inside its high white walls, and the doors of houses looked around, worrying, as if knowing that their king did not properly honor the sacred places.

I played with all the animals, especially the dogs, but I never had one of my own again. On our island, people slept on raised platforms in the same room as their sheep, so they were always warm, although a bit smelly. But in Siphnos town, the doors on the ground floor led to separate rooms for animals, while families entered their homes from the porches in the air.

Whenever I could, I went to the stable to admire the king's horses. "You have more horses than anybody, don't you?" I said to him one day when we were feeding them windfall apples.

Nicander laughed. "I have six horses. Menelaus, the king of Sparta, has fifty. And in Troy—they have a thousand horses twice the size of mine. They scorn our horses and call them ponies. Trojans tame wild horses and ride on them."

"No, they don't," I said. "Men don't ride on horses."

"In Troy they do. And farther east, around the Third Sea, the one called Black, all the people ride horses. Even the women and children."

I could not believe that. Horses went too fast. You would fall off. And how could you get up on a horse to start with?

"The Trojans stand on a stone," Nicander explained, "so they're high enough to swing a leg over the horse's back. The rider clings with his knees and knots his hands in the mane. The horse goes so fast a man's hair streams out behind him."

A donkey won't go any faster than you could walk. What would it be like to move so swiftly that your hair streamed out behind you? My father, Chrysaor, had long honey-colored hair. He preferred it loose, but when he was fighting, his slave braided it.

Every memory of my father made my heart peel away from my ribs and thump in a lonely place. "Anyway, horses eat far too much grain," I told the king, with the voice used by the queen when she scolded him for keeping six useless creatures. "How could those Trojans feed a thousand of them?"

"Around Troy the grain fields stretch for miles, uninterrupted by rock and cliff. Troy does not have to buy wheat. They really can feed a thousand horses."

Talk of Troy made men's eyes distant and full of memory. "Troy's walls," Nicander said, "are as high as a cliff. The houses are three stories high and the watchtowers two stories higher than that. I have one main gate; Troy has four. I have a brook that runs only in the spring; Troy has two rivers of her own and the Hellespont as well. I have two thousand sheep; Troy has a hundred flocks that large."

I pressed my cheek against the horse's beautiful neck. I did not believe any horse could be twice her size.

"I have never been inside the gates of Troy," said Nicander. "They are careful of their gates."

"Because the city is so full of treasure," I said eagerly. "What if a sea captain like you refused to give them a share of his cargo?"

"You could not outrow or outsail Troy's warships. They'd ram you. Then they'd have your cargo, your ship and you."

"Could Troy be taken?" I asked.

"What a little warrior you are. Chrysaor must have grieved that you were born a girl. Taking Troy would require a vast fleet. Every king on the Main Land and every king from every island would have to join the attack. Such a thing has never happened. And an attack must have a general. To what man would kings submit? And even if such an army were put together, Troy would just sit behind her walls and wait till winter came."

"You could fight all winter and starve them out."

"Where would you get your own food? Your own firewood? You can't sail during the winter, so you couldn't go get what you needed. How many shiploads of supplies would it take for so huge an army? How could you man all those ships? If you built winter quarters, you'd have to bring tents and lumber, grain for flour, women to bake the bread. And what about the families you left behind, unguarded? While you froze on the beaches of Troy, your people would run out of food and be attacked by some other enemy."

I was impatient with details. "But these Trojans who ride horses," I demanded, "are they good warriors or do they just have a good place on the water? Could you whip them?"

Nicander grinned. "I would love to bring sobs and groaning to Trojan wives. But I do not think that I or anyone else can whip Troy."

Shortly after that, Nicander took half his fleet and sailed for the Third Sea, the one called Black. The queen said it was because I had talked too much about Troy.

Then she found out that the shepherds had taught me to use a sling.

The sling is a tiny leather hammock with two cords the length of your arm. You place a small smooth stone in the

18

sling, swing it in hard fast circles and release the cord. The stone flies with great force.

A shepherd could bring down a partridge for dinner with his sling. In war, of course, a good shot between the enemy's eyes would kill him. It took me a year to learn how to aim at all. But to aim well—to bring back a wandering sheep by kicking up the dust in front of its grazing face— this is a great skill.

The queen was not impressed and ordered me to the women's wing for good. There I sat, as the women worked looms and the girls spun. A whole day's spinning makes thread for only one hour of weaving. I liked the rhythm, tossing my spindle into the air, feeding fiber into the twist. My spindle was a gift from Petra, polished and painted. Petra said that Helen, wife of King Menelaus, had a spindle made of solid gold. Petra loved to speak of Queen Helen, the most beautiful woman in the world, and of the one time they had met.

"A gold spindle would be too heavy to use," I objected.

"Anyway," said Callisto, "I don't believe a queen such as Helen ever actually spins. Helen is the daughter of a god."

"Every woman spins," said Petra, "god child or no."

When we weren't spinning or weaving, Callisto and I played with dolls. A girl plays with her dolls until she is married. Callisto and I never admitted it, but both of us would play with dolls forever. Marrying Callisto, only child of the king of Siphnos, would bring a man power, but no children, for Callisto was too weak to bear them. No man wants wealth more than sons. As for me, a hostage whose family no longer cared to redeem me, I had nothing to offer any husband and never would.

The king was gone for a year. The queen heard petitioners, helped the poor and settled estates. The throne was plastered into the floor to show that the king was attached to his world. Petra never sat on the throne.

When Nicander came home at last, he brought back the usual treasure: grain, women, lumber; a necklace of deep mysterious blue for Callisto, strange shimmery cloth for Petra, a vase painted with Trojan horses for me, and for himself, a mining engineer.

"No, Nicander," said Petra. "Please do not return to that mine."

The king laughed. He was very excited. He could hardly wait to show the engineer the old mine shaft. "I made my peace with Apollo," he told his wife. "Now it merely remains to find a new entrance to the gold."

She caught his arm, but he shook her off and with long strides set off for his ruined mine.

Almost immediately, the sky blackened at the edges. The air took on a strange smell, as if we were biting tin. But the king and his engineer walked on.

The earthquake hit just as they reached the old shaft. They were thrown to the ground, but not into the hole. The kitchen wing of the palace fell in, and five slaves died. The horses were in the paddock but they broke through the gate. Five ran safely into the fields, but the sixth in his terror galloped off the cliff.

How the king and queen argued over the meaning of that horse's death!

"Apollo wants his gold left alone," said Petra, furious and afraid.

"Now, my dear," said Nicander. "Sometimes an earthquake is just an earthquake. It is my gold and I am taking it."

III

THE DAY CAME WHEN half my life had been spent on Siphnos, and most of that in the prison of the women's wing. That morning, Petra and Callisto were braiding flowers of beaten gold into each other's hair. They had hair as dark and beautiful as pines in shadow. I remembered suddenly how fondly my mother used to tell me that my hair was the color of a wild hyacinth.

I drifted out of the room and slipped down the stairs to the courtyard.

There were no men around. Half the men were pirating with Lykos and the other half were digging yet another entrance to the gold mines. They'd gotten down some twenty feet into the rock, but water was seeping up to meet them. Nicander had not given up, although the queen had asked him to. Every day he marched a mile north of Siphnos town in the hope of gold.

I went out the Curved Gate and headed for the hills. I threaded through the apple orchard, where orchardmen were painstakingly watering each tree. I leaped over stone walls and scrabbled up a sloping field where longhaired sheep grazed, and I waved to their shepherd, a boy of six. There were no wolves on Siphnos, so the task of a shepherd was to keep his flock from falling off cliffs. We did not waste grown men on this task.

I climbed even higher than the ancient olive, up a crag that broke under my fingers like dry sand and twice sent me tumbling almost to my death. I wanted to reach the highest place on Siphnos, for places closer to the gods are sacred. When I reached it, sweating and gasping, I kissed the feet of the ancient idol there and faced the dot in the sea I believed to be my island. I knew in my heart that there were many islands tilting in the Aegean, and that the isle of my birth was four days' sail and far over the horizon. Nevertheless, I waved to my mother and father, as if a wave of the hand could cross the waves of the sea.

A row of little red oblong sails bobbed in the water like flowers. Our fleet was returning. There were more ships than had sailed away a few months ago. This meant that our men had commandeered ships from some other harbor, and we were richer, and Nicander was stronger.

My hostage father did not actually care for trade, although his men did exchange leather for wheat and purple dye for bronze. There is no honor in trade. What poet can sing of your excellent exchange of pottery for rope? Whereas, were you to pirate some great city like Smyrna or Antissa, what songs would be sung of your valor!

I made my way down to the sunburned meadow and my tree as old as time and called a prayer to my goddess. On Siphnos, gods possessed names. The king and queen prayed to Athena and Apollo, to Demeter and Dionysus, to Poseidon and Zeus. On my birth island, we were distant from the knowledge of so many gods and goddesses.

I stood on tiptoe on the old stump and reached into the

small hole where I kept my mother's jewels. Yes, they were still there. They would always be there. Nobody but me dared poke bare fingers into Medusa's scream. Then I climbed up a fat and twisty branch to curl myself in the very best arm of the tree. I dropped my sandals onto the stump table and wiggled my bare toes.

Out of the silence of the lonely meadow came a whisper.

I sat very still, remembering that sensible men never came near this tree.

Across the blue kettle of the sea raced the ships. Nicander's white octopus was now visible on the closest sail. The sails of the conquered ships, also red, wore a different sign, but from this distance, I could not make it out.

Suddenly every ship lowered sail at the same instant, and out came the oars, and their white shafts feathered the water. Oars control a ship better than sails. It struck me as odd that the ships were approaching so quickly. The harbor itself wasn't on this side of the island and ships heavy with plunder should have been going to the harbor where donkeys and carts awaited. But they were rowing full speed toward the palace side, where cliffs fell hundreds of feet and the only way up from the sliver of beach was a narrow twisting footpath.

Again came the whisper. It was not a voice. It was snakes.

Medusa did not come from this island, but she might have. We were an island of snakes. Some bit with poison and some did not. I looked up. Hanging from the branch above my face, a dozen snakes had twisted into a knot and were leaning toward me.

Medusa is the Shriek made Woman, and although I was not yet a woman, I could shriek as loud as Medusa ever did.

But one snake dropped through my hair and onto my sandals, so I wasted no time on a scream but leaped out of the tree, tumbled to the stony ground, rolled to my feet, ran a hundred yards and stopped.

The wind ruffled my dress like a thin curtain.

Again the meadow was silent. Not even the cicadas rasped.

I looked out to the sea instead of back at the snakes and saw that the ships were rowing right up onto the sand.

That is how you attack.

Boats coming home would stop in deeper water and ship the oars.

Yet these were our ships. How could they be attacking?

But Lykos had spent his life at sea. He must know what he was doing. He would have brought me a present, although not the present I actually wanted, which was a puppy.

I looked back at the olive. Silver leaves hid the snakes. I would borrow the long hooked staff of the six-year-old shepherd and use it to pull my sandals out. At the edge of the meadow I leaned over the crag to see where he was.

Far below me, the little shepherd had left his flock, a thing unheard of; a thing that even at six he would be beaten for. He was running—skidding—slipping—down the rocky path toward town. An orchardman dropped his bucket of water—precious scarce fresh water—and also ran, pausing to scoop a toddler into his arms. Old women rushed from huts. Dogs barked and field hands dropped their tools.

Men were vaulting off the red-sailed ships. They carried spears and swords. They swung shields. They had bows and arrows and they had darts.

Too late I understood. Our men had not conquered and

sacked a foreign city. They had *been* conquered. Sailing our ships as well as their own, foreigners had arrived to attack us.

It is how we live, here by the sea. We take, and we are taken.

None of Nicander's men who had sailed away could be alive. Lykos, the captain, was dead, and all his crew, their bodies hurled into some distant sea; their oars and blankets the property of pirates; their hopes and plans as dead as their bodies.

O my king. You should never have betrayed Apollo.

The enemy raced up the zigzag path. From the watchtowers of the palace came no shout of warning. From the mines came no outpouring of men to save us. But the people did not know they were undefended. They ran for the safety of the town.

Siphnos town was designed to fend off the wicked. The high wall was unbroken by windows, the great gate curved to slow an enemy. He would emerge at an angle from which he could aim no arrow. And he could not enter the gate to start with, because its thick wooden doors are braced with bronze.

But on this day, the gate lay open. The men with sufficient strength to close the doors were not there. The soldiers who knew how to fight were down the wet shaft of a failed mine.

The snakes had been a sign from my goddess. I had called her name, and yet not listened when she whispered to me.

I too was running now. My bare feet were shredded by the sharp rubble. Below me, people were pouring into the town in the hope of safety, but the enemy was pouring in at the same time, cutting the people down.

Now the gold miners began climbing desperately out of the rocks. They massed together, running toward the town. They were unarmed. The pirates were between them and their weapons. They would have to fight with their hands or their mining tools.

And so they did: pickax against sword.

I could hear the singing zip of darts and the death whistle of arrows. Our men ran uphill while the pirates took easy shots down on them. How quickly the bodies began to fall!

From inside the walls, a few men leaped to the parapet. Each carried an armload of spears and swords. They did not attempt a defense, but threw themselves and the weapons over the wall and ran to aid their brothers. The fall was far enough that one man broke a leg and was cut down in some amusement by the enemy. But the rest gathered up the weapons and raced downhill to arm the miners.

Not one made it.

The enemy darters threw mercilessly, and the sharp points of those light weapons pierced the backs of our men, who fell upon their own stacked spears.

"O my goddess," I cried. "Let me save Callisto, who cannot save herself."

I would circle the palace walls and go in by the cypress garden, where a strong vine climbed up a pillar. I could pull myself up onto the second-floor balcony. I had done it before, escaping the princess prison into which my hostage life had put me.

The pirates would be after treasure, which they would expect to find deep in the palace, in a thick-walled room with no windows and a massive lock. Only my father had kept his treasure beneath the sea. The pirates would have axes to chop through the doors, but they would rather find

26

the queen and put a knife to her throat. She would soon enough hand over the key. Petra might even run to meet them, hoping to delay their finding Callisto; hoping to give Nicander time to destroy the foe in spite of such terrible odds.

I leaped down a terrace wall, ran between apple trees, vaulted down the next terrace and flattened the high stalks of onions.

I would yank Callisto out of bed and push her onto the balcony. We'd jump. I'd carry her into the hills or drag her.

Three pirates were headed my way, but I did not think they saw me. Their eyes were on a big flock of sheep enclosed in the stone fold. Nicander had been planning to sacrifice a hundred sheep to Apollo upon the safe return of these very ships.

O my king.

I swerved from the path, slipping behind cypresses, whose green tips stabbed the sky, and followed a narrow twisty track to the rear of the palace. To the left were laurel thickets and the pillar I planned to climb. To the right, the cliff.

Far below was very deep water. It was the thing with boys to prove their bravery and jump off the cliff. They would get a running start, leap into the air, ball themselves up and hit the water with an impressive splash. Mostly they were fine, just bruised, but a few years before, a boy had died, and the king had frowned upon cliff-jumping since then.

Through the greenery, I saw that the side gate of the palace also lay open.

Piled by this gate were immense two-handled jars, higher than my waist. All were filled with olive oil, stamped with the king's octopus seal, ready to be shipped. Pirates came from both directions through the side gate, saluting one another as they took Siphnos. For the fun of it they smashed every jar spout. Cracked sharp pottery cluttered the stone walk and golden olive oil puddled everywhere.

The next pirate carried a torch to light his way down whatever dark passage led to the treasury.

In the heat of excitement, men forget themselves.

And so with this rejoicing pirate. He set fire to the shattered containers of oil. Flames exploded. In a flash, the side gate was blocked. No man could pass through such fire.

The palace rooms adjoined. Indoor and outdoor halls and balconies were connected by open wooden stairs. The support timbers of the palace were not plastered over, because beams were handy for driving in pegs from which to hang things.

In moments every wall and ceiling was ablaze; every curtain and tapestry. Fire shriveled the vine I had planned to climb; fire took the trellis and charred the pillar.

O my princess. I cannot reach you, Callisto.

The enemy, of course, had planned to burn the town *after* they got the treasure. They raged, but they too were driven out by the burning heat and they drove the villagers ahead of them.

Our own men were still on the rocks, fighting or dying. Mostly dying.

More pirates were coming toward the Curved Gate, having finished off most of the unarmed miners. The peasants, caught between, were cut to pieces. The six-year-old shepherd, who could have stayed in the hills and saved himself, fell to the sword. The sheep were herded over the bodies of the fallen and down to the ships, so the pirates could feast after their victory. Some sheep panicked and fell off, baaing until they hit the rocks.

The three marauders who had found my path now found me. The first man drew back his spear. I was close enough to see that he was missing teeth and his beard was filthy and his muscles strong. I bolted to the dizzying edge of the cliff and stepped off.

I had not done it correctly.

I had not thrown myself away from the jagged edges, but just tipped over. I would be torn to pieces on jutting rocks and finished off when I snapped my neck hitting the water. But just in case, I tucked myself into a ball and hit the water kneecaps first and sank like an anchor stone. The smack of the sea was as blunt and flat as the slap of an angry hand. I felt broken.

Down and down I went, and then I opened myself up and began swimming. Pain was present, and terror, but the desire for air was greater than these. I broke the surface, gasping in blessed air and blinking salt water out of my eyes.

There was a sharp *squiff,* like snakes. An arrow pierced the water at my side.

Squinting in the brassy glare of sun, I looked up. The three pirates stood on the cliff edge, laughing down on me and stringing their bows.

I dove underwater, forcing myself to swim toward the pirates. If I could get close to the cliff, I could shelter beneath the rocky overhang, like an octopus in its cave. I used my arms to shovel the water away from my face and push it behind me, in a stroke the shell divers had taught me.

When I came up, I was not entirely sheltered and had to

dive a second time. I waited in the shade of the rocks for some time before I ventured a peek. The cliff edge was empty. I was safe.

Siphnos was burning. The stench of the fire as it took flesh and oil was equaled in horror only by the screams of the wounded.

Then from the sand where the ships were beached came a triumphant yell. "I see him! He's over there! In the shallows below the cliff! He's mine!"

I was a her, not a him, but a girl of twelve is easily mistaken for a boy of twelve when both wear simple tunics. And few girls willingly throw themselves off cliffs.

"Let him drown!" yelled somebody else. "One boy doesn't matter. There are still men to fight!"

I strained to comprehend their Greek, which was heavy and sluggish.

The first voice moved closer. "Nobody gets away from me."

Medusa was killed on an island near Siphnos. I do not have Medusa's blood, but I wished I did. I would have turned this barbarian to stone with a scream and the force of my eyes.

Luckily I knew the waters well. There were rocks piled where once, long before, a stone jetty had stretched. Earthquakes destroyed it in the time of my king's grandfather. I didn't like it out there because there were so many octopuses. The boys liked to walk all the way out the sunken jetty—looking as if they could walk on water—and fish for octopus.

Weaving in and out of the fallen stones, I swam underwater, eyes open and lungs bursting. When I reached the only two stones that still protruded from the water, I came up for air, praying to my goddess that I would not be seen.

If I had hair as dark as Callisto's, I would look like a rock or a seal. But my red-gold hair was no asset here.

The pirate hunted for me, but did not find the sunken path he could have walked on. "I must have killed him," said the pirate sadly, as if he had hoped to do something worse than kill. Indeed, had he found me alive and a girl, he would have.

I floated.

The battle went on.

I was too close to the enemy ships but I had no choice. On their red sails was stitched a twisted blue fish. It was ugly and unforgettable.

Standing high on one deck was a watcher, the enemy poet, I guessed, taking note of the action so he could sing later of deeds and valor. Men pirate for treasure, of course, for women and horses and armor. But they also pirate for fame.

What is better entertainment in the evening than a song about you? Who does not hope for a story so rich that it is sung year after year, and even your grandchildren learn it?

I peered between the rocks.

There was still some fighting on the sand. A few miners had run up the beaches to attack the enemy instead of heading for high ground. Among them was our king. Had he glanced up from his ruined mine and assumed, as I had, that these red-sailed ships were his own?

Our harbor master, badly wounded, was thrown to the ground. The pirate placed a boot on his head, holding down the skull and getting it at the right angle. Then he slit the throat as easily as a priest slits the throat of a lamb.

But my hostage father the king would not surrender. He had a shield, presumably ripped from the body of a pirate he had killed. It was not as large as his own shield. He had a sword also, and whether it was his or another's I did not know.

Most of the pirates wore helmets whose horsehair plumes ran front to rear, extending the line of the nose back to the tip of the spine. But this warrior who fought my hostage father had plumes from side to side, arching around his head like a rising sun. The front of his helmet bulged out in a great metal nose, and the eye openings were vertical slices, like ravines in a mountain.

Nicander was the only one of our people left on his feet. He wore no armor. He had been cut several times.

Of course the pirates could have surrounded the king and done away with him easily. But he wished to die well and they wished to kill well, so the enemy did not interfere with the duel, but paused to admire.

I sang my king's praises in my heart: how he thrust and forced himself forward. He had badly wounded the foe, goring him in the side. Blood cascaded down the man's legs. The foe was weakening. My hostage father would win.

It would not change the battle and it would not keep him alive, for another of the enemy would continue the duel, but at least Nicander would die in glory.

And then a pirate stabbed the king in the back, denying him the chance to die as a warrior. He died as a slave dies.

Even the pirates were furious, especially the cross-plumed warrior. "You had no right! He was my man!"

"My brother, you are badly hurt. I cannot let you be killed." The backstabber yanked his dagger out of my king's back. Tearing strips from his own cape, he bound up his brother's gashes.

No poet can sing of the foe being stabbed in the back. The bard threw up his hands in disgust. His song was ruined. "It is a shivery thing to kill a prince of royal blood that way," he shouted from the ship. "You will call down the gods' wrath."

The backstabber shrugged, although it is not good to shrug when gods are mentioned.

The battle ended. There were none of us left to fight. The town burned. The pirates waited for the fire to die down so they could go back for Nicander's treasure. Some of them sat in the sand, cleaning blood and gore off armor and weapons. Others gathered their own dead for a pyre. They sank several ships, which puzzled me until I decided that enough of their men had been killed that they were short on rowers. They were not leaving any ship for survivors to use.

In dories they rowed out those women they were taking captive. They made Queen Petra walk over her husband's body. They did not have Callisto.

The sun slid low in the sky, and the sky turned gaudy red. Great black shadows shot behind the ships.

Grinning, the backstabber kicked Nicander's body. He knew the dead man was a king. He knew kings are sacred. He knew and was glad that a king's body would go unburied, a terrible ending for a fine life.

In the water, circling my legs, was an octopus.

It was not one of the small dainty ones. It was one of the big strong ones, its legs as long as I am tall.

I had a horror of the octopus—its soft swollen body, its hundreds of fleshy sucking cups, its eyes staring in different directions. I wouldn't eat it, although everyone else loved sliced octopus, fried in oil and served hot and salty with rosemary and thyme.

They say Medusa's hair was made of snakes, but on my idol it is clear that Medusa wore an octopus in her hair, letting the dreadful arms swing about and cling to her skin with their little sticky cups.

As a wanderer on the shore would kick a dead fish into the waves to get rid of the stink, the pirate was kicking the sacred body of my hostage father the king.

I took a deep breath, closed my eyes so no sucker would fasten on them and blind me, and sank down beneath the octopus. Gripping the swirling arms of the hideous creature, I put its cool bloated body right on my head and stood up on the rocks screaming.

I was walking on water, gilded by the setting sun.

Medusa.

"I am Medusa!" I shrieked, in their heavy ugly accent. "I come to take your lives!" With one hand I held the octopus and with the other hand I shielded my eyes to catch the pirates in my stare. Hundreds of men stopped what they were doing and stared in horror.

"Look upon me!" I screamed. "Look upon me and die!"

I thought the pirate kicking Nicander might actually die. He slipped on the rocks, whimpering, and scrabbled away as a snail scuttles from the gull.

My snake hair—my octopus—waved.

From the sand the men leaped up, lifting shields to protect their eyes. Frantic, they shoved the last dory into the water and paddled for the safety of the ships.

"You die!" I screamed. "May your eyeballs be eaten by fish when Zeus holds you underwater!"

The legs of the octopus flailed in the breeze, for the octopus hated air. Its legs found places on my bare skin to grip. Curses poured out of me like lava from the spout of a god. "May the waves hold your face downward and your lungs be filled with sand! May your corpse be cast ashore naked and chewed by dogs!"

Men abandoned everything, flinging themselves into the waves, struggling to reach ships that were already sailing away. Their legs churned the water and those who did not know how to swim learned.

I shook my fist, which itself was clasped by two legs of the octopus. "Die!" I shrieked.

But they sailed safely away, every one of them, even the backstabber, and I stood among the dead.

I sank down into the water.

The octopus let go and swam off.

I was alone.

A full moon came out, casting silver light upon my task. Diving underwater time and time again, I retrieved the sail of a sunken ship. It was surprising that the pirates had not taken the sails. Cloth is harder to come by than wood.

With difficulty I hauled the big soaking piece to shore. In this I wrapped my hostage father's body.

Lying in the sand were shovels from the gold mines, brought by men with no other choice of weapon. I dragged the corpse high on the beach and dug a hole as deep as I could. The same seawater that had ruined the king's gold mine now filled his shallow grave. After I covered him, I swam back out and retrieved an oar. It was not the king's oar, beautifully painted and retired to a position of honor in his throne room. It was just an oar.

I stabbed it into the sand to mark his grave.

So here I stand in the ruins.

Every song must be dedicated to the powers above, and I dedicate this song to the goddess of my birth island.

But it is a song not finished. I swear to my goddess and to Medusa: I shall take my revenge upon the men of the twisted fish.

IV

THE DAY AFTER THE PIRATES attacked Siphnos, I retrieved a second sail and created a tent to shelter myself from the heat. I could not leave the narrow beach. I was trapped there by piles of the dead; by eagles and vultures and gulls come to feast on them.

I kept track of the days by marking a stone with a bit of charcoal that had once been some treasure made of wood. I ate bread and oil from supplies abandoned on shore when the pirates saw Medusa. There was even plenty of fresh water, the pirates having planned to restock their ships with our jars.

By the fifth day, I was out of food.

Rain began on the eighth day, surprising me very much, for it generally does not rain until autumn. We had not had rain in months and the earth would not accept it. Rain ran in sheets down the terraced fields, pulling walls over, flooding the ruined town, changing the ashes of the palace to mud, which slid over the cliff and dissolved in the sea.

Rain to a farmer is joy. Rain to a sailor is the gods pissing through a sieve. I agreed with the sailors. It rained hard all day and all night, but on the ninth dawn, it slowed to a drizzle.

Three is of course a magic number. It is best to call upon

three gods or to call upon one god three times. But on the third day after the attack, I had had no taste for gods who abandoned us. Nine being an even holier number than three, however, on the ninth morning I gathered my courage.

I walked uphill and forced myself to pass through the stumps of the Curved Gate. The courtyard was packed with bodies in various states of decay, all the insects that live on meat feasting on what had once been people. I breathed through my apron.

The pirates had taken the sheep. The goats had vanished into the hills. With practice, perhaps I could get back the skill I had lost weaving in a princess prison and bring down a rabbit. I scavenged among the bodies of fighters to find a sling, a pouch of shot and a knife for skinning and then I went back out the Curved Gate.

The climb was not the usual dusty scrabble. I slipped continually in mud. Part of the path to the ancient olive had been destroyed and I had to walk much farther to get there.

The rain increased.

I faced into the wind and washed my hands in the falling drops. If you do not purify yourself first, the gods will spit back your prayers. "O goddess of yesterday," I said sadly. "Be with me, for I am full of fear and sorrow."

I did not know what to do.

I could cross the spine of sharp hills and descend to the opposite coast. Find another village. Beg for help. But a young girl alone is a target. I had no important name to impress strangers. In fact, people would wonder why I still breathed, when no one else survived. Had the will of the gods been sidestepped?

Strangers might finish me off without giving me time to explain. They might not believe the explanation anyway.

How indeed could a twelve-year-old girl drive away a horde of pirates in their swift ships?

O goddess, again I have no family. Again I have no home.

I wondered if the queen was still alive. I wondered if she would rather be dead.

"Goddess," I whispered.

The rain slackened and became mist, and the sun floated on each drop and a rainbow lifted in the sky.

A nightingale began to sing.

Nightingales will sing both day and night, unceasing, but usually in spring, when finding mates and raising young. I searched for the plain little bird with the beautiful voice, but could not see him. The song seemed to come right out of the sky.

Slowly, I realized that it did come out of the sky. It was the voice of my goddess.

I raised my voice to sing with her, and our voices mingled and my hair began to dry and my hopes to lift.

"I give you all my jewels now, O goddess," I told her. "I keep none for myself. Be grateful for this, goddess, and care for me properly now."

Slowly I went back down the hills, walking on the tops of terrace walls to stay out of the mud. I went in the scorched and collapsed side entrance of the palace. Both roof and balcony of the women's quarters had collapsed into a pile of timbers and broken beds. I kicked the ashes, wishing I could kick the pirate who had stabbed my hostage father in the back; wishing I could kick Fate.

And there in the ashes was my Medusa.

Few humans smile at Medusa, but I cried out in joy, kissed and embraced her.

She is but seven inches high. She was darker from the

fire, but unhurt. The nightingale sang on and I turned my back on the carnage and looked at the noble sea.

There were sails scudding toward Siphnos.

Even from so far away, the sailors would know what had happened here. Flags and banners no longer waved from a tower that no longer stood. Walls that had been as white as clouds were black with soot. No ship was moored in the harbor; no women mended nets on the shore.

Whose sails were these?

Good men, allies of Nicander?

Or the very same ships of the very same pirates? Coming back for the loot they had left behind when they were frightened away by a girl and an octopus?

Should I run or should I hope?

If I was to run, the time was now. I could follow a goat path and lose myself in the crags and folds of the island.

Instead, I walked down the narrow path strewn with corpses unburied and treasure uncarried. I put my Medusa in the basket of my apron. I was caked with mud, my clothes stained with ash and gore.

I stood beside the oar of my hostage father's marker. If these were pirates, they would kill me where I stood.

But these sails were black with a white horse—the very famous mark of a greater king than Nicander. The ships of Menelaus, the red-haired king of Sparta, Lord of the Main Land, to whom Nicander himself paid tribute.

The Main Land was a place not surrounded by the sea. I had never seen it. I could not quite imagine it.

Menelaus would not kill me. But he would want to know why I lived, when my king and princess had died; why I was safe, when my queen had been taken into slavery. Who are you? the red-haired king would demand.

40

I am nobody, I would have to say. Only the unwanted hostage daughter of a minor chieftain on a rocky isle.

It was too much to hope that the king would have me serve gently in his own household. A filthy stinking half-clothed twelve-year-old girl without family has no value. Perhaps Menelaus would parcel me out to a sailor who was short on loot. Although who would consider me a treasure, I could not imagine.

Or would Menelaus send me back to the mother and father who had never spoken my name again? I no longer remembered what Chrysaor and Iris looked like. My brothers would be men. They might be married. They might have children. I might be an aunt.

Would Chrysaor and Iris take me in? Or send their forgotten daughter to live in a shepherd's hut and marry a farmhand?

But perhaps the isle of my birth had been sacked as fully and viciously as Siphnos. Perhaps none of them were alive either.

Chrysaor and Iris were so remote. It was Nicander whom I loved, and his wife and daughter for whom I grieved.

The ships of Sparta drew near. The black sails were taken down, the anchor stones dropped into the water.

I stood as straight as I could, clasping the long slim handle of the oar as if it were a spear and I its warrior. I would not show fear. I would not call out. I would stand my ground.

Slowly the men waded toward me. They looked ordinary, so I remained silent. I would not speak except to a captain. Unblinking, I stared beyond them, waiting. Each sailor paused, nervous at my demeanor.

Well, that was not surprising, since I had recently been

Medusa. I suspected that was a trick which would not work twice.

The men encircled me and I thought of death.

From one of the ships, a dory was lowered into the water. A red-haired man, assisted from above and from below, that he might not get wet or stumble, stepped in. Two rowers brought him through the shallows.

He was brawny but not tall, a barrel of a man who gleamed with oil. His beard was very curly. Fashion required a neat projectile, extending a man's chin straight out in front of him, but this man's beard raged over his cheeks and jaw like a bad temper. He was not handsome. His hair was red as a poppy, having no gold in it like my own.

It could only be the king of Sparta himself. Lord of the Main Land. A man to whom a king such as Nicander was merely a commander. And I—what was I to such a king?

Menelaus stepped out onto dry land.

I clung to the oar. I had not been strong enough to dig a deep hole. Every day I had mounded the sand back to keep the body covered. There was no mistaking the shape of what I stood beside.

The king approached me slowly, boots sinking in the soft sand. "Lady," he said courteously, "stranger-friend. Tell me what has passed here."

I am acquainted with many languages, since our slave women come from so many places. Not all languages treat the word "stranger" and the word "friend" as one, but in our tongue, the words tangle. You must wait out a conversation to see into which category you and the other will fall. Not all strangers are friends, but such must be your hope.

That the king of Sparta would accord me such courtesy weakened me. I felt tears rising and my throat thickening. I tried to speak, but the horror of what had passed would not land on my tongue. The king laid a hand of comfort on my shoulder to encourage me.

"They stabbed him in the back," I said finally, and my voice broke. "The pirates who destroyed our town. I buried him here. My father the king. Nicander. All the rest are dead."

The king of the Main Land put his arms around me and kissed my ruined hair. "Poor princess. I am so sorry. How proud your father the king would be that you found the strength to bury him properly. That you marked his grave with a fine oar. That you stand by his resting place as a priestess by her altar."

I had referred to Nicander as my father only to honor him. It was a figure of speech used by many, for a king is father to his people. It did not follow that I was his daughter. Yet so Menelaus assumed.

My fingers grew tight and stiff on the shaft of the oar.

I did not correct the king of the Main Land.

Nicander had cared more about gold than about gods. And it seemed that I cared more about staying alive than being true.

Menelaus had women with him, booty from his own expedition. Two of these were brought ashore to bathe and dress me while the warriors of Menelaus began the terrible task of cleaning up bodies. We do not burn our dead as a rule, but burning was the only choice now. Great pyres were built on the sand, on the path, by the gates, and in the courtyard. The dead were dragged to each heap.

"Truly," said Menelaus sadly, "they went through your town with a net."

It is a fishing term: When fishermen fling their nets into

the sea, they hope to enclose an entire school of fish, drag it back and eat every one.

"Yes," I said, thinking of Callisto and of the six-year-old shepherd.

The women drew water from the well and the men brought a cauldron to heat it, and from the ships came towels and fresh clothing. It was an extraordinary relief to be clean. But an even greater relief was to be cuddled in the soft arms of plump women. They spoke no language that I knew, but they were mothers, and for a moment, they were my mother. Their towns too must have been slashed and burned; their daughters lay dead and their sons murdered; their futures now terrifying and unknown.

I buried my face in the bosom of a woman newly made slave, while she worked with a comb to get the tangles out. When I was clean and my hair drying in the sun, each red-gold curl springing up, the king came back. "You *are* a princess," he said approvingly. "Hair like the sunset. Eyes like the sea. Though I do not recall that Nicander had either red hair or blue eyes."

No. And no one else would recall that either, since the real daughter of Nicander had had hair as black as night, and eyes dark as deep wells. "My father the king's hair was black as the pines after the sun goes down," I said, hoping poetry might distract the king. "Thank you for this lovely gown, sir."

He had not noticed what I was wearing and looked blankly at the gown. It was for a girl much older than I, pale pink, embroidered with roses and bordered in white. It was loot. I thought about loot. Why be loot if such could be avoided? Why be a slave?

If Chrysaor and Iris never admitted that I existed—well, then, I would not admit they existed.

To deny one's father and mother is probably a very bad thing and it is no doubt worse to pretend another set of parents altogether. Kind as they had been, Nicander and Petra had never called me daughter. Friends though we were, Callisto had never called me sister. But I required a lineage and theirs was excellent.

I said to the king of the Main Land, "Fire chased the pirates out of my palace before they reached our treasury. I think all our treasure still lies within." For Nicander had been a successful sacker of cities since paying off Apollo. "I trust that you will keep my treasure safe for me, O king, so that when I am grown and you give me in marriage to a noble, I will have an island and much gold to bestow upon my husband."

The king's men stood tensely awaiting his answer. Of course they hoped he would laugh at a little girl. They wanted that gold divided among themselves.

I fixed my eyes upon the king's.

"You have guarded your treasure well, little princess," said Menelaus. "I give you my word. I will keep it in trust for you."

"Thank you, my king," I said, as if I had expected nothing less. "Will you leave a man here to take care of me?"

Menelaus was astonished. "My dear princess, you cannot possibly stay here. It will take a year to rebuild your palace and you have no flocks and no people. You will come home with me. I have a daughter with whom you will be friends. She is younger than you. She's nine, while you look about twelve. I recall that none of Nicander's sons lived. I should

45

remember the name of his precious daughter, but I do not. Please give me your name."

I dislike silent prayer. The mind of a human is too small for a god to listen to. To be heard from the sky, a human must call out. But I had no choice.

O goddess! Hear me even in silence. Is it evil to claim the name and lineage and island of Callisto?

I heard my goddess clearly.

I am with you.

So I had been wrong. The gods could hear a silent prayer.

"My name," I said to the king of the Main Land, "is Callisto. It means 'the fairest.' "

Menelaus smiled at me. "And the right name for you, my princess. You are fair indeed."

And so, for the second time in my life, a king carried me across the water and brought me to his house to be companion to his daughter. Again I sat on a decked ship to listen to the stories of a king.

Menelaus loaded my treasure into his vessels to be taken to his own palace, where it would be stored apart, Menelaus assured me, and saved for my dowry.

"But I am surprised you have room in the hollow ships for yet more treasure," I said to him. "You must have great booty from your latest expedition." I thought that I would chat with him for a while and then mention the sails of the twisted fish; I would tell him of my plans for revenge and seek his help. He was a great king who had traveled much of the world. He might know who those pirates had been.

"I collected a little tribute," said Menelaus, "but I did

not sail to sack cities. You see, Callisto, my kingdom, my beloved Sparta, has been ravaged for two winters with a horrible illness. People get a raging fever, and just as they seem to get well, the stomach bursts and they die. We have lost hundreds to this, even strong men and young wives. I went to Delphi to ask the Lord Apollo how to stop this plague that he had sent. His oracle told me to cross the sea to Troy, which has a very important altar, and make offerings to the Palladium."

The very same god had taken all those baby sons from Nicander. Now I learned that he would kill hundreds of strong men and young wives. How could men worship this god? On the other hand—how could they not?

O my king! I thought, but the king in my heart was Nicander.

"You weep," said Menelaus gently.

"For my father," I said, and it was only half a lie. I opened my mouth to tell Menelaus about the twisted fish when it occurred to me that the pirates might be his allies, having just paid tribute themselves. Menelaus might care more about them than about me.

Besides, the real Callisto would never have considered taking revenge. The living Petra probably was not considering it now. She was a lady. Even in the suffering of slavery, she would not think of using a weapon, shoving sharp bronze between ribs and into a heart. Although I considered myself as hard as the soles of my feet had once been, I too must be soft.

So I said, "What is the Palladium?"

"The most ancient form of the goddess Athena. I shivered to be near it. She came as a huge stone from the sky, pocked and pitted and very strange."

A stone goddess out of the sky? "I wish I could have seen that!" I told him.

"It was long ago. But some were there to see her come. They brought her to the pinnacle of Troy and built a temple around her. The sacred place is open to the heavens, so the goddess need not lose sight of home. I knelt and drew on that power, to save Sparta from plague."

"And did the goddess answer? Is the plague over and gone?"

He took a long slow breath. "I do not yet know. Kinados, my captain, changed course when he saw the blackened height of Siphnos town. Many of my ships continued on to the Main Land. When we arrive at Gythion, therefore, my people will be expecting me, streaming down from Amyklai and Sparta to welcome me home, and they will tell me, and then I will know."

I listened carefully.

He called everything "mine." *My* people. *My* captain. I too, now a princess, must refer to *my* people, *my* palace. Anaxandra never existed, I said to myself. I am Callisto. Princess. Daughter of Nicander and Petra. Heiress to the Isle of Siphnos.

"I am not quite sure of your many place names, O king," I told him, omitting that I had grown up in a place without any name at all. "Sparta. Amyklai. Gythion. Will you tell me about your Main Land?"

"The Main Land is very great and divided into many kingdoms. The largest kingdom belongs to my brother, Agamemnon. My part of the Main Land is Sparta, which is both kingdom and city. But I do not live in the city. I live in my palace, Amyklai, several miles south of Sparta town. First we will land at my port, Gythion."

Menelaus and his people had very different Greek from the speech of the pirates. The king made long puffs of air around each consonant, giving each word its own breeze. Every *khhhh* and *phhhh* and *quhhh* made his speech slower than mine. In comparison, my words tumbled harshly like pebbles. I expanded my syllables with "h"s. "What gift could be fine enough for the Palladium goddess?" I wanted to know.

"I gave my best statues of marble and ivory, cloaked in purple wool embroidered by my wife, Helen, who is a brilliant needlewoman. I gave alabaster urns, gold cups, silver vases. Anything, in short, that could not be turned into a weapon."

"Would they have fought you?" I said excitedly.

"Troy would fight anybody. Troy can make weapons without end. They cannot be beaten in war. They possess so much tin they don't even work it, but just leave it lying around in warehouses."

Everything I heard about Troy was so hard to believe. Copper is an easy sail away, being mined out of the island of Cyprus. But bronze requires tin, very hard to come by. No one even knows where tin is mined, because it has to pass through so many merchants on so many ships. "Is it true that Trojan horses are twice the size of ours?"

"It is true. You'll see when you reach my palace at Amyklai, for I bought six Trojan stallions and fourteen mares. It is no easy thing to get a stallion into a boat and less easy to keep him there. Those ships I pray have already reached the Main Land. Their captains were eager to unload such difficult cargo. I shall tell you an amazing thing, Callisto." Menelaus began laughing. His captain Kinados sat beside us for a moment and shared the laughter.

49

I did not laugh. He had called me Callisto. It is a shivery thing to seize the name of another. It is a shivery thing to cease being oneself. If this king and this captain found out, what would they do to me?

"In Troy," said Menelaus, "they sit upon the backs of their horses as we do on mules and donkeys."

I did not tell the king I already knew about this. "How do they hold on?"

"Tightly," said Menelaus, and the three of us laughed together.

"Did you try, my king?" I asked.

He shook his head. "They offered me a gentle one and said I would have no trouble, but I could not see the point."

Kings were not stable boys, to handle animals. In parade, Menelaus would ride in a carved and painted cart, sitting on cushions his queen had embroidered, while his driver managed the horse. In battle, Menelaus in his armor would stand up in the chariot while the driver held the reins. I could not imagine Menelaus with his feet sticking out on either side of a rearing stallion, but I imagined myself. My stallion would gallop as I clung to his mane. Together we would leap over stone walls and my stallion would paw the air with his front hooves.

"Oddly enough," said Menelaus, "Troy will soon be sending a delegation to me, for almost the same reason I went to Troy. The king of Troy, whose name is Priam, has a son named Paris."

"The king of Troy," interrupted the captain, "has *fifty* sons."

"No, he doesn't." I was laughing. "No woman could bear fifty sons."

"True," said Menelaus. "But Priam has many wives. I have

50

never seen such a thing and I have traveled much of the world. My wife, Helen, would not be amused were I to wed time and again."

"And were you to keep every one of those wives in the same palace with her," said Kinados, "Helen would put a knife through you."

He and Menelaus laughed.

"I myself have three sons," Menelaus told me, "and think myself lucky. Two of my boys are older than Hermione, the daughter with whom you will play, and one little more than a babe. But imagine having fifty sons! Anyway, Priam's son Paris is careless and wild and spoiled. He was playing with the child of one of his father's generals and got too rough. He accidentally stabbed the little boy with his sword."

I hated stories where children died. "Was the little boy all right?"

"No. He died in anguish when the wound turned putrid. Myrrh was brought, and packed into the depths of the cut, and even myrrh had no effect."

Myrrh is rare and costly. I have never seen it myself. I believe it to be the resin of the tree of life. Nicander once told me that myrrh is so far away, the man who harvests it must walk on land for an entire year before he reaches the Aegean Sea.

"Of course Paris paid the family a large death duty," said Menelaus, "but he is stained by his deed and must cleanse himself. Now it is I who can offer the remedy. My temple of Apollo was built long ago in honor of Hyacinth, a boy whom the god Apollo—in similar fashion—killed by mistake."

I had not known that gods made mistakes. Were they not less god for having done so? And if gods made mistakes, why were they not kinder to men who made mistakes? If Apollo killed Hyacinth by mistake, why didn't he forgive Nicander, who had given Apollo a leaden egg by mistake?

But of course, Nicander had made no mistake. He had just cheated. And while Menelaus was making a mistake thinking that I was the daughter of Nicander, I was not making a mistake claiming it. I was cheating.

I wondered how a god as cruel as Apollo would make me pay.

"I am chief priest of Apollo's sanctuary," said Menelaus, "so I will cleanse the Trojan prince."

"Are you not worried that this prince Paris, when he comes, will look around and see how *your* kingdom might be attacked?"

"Couldn't be done. Sparta is inland, wrapped in mountain ranges impossible to penetrate. Attackers would have to land at Gythion, leave their ships and walk two days through a land they do not know. It's difficult land, ledge and crag and hidden glens—where my men can lie in ambush. Along the way I have a dozen watchtowers. It would not matter how much tin sits in a Trojan storeroom across the sea. Invaders would have no hope. Indeed," said the king of Sparta, "I look forward to showing a prince of Troy that I too cannot be beaten."

Quickly he threw wine into the sea to placate any listening god, for it not good for a man to utter such a boast.

All men can be beaten.

V

AND SO WE LANDED in Gythion, where wharves stretched into the blue cauldron of a vast bay and the slate roofs of storehouses and workshops were strewn for a mile.

Upon the sand, seagoing craft of all sizes were beached. Men were blackening hulls with pitch, making rope for rigging, and carving oars. Women were sewing together the many patches of linen required to make a sail, for no loom can weave so wide a cloth. Shipbuilders were hewing beams. Open-fronted potteries held thousands of bowls in towering stacks. Immense enclosures for sheep and cattle soon to be sold or slaughtered filled the air with the rich scent of manure and hide.

All these lay abandoned as the people sprang forward to welcome their king and tell him the good news that the plague was over.

It was a day of terrible heat. The sun leaned down to burn the skin and blind the eye. Menelaus had been oiled by his slaves so his skin would gleam, for the face of a god shines, and a king is arm to the gods. On his red hair sat a helmet cut through with holy shapes. From his shoulders hung an ivory-hilted sword, useless in battle, breathtaking in parade. His cape was embroidered with hundreds of arrows flying in all directions, the back panel woven with stallions chasing the wind while apple green oceans lay under blood-red skies. Queen Helen had made it, the captain Kinados told me.

Men waiting on shore gave Menelaus the right hand of friendship and clasped his shoulder. Women knelt to embrace his knees. They all came: salt merchants and elegant ladies, little boys and sagging grandmothers and potters with clay-stained hands.

We waded through crowds as deep as the water we had just left.

Every citizen needed to touch him or his garments. I knew that kings were holy, but I had not seen a people worship their king. How proud Helen must be of such a husband. How eager to see him after so long a separation. How excited his four children, who would soon embrace a father returned in honor. A king whose prayers end plague is held in the cup of the gods' love.

Gythion was *unwalled*. How strange to be inside a town and yet be able to look out. Gythion did not have the tight huddled anxiety of Siphnos. It was noisy and relaxed. Its central square was not square at all, but just an openness, called an agora, with a stone floor and stone benches. Trellises gave shade, black poplars stood behind a splashing fountain, and red flowers bloomed in great clay jugs.

The priests had already begun the roasting of the gods' portion from the many sacrifices, and slaves carried forth the feast. There were fat twisted loaves of bread and bowls of black olives and stiff cool celery. There were casseroles of barley, cheese and onions, into which people dipped fingers or bread. There were poppy seed cakes and honey cakes with currants.

And there was shopping.

On Siphnos, we traded. Villagers brought cheese from their sheep or yogurt from their goats; fishermen came with their catch; traders landed with wheat and rope and furniture. These were laid out on canvas or dropped on the sand. Now and then a vendor might erect an awning to keep the sun off fresh berries.

But Gythion had buildings for no purpose except the exchange of goods. These were arranged row upon row, their fronts open to the air, but their roofs permanent. Hundreds of people gawked and traded, arguing furiously about a fair exchange.

There were perfumes and rouge, eye color and lip balm. Rings of gold and anklets inlaid with carnelian. Razors and combs, an ostrich egg and the ivory tusks of some great creature. Swords and daggers, double axes and arrowheads.

There were leeks and scallions, pomegranates and figs, and salt in great barrels; cassia to control the bowel and hyssop to cure leprosy.

There were mirrors and vases, idols and statues. Painted tables, sturdy stools. Feathered caps and bronze scimitars. Flutes of wood and lyres of tortoiseshell.

There was a slave market.

One does not normally give slaves a thought. But a very pretty pair of girls my own age were lifted up on the sale table.

If Menelaus found out that I whom he rescued had stolen a birthright, slavery would be the best I could expect. Being flung off a cliff like a newborn unworthy of its father was more likely.

I was surrounded by trembling slaves, fearful of who

might purchase them and for what use. Fine strong men in shackles awaited the field or salt mine. Young women nursed babies, which would be taken from them so the breast could be used for the master's child. There were weavers for sale, potters and jewelers, holding up examples of their accomplishments, that they might be judged worthy.

I entered the nearest booth and examined vests and kilts made of thick leather for men who could not afford armor. These were an unlikely purchase for me so I moved on. Sponges were available at many stands. One needs a sponge for hygiene. I picked them over.

Behind me, the slave trader called out the final bid on the twins.

A princess, I said to myself, does not notice slaves. I am Callisto of Siphnos. I do not give slaves a thought.

In the next booth were dyes in copper vats: arsenic to make bright yellow and madder for dark red.

I thought of color. How many people knew that Callisto had had black hair? That Callisto had been crippled?

From booth to booth I walked in a daze, thinking of all that could go wrong; of all, indeed, that was wrong with the whole undertaking.

And yet, my goddess had agreed with me. I must hold on to that.

In a jewelry booth, I found something I could not identify. It was a tiny jar, the length of my finger, and hardly twice as wide.

I forgot everything as I held this amazing jar. *I could see through it.* The merchant dropped a shiny red bead into the jar *and I could still see the bead.* It broke all the rules of a container. It contained, but did not hide.

"What treasure have you found, my princess?" said Menelaus, smiling down.

"A magic jar," I told him.

"Not magic, but glass. It comes from Egypt. I have sailed there twice and met their king. They are a very strange people."

"Glass," I whispered, stroking the smooth surface of the magic jar.

Menelaus bought it for me.

The merchant lowered my glass into a bag of soft kidskin, and told me never to drop the glass or let it tip over, because it broke more easily than hearts.

"She is too young to know about broken hearts," said Menelaus. I saw that he had not really been smiling at me. He was smiling at the world. He was home. His queen, beautiful Helen, would have ruled in his stead, as had Petra in Nicander's absence. She would have planned a storm of joy to welcome him back.

I held tightly to my new treasure.

And there was also the treasure of Nicander to consider. Did I now own everything Nicander owned?

If so, I was a greater pirate than anyone on earth.

For I had stolen an island.

We were to spend the night in the house of a noble named Axon. The house of Axon was larger than the palace of Nicander. Yet it was spare and unwelcoming. No tapestry brought warmth to the walls and no clay pot spilled over with flowers. I saw no altar. I shivered to come and go from a dwelling where no god watched the threshold.

After Menelaus and Axon exchanged greetings and gifts, I

was brought forward. "This," said Menelaus, putting a hand on my head, "is the only surviving child of Nicander of Siphnos. Every ship and farmer, every sheep and slave she owned is gone. Yet the pirates fled before reaching the treasury."

"So her dowry includes an island and Nicander's treasure," said Axon thoughtfully. He seemed puzzled. "I was a great friend of your father, little princess," he said slowly. "Of course he loved you so."

I could think of nothing safe to say to Axon, but a silent girl is a good girl. I kept my eyes down. His toes were so long they lapped over the edges of his sandals like misplaced fingers. His hairy ankles bulged with blue veins. The torchlight made a cruel shadow of his potbelly. "You grace your father's name," said Axon. "Yet I know your father Nicander feared for your health."

Children recovered from sickness. I, Callisto, could recover from being crippled. "My parents offered many prayers during my long illness," I said, "sacrificing often. The goddess healed me. Where I was weak, now I am strong."

"How wonderful," said Axon, but he was still puzzled. He took a lock of my hair in his fingers.

It was good he had not touched my hand, for my flesh had gone as cold as winter. I raised my face and smiled into the man's eyes. "My mother the queen often said that my hair is like rose petals," I told Axon. "She said red hair is an uncommon gift from the gods, and she often gave thanks."

"And so do we all," said Axon, smiling and relaxed. "Who could not rejoice in such beauty?"

Twelve is a gawky skinny age. Only my hair was beautiful. I wondered what color Hermione's hair was, daughter of golden Helen and flaming Menelaus.

The two slave women came with me to my room and

when it was time to wash, I gestured that they might also bathe, and we had a happy time of it, for cleanliness is joy to a woman. Afterward, we used fragrant oil on our skin. The women knelt to me, holding up their hands and beseeching in their own language. They hoped not to be sold in the market. I held them by the back of the neck, they in submission and I in ownership.

In the morning, I thought, I will beg the king's permission to keep these two.

Then I remembered that I was a princess. In the morning, I would inform Menelaus of my decision.

Axon's courtyard was grim and cold in the hour before sunrise. I was wildly excited and also afraid, for I did not know how far on top of the Main Land my goddess could come.

I wanted to cling to my women's hands, and the real Callisto would have, but I wished to be a different Callisto. A stronger, more regal Callisto. So I did not hold a slave's hand. I stood as straight as the oar of Nicander's grave.

Menelaus drew me aside. He looked very stern. The half-light of dawn cast harsh shadows over his face. His eyes, sharp now, not gentle, examined me from hair to sandals. Then he took my right hand and studied my palm, tracing the life line.

Axon had told the king his suspicions. Menelaus knew now that the princess Callisto ought to be crippled and dark-haired. He who had so kindly bought me a magic jar would despise me. I was a cheat and a liar, to be sold on the table like the twins who had trembled before their buyers.

"Little princess," said Menelaus, "Axon has offered to marry you. It is a good offer. He will fortify your father's island and resettle it. He will care for your inheritance and make it grow. Your sons will enter the world with a fine lineage."

Even though I had spoken the word "dowry" to coax Menelaus to guard the treasure, and even though last night Axon had used that same word, twelve-year-olds do not think of marriage.

No doubt possession of an island helped my looks. No doubt I would appear beautiful to any man in need of treasure. But Axon was old. Older than Menelaus. He was fat and wrinkled and his toes were too long. He did not even have an altar at his front door so that gods could come and go.

But the danger was more profound. Marriage is a vow. Dared I, in the company of gods, take a vow in the name of Callisto? I, Anaxandra?

It is an offense to the gods to throw away your lineage, since the gods chose it for you. I had offended and did not shrink from the offense. I had stolen a birthright and did not shrink from that either. But steal a marriage? Axon would want sons. He would believe those sons to carry the blood of Nicander. But they would not.

"Axon tells me Nicander's daughter is fifteen," said Menelaus. "I would not have guessed this. You are nearly as small as my Hermione, who is nine."

Actually I was shaped like twig off a tree and probably looked precisely like Hermione. If I said I was fifteen, Menelaus would make the dowry arrangements immediately and I would be Axon's wife by nightfall. But if I admitted to being twelve, I would be unmasked.

"I am fifteen, but because of my lengthy illness," I said, "I am behindhand and have not yet become a woman."

A potential husband would think twice when he learned that. Suppose his bride were barren. Suppose she could not give him sons. Of what use was such a woman, even with an island?

"I see," said the king. "Axon and I will discuss it further. Meanwhile, you will come home with me and play with Hermione. Come. We set off for Amyklai."

I had been told that it was two days' walk to Amyklai, a thing I could not imagine, since the hike across Siphnos at its very widest took but two hours. "Wouldn't it be quicker to sail?" I asked.

"There is no water. We are leaving the sea behind." And with that impossible remark, Menelaus put me in the care of the two serving women, and all three of us in the care of a male slave named Tenedos.

Tenedos led us through the alleys of Gythion and north of the town. We never passed through a gate and we never saw a wall. If I were attacking Menelaus, I thought, I would sail quietly up the far coast and seize all the tiny villages in every tiny inlet, and then I would approach Gythion from behind and take it by land instead of by sea.

But these were the thoughts of a pirate, not a princess. I had to think of other things. And then I laughed aloud, for there indeed were other things.

The Trojan horses.

Their great rippling flanks gleamed where grooms had brushed them. Into their long tossing manes had been tied ribbons and on their traces were medallions, glittering in the first rays of sun. One matched pair was black as starless night. Another pair was sable and several were white. The horses were very nervous and people stayed well back when one stallion reared and snorted. He was dark creamy gold, like topaz. A strike from his great hoof would break your leg. His groom spoke tenderly to him. "Good boy, Sea Belt," crooned the groom, and slowly the horse calmed, although it continued to mutter under its breath.

The eldest son of Troy's king Priam, Hector, was famous as a tamer of horses. I had not understood how a man could achieve fame for putting reins on a horse. Now I knew. I edged closer.

The groom smiled at me. "You like horses?"

"I love horses," I told him.

He put an apple core in my hand. The topaz horse whickered softly and lowered its great head into my palm to take the treat. Then the stallion nodded its head up and down as if saying thanks.

"Trojans speak Greek," said the groom, "although with strange accents. But it means that I can use the same names for these horses that their trainers used. This is Sea Belt. The black pair with stars between their eyes are Sea Star and Sea Reach."

"I had a puppy once named Seaweed," I told him.

"Isn't that interesting? I ran into a captain last year whose ship dog was named Seaweed."

My heart was sundered. Should I ask for the name of that captain? The age of his dog, Seaweed? The names of that captain's sons . . . and daughter?

The topaz horse nibbled the grass at my feet and I pressed my face into its long windblown mane.

Tenedos said, "Little princess, you must stay beside me. Take my hand, please."

I turned my back on the groom, who had perhaps listened to the bark of my puppy, Seaweed, and shared a cup with my father, Chrysaor. I put them out of my mind, for mine must be the mind of Callisto.

Behind the Trojan horses were carts filled with Trojan gifts and Siphnos treasure. My dowry.

On my birth island, there had been one or two carts. Their wheels were always breaking from jouncing over stones, so everyone preferred donkeys. On Siphnos, there had been several carts, whose proud owners painted them in vivid colors. But wheels remained a problem, for the punishment taken by wheels quickly destroys them.

These carts were different. Some had not two wheels, but four. Some were pulled not by one mule, but by a pair of oxen. One immense wagon had four oxen. The wheels of this cart were bound in bronze. It kept the wheels alive longer, Tenedos explained.

For this journey, the king himself would stand up in a chariot until he had left the crowds behind, while Axon and the other Gythion nobles walked alongside, spilling wine to keep the feet of the king safe on his journey.

The path was so wide that two carts could pass each other, and it was not simply made of beaten dirt, but spread with gravel. "What a remarkable path," I said to Tenedos.

"It is called a road. The gravel makes the way smooth for wheels. When it rains upon such a road, there are no ruts and no mud. And when we reach the king's palace, the road will be paved."

"What does that mean?"

"Slabs of stone," said Tenedos, "as if the palace courtyard extended out beyond the walls, all the way down the citadel ramp and far into the valley."

"The king must have many men, if they can be spared to lift stones into place for a cart track."

"Menelaus' kingdom is far flung," said Tenedos in a tired

voice. Perhaps he had once thought himself safe from the far-flung power of Menelaus. Perhaps he had once been free. "There are about three thousand people in Amyklai," Tenedos told me, "and Menelaus owns a dozen such cities."

My jaw dropped at the thought of so many people on earth. And had not Menelaus himself told me that his brother Agamemnon had an even larger kingdom? And had not everybody said Troy was the largest of all? How many people lived and breathed in this world?

"In his palace of Amyklai alone," Tenedos went on, "are five hundred female slaves and about that many slave children."

He himself must have been a child when captured, for if he had been an adult, he would have been killed.

When we had left the city behind, the king stepped out of his chariot. His men removed the wheels, folded up the basket and set it on top of the four-ox wagon and the king walked, as did we all. A white mule with exceptionally long ears walked placidly near him, in case he should wish to ride, but I knew that he would not. I have heard that in some parts of the world, people do not use their legs. I would not want to abandon my body like that and a king among his troops would never do so.

A slave named Pyros jogged back and forth along the line, making sure every cart rolled smoothly, every slave walked swiftly and every order was obeyed. "Pyros" means "fire," but in the overseer's case, it was not the comforting fire of the hearth. The slaves were afraid of Pyros and it infected me. When Pyros whipped a laggard on both cheeks with a leather-bound rod, my fingers tightened convulsively on Tenedos' hand.

"It's all right, princess," said Tenedos softly. "The over-seer will not scold you."

"Isn't your name, Tenedos, the name of an island?"

"Yes, lady. Tenedos is the island of my birth. It is not far from Troy, but we were never Trojan allies. We thought our-selves neutral and a friend to all. We were wrong. When Tenedos was sacked, we younger boys were taken as slaves, but none of us were permitted to keep our names, as it was too much trouble. We are all just called Tenedos."

I knew what it was to be sacked. I knew the number of bodies left unburied and the sobs of women in the boats. "When was this?" I asked, wondering how old he was. House slaves last better than field slaves.

"When I was ten, which—"

Pyros thrashed Tenedos on the back of the neck, where the spine ends, and hit him a second time on the side of his head, just above the ear. Tenedos staggered slightly.

"Do not bother a princess with your past!" snapped Pyros. "You are nothing. Your past does not matter."

Tenedos apologized to me.

I spoke as a princess would. "I will decide whether a slave requires punishment," I said sharply to Pyros. But per-haps a princess would not say that, because she would not notice how a slave was treated. I had much to consider.

Without warning, and although it was midday, we en-tered a shocking darkness. It was black yet green, filling the world from earth to sky. It was the dark of trees and yet not of trees. It was evil. "What is this?" I whispered. I wound my fingers around each other to keep from grabbing the hand of Tenedos yet again.

"It is called a forest, my princess. Many trees in one

place, so dense they blot out the sky, like the evil message of an eclipse. I too hate the forest. On my island, like yours, few trees stand together. We will walk for an hour among these pines before the forest ends."

Nicander's bard used to sing a poem:

> *Seven ways of terror*
> *in a forest all of pine.*
> > *The empty.*

Now I understood the words.

"Do not leave the path," said Tenedos, as if I had considered this for one moment. "The leaves that brush your face are the souls of those who died unburied."

But Pyros heard this and hit him again. "Don't talk nonsense, slave. Princess, the trees are just firewood. One day men will cut it all down. Anyway, we are armed. Neither man nor beast will hurt you."

Tenedos and I were not worried about man or beast. When the overseer moved on, Tenedos hissed to scare away spirits. "May the daimon of this grove take Pyros and—" With an effort, Tenedos stopped himself from cursing in my presence. I was sorry, because a good collection of curses is a useful thing, and Tenedos probably knew some I had not yet heard. I almost told Tenedos that I agreed with him, Pyros was just a dog tick, but remembered in time that I was the princess Callisto.

At last we broke out from the evil shade.

Before us lay tilted fields sliced apart by dark hollows and rocky gorges. The Sparta before us was an unquiet land, skeletal, spines of rock and ribs of stone. White and black and brown sheep wandered, too many to count even with the word "thousand." Flocks of wild doves burst out of bushes. Before us were mountains so high they invaded the gods' sky.

So this was the Main Land. How could the people of Menelaus bear to live under these great mountains, close to the dark of that awful forest?

But they did not live close, I discovered, for we walked on and on.

We passed fields of flax being harvested with scythes. I had never seen this, and I found the rhythm and the gleam of the curved blades quite beautiful. Having set in motion my new life, could I keep it swinging back and forth, like a scythe? Or like a scythe, would it cut my throat?

We came upon slaves knee-deep in pools of water, treading on the flax to soften the stalks so that the linen thread could be removed. It was strange water, having motion but not waves.

"The Eurotas River," Tenedos told me. "It runs even in the heat of summer."

I had never seen a river, only seasonal brooks from spring rains. And in all my life I had heard of only one river, the river at Troy, the great Hellespont. Since his birth island was close to Troy, Tenedos must have seen that. "Is this what the Hellespont is like?" I said eagerly.

He nearly laughed out loud. "No. Up this little stream, one man could pole a boat. In the Hellespont, forty rowers could row till their hearts burst and hardly make progress against the current."

We passed through fields of clover and red wheat, olive orchards frothing silver leaves like the foamy sea and clusters of tiny stone houses. At the doorstep of a cottage, an old woman milking her goat let me drink out of the pail. It was warm and thick.

"This Main Land," I said to Tenedos, "is a wondrous place. I did not know there were mountains as high as gods. I never dreamed of roads, or roads made of stone. You know, the first time I saw stairs—" I chopped off my statement. It was Anaxandra who could remember the first time she saw stairs. Callisto had been born into a house with stairs. "Tell me about the family of King Menelaus," I ordered him.

Tenedos broke off high slender grass and chewed the end of it. "The household is confusing. Menelaus married Helen, a daughter of the king of Sparta. From this marriage, Menelaus' land greatly increased. All you see within the embrace of those distant mountain ranges and all the way back behind us to the sea is the kingdom of Menelaus. Now, Helen also has twin brothers, much older than she, named Castor and Pollux, who also possess much land."

"I know about Castor and Pollux," I said delightedly. "They sailed with Jason on the *Argo* to bring back the Golden Fleece. Every bard who ever visited Siphnos sang of Jason's voyage."

"You will hear them sing even more now," said Tenedos dryly. "Castor and Pollux never tire of hearing how wonderful they are. The twins have even coaxed the astronomers at the palace to name stars in their honor."

A princess should not let a slave speak badly of his betters. I should have Pyros use his whip. But I wanted Tenedos silent about my stair mistake, so I let it pass. I said, "I have never heard of the naming of stars."

He stared at me. "But how do you study them, as they

68

cross the sky every night?" When I had no answer to this, Tenedos chewed down hard on his grass and said, "Queen Helen has a sister Clytemnestra, and Clytemnestra married the older brother of Menelaus, who is Agamemnon, strongest king in the world. So two sisters married two brothers. Agamemnon's far-flung lands are beyond those mountains on the north. When the brothers visit each other, they do not cross the mountain range, for the pass is fit only for wild goats. Each king returns to the sea and sails to his brother's port."

I drew a picture in my head of marriage lines between the brothers. I drew lines down for the children of each king. With a sickening thud in my heart, I realized that I had paid little attention to the genealogy of Callisto. No noble child exists who cannot preach the family genealogy. I would be expected to recite it back ten generations. I began piecing together the lineage. I knew the parents and grandparents of both Petra and Nicander. Could I recall anything more than that?

"The sisters Helen and Clytemnestra are the most beautiful women in the world," said Tenedos. "Helen is so lovely that goddesses are jealous. But even the jealousy of a goddess cannot hurt Helen. In fact, nothing can hurt Helen, for she does not have an earthly father. She is the daughter of the Lord God Zeus."

I had known this, of course; all the world knew. But now I would meet her. Was Helen fully human or would I be able to tell that she was half god? Was her blood red like mine? Would she know things, the way immortal gods did? Would she know, for example, that I was not Callisto? "What did Zeus look like?" I asked. "Did Helen's earthly mother tell anybody? Was he a giant with huge muscles and a curly beard?"

Tenedos shook his head. "Zeus came to Helen's mother in the form of a swan."

"Oh." I was blank. "What is a swan?"

Tenedos sucked in his breath and held it.

In his silence, I heard a thousand noises: the creak of wheels and axles; the panting and wheezing of donkeys and mules; the clopping feet of oxen and horses; the slap of sandals; the talk and laughter of men.

"Little princess," said the slave softly, "the court of Menelaus and Helen is sophisticated, and you have been isolated. You have never seen glass, don't know what a river is, have never walked on a road, do not know the names of stars, have never seen a swan. Here is my advice to you. Stay silent. Be fearful of Helen. The daughter of a god pays no price for any action she takes. She cannot suffer and so does not discern the suffering of others."

How dare a slave speak like that of his queen? I was angry with him.

But—*Listen carefully,* said my goddess. *You enter a strange world under a false name. He is an ally. Be thankful.*

Pyros missed nothing. He was beside us in an instant, eager to inflict pain. "The slave has offended you?" he asked me eagerly, flourishing his whip. I thought I knew how he had come by the name Fire. He burned to hurt Tenedos.

And then I saw sailing on the Eurotas River several large and beautiful birds whose slender heads turned on remarkable long thin white necks to study me. "In the river," I said to Pyros. "What are those?"

Pyros turned but saw nothing worthy of comment.

"Those are swans, princess," said Tenedos.

In such a shape had Zeus visited the mother of Helen.

How white Helen's skin must be. How long and slender her throat. How graceful her profile.

We walked on. I dreamed of swans and cold clear gods.

"Swans are vicious," said Tenedos. "Be careful of swans, my princess."

VI

THE WALLS OF SIPHNOS were a sheepfold compared to the walls of Amyklai.

Men standing on the shoulders of men standing on the shoulders of men could not have touched the top of Menelaus' wall. Above his immense gate, stone lions snarled at one another. They were not painted the tawny color of the wild, but scarlet. Their eyes and fangs and claws were laid with gold leaf.

Had I been six years old, and newly come from a primitive rock, I would have thought the lions frozen where they fought, forced to stand forever with fangs bared and claws drawn. I knew now that the hand of man had sculpted them. And yet the lions had such strength I could readily believe that one day they would leap down and tear to pieces those who tried to pass beneath them.

That night I met the lion.

Her name was Helen.

O Helen.

Think of hot gold infused on icy silver.

Think of a soft blue sky over an iron-hard sea.

The warmest sun and the coldest marble.

Helen. Swan and goddess.

But Menelaus did not notice. He gave his wife a mild hug, as if she were his sister. She in turn smiled briefly and returned to her embroidery. Her yarn was green shot through with sun, like the sea underwater. Elderly maids sat by her side, on stools so low their knees touched their chins, and threaded her needle for her.

Menelaus boxed fondly with his older sons, Aethiolas and Maraphius, who looked about ten and twelve. They were hopping up and down with the joy of having their father home. "Don't go anywhere without us next time, Father."

"Let's go hunting, Father!"

"We've trained new dogs, Father! Wait till you see."

"Father, let's—" and they had a great list of things to do together: wrestling, chariot racing, ball games, hunting boars, running the hounds.

Menelaus tossed his baby boy Pleisthenes into the air and a cascade of giggles came from the pretty child.

With Hermione, a fragile copy of her beautiful mother, the king was gentle, but Hermione was as wildly excited as her brothers. "I'm so glad you're home, Father!" she cried, wrapping her arms around him and tugging on his flaming beard. "I missed you so. Nobody else will play checkers or pegs or kings with me."

"That's because you can't bear to lose," said her father affectionately. "And nobody but me can tolerate your tears."

"I've outgrown tears," said Hermione haughtily. "I have not cried at the end of a board game in months."

"Because you haven't played in months, Hermione," said her brother Maraphius. "You're still a crybaby."

Hermione flew at her brother, her frail fists as effective as dust kittens.

Helen's long slender fingers searched among the bright

yarns spilling out of a silver basket. How fair of skin Helen was. Like the last mother and daughter I had known, Helen and Hermione seemed never to have been under the sun, which was what kept their skin white, but would also keep their lives dull. I expected that they had never seen a swan either, nor trembled in a forest, nor drunk warm milk from a pail.

For the boys, Menelaus brought out sets of toy Trojan soldiers, with shields and spears and even toy greyhounds and horses and chariots.

For Hermione, the king had chosen strange top-heavy dolls. I did not like them.

Hecuba, queen of Troy, whose name I liked, for it had to do with moons and arrows, had sent Hermione a miniature tiara: roses, leaves and thorns beaten out of gold. Hermione's nurse set it gently on the little princess's head and laced her hair through it.

For Helen, Menelaus had brought a silver-rimmed bathtub. It was high and round, just enough room for one person to sit with her knees drawn up as warm water was poured down over her shoulders, to make a lake around her so she might relax her tired limbs. Helen did not look like a person who ever did enough to be that tired. In any event, she hardly glanced at the silver bath, but took another stitch.

The day I was brought to Siphnos, Nicander had forgotten about me, but Menelaus was a greater king and forgot nothing. He took my hand tenderly. "This," said Menelaus, "is a little lost princess. Her name is Callisto. Her father, King Nicander of Siphnos, was killed by pirates as she watched and her mother, Queen Petra, was made a slave, while the palace burned to the ground."

"Oh, how sad!" said Hermione, rushing over to kiss and sorrow with me. "You saw it happen? Callisto, how dreadful. I am glad you are here where it is safe."

"Callisto will be a sister to you, Hermione," said Menelaus. "She will play pegs or kings with you."

I was stunned. Nicander had explained to his family that I was a hostage whose value was gone . . . but this king announced that I was a sister.

And because of my lies.

Hermione clapped so gently that her hands made no sound. "I have two wonderful girl cousins," she confided. "Iphigenia and Electra. They were here all last summer. I loved them. But they aren't coming this year. I'm so glad to have you instead. You must sleep in my room so we never have to stop talking."

"I would be honored to sleep in your room, princess."

"Oh, good. How old are you? I'm nine. Your hair is beautiful but you wear it so plain. Do the ladies on your island not braid their hair?"

I ignored the question about my age. "My mother the queen liked my hair loose. She said it looked like rose petals."

Helen paused in her needlework. Everyone in the room—family, squires, maids, noblemen awaiting assignments—was aware of the change in her. I realized suddenly that the courtiers and servants in this large room had hardly been aware of the touching reunion between father and his children. They watched only Helen. They breathed in her rhythm and looked where her eyes looked.

I too felt the god in her and ached for her approval. When she turned and looked at me at last, an uncertain smile fluttered inside my mouth, eager to jump out and spread my lips and show my joy. I was breathless waiting for her permission to be happy.

"We once entertained Petra and Nicander," said Helen. Her voice had no inflection. It had no wrath, it had no sympathy, it had nothing. It was merely air. "Petra and Nicander attended a festival at our temple of Apollo. They were dark haired." Helen looked me up and down as one examines a slave on the table. The courtiers looked me up and down as one examines a slave on the table. My smile stuck inside.

"Usually," she said, "a child resembles one of her parents."

Fear sucked on me like an octopus.

"None of us has red hair, Mother," Hermione pointed out. "You would think with four children at least one of us would have Father's hair."

"How old are you, girl?" said Helen. Her face showed no more emotion than a statue. The god part of her was made of stone, not swan.

"I am fifteen," I said. "I know I look younger. I had much illness as a child."

"Are you betrothed?" Hermione wanted to know.

"I am not."

"How strange," said Helen. Her eyes hooked mine, as a sharp hook will fasten to a fish. "A king's only child is fifteen years of age and yet that king arranged no betrothal?"

She was right, of course. It was unheard of. What king would allow chance to decide his heir? I could not explain that since Callisto was crippled and likely to be barren, no one wanted her, because now I was Callisto.

I said nothing, and it was the right course, for Helen had arrived at a favorite topic. "I myself at fifteen," said Helen, her voice growing rich and pleased, "had a palace full of suitors."

She was famous for those suitors. There had been so many eager to wed her. As men in athletic competition will become fierce, trying to prove day after day who is strongest and best, so the suitors turned to dueling. Helen's earthly father, the old king of Sparta, did an extraordinary thing to stop the suitors from killing each other. He brought forth his finest stallion, sliced its throat, and made every suitor stand in the blood of the horse. Then they had to swear the most terrible oath known in our times: that the man Helen chose in marriage would forever have the loyalty of all the rest.

The sacrifice of a horse was shocking, because men do not eat horse meat, and a sacrifice is also a feast, and every citizen will partake in the great meal that follows. To make a horse holy is very powerful and strange, as its meat will not be put upon the coals. It must be buried, and the earth around it becomes sacred.

I had heard bards sing about the oath of the horse as many times as I had heard them sing of Jason and the Golden Fleece. I never liked thinking of those young men with their bare feet soaked in blood, but when I looked at Helen, I imagined something more terrible: Helen watching them.

Now she watched me.

The room watched me.

"Recite for me," said Helen, "the genealogy of Petra."

I froze like the boy in Nicander's courtyard. I could not remember one name from that family not my own.

"Petra was distantly related to me," said Helen. "We share the same grandmother five generations back."

Desperation pierced my heart and spread outward into my limbs, as one poisoned by hemlock would die. I clung to my magic jar. I wet my lips.

But it was not magic that saved me. It was a real princess.

"Isn't that good news, Callisto?" cried Hermione. "You and I are cousins then. But I am so sad for you. Your dear father dead and your mother now a slave." Hermione pointed to the maid on Helen's left, a very old woman, hair of silver, hands gnarled and trembling, cheeks wrinkled like last year's apple. One eye was white with the blindness that seals up the sight of the very old. She held her sewing up close to her good eye. She had an enormous workbasket to complete. "Aethra was once a queen," Hermione said. "She belongs to Mother now."

A queen. Hemming sheets instead of resting on them.

"Yes," said Helen. She was pleased at the sight of a queen brought low. "My dear brothers Castor and Pollux brought Aethra to me." Helen put her wool into the silver basket. "Fetch my other embroidery, Aethra. It's upstairs."

The slave woman's stool was low and her body old and stiff. Aethra struggled to her feet. Helen watched bright-eyed, as if enjoying jugglers or gymnasts. When the old queen had made it out of the room, her swollen fingers touching the wall for balance, Helen turned toward me again in her slow considering way. Hers was a remarkably still face, as if halfway between living and dead. "When Queen Petra visited, she told me of the crippled state of her daughter. She showed me the lock of her daughter's hair that she planned to set on the altar of Apollo. It was black."

"You've just gotten Petra and Nicander mixed up with somebody else, Mother," said Hermione.

I should have accepted Axon, I thought. I said, "And

Apollo answered her prayers, O queen, for I am no longer crippled."

The baby boy had been set down. He toddled with the headlong dash of the very small child who cannot stop except by falling. I swung him up to kiss him, praying I could distract Helen. "Hello, Pleisthenes," I said. A long name for a little boy, but it means "strength," and such a virtue requires many syllables.

He beamed at me.

"My name is Callisto," I said to the little boy. The name did not come easily to my tongue. I knew Helen knew I was lying. Because she's half god, I thought. The seeing half.

"We call him Pleis," Hermione told me, poking a sharp finger into her brother's ribs to make him squeal with laughter. "He's just starting to talk. He can say about ten words. Pleis," she crooned, "this is Callisto. Say 'Calli,' Pleis."

The baby grabbed one of my curls and chewed on it. "Calli," he said softly. His chubby arms tightened around my neck and he gave me a wet squashy kiss. My heart flew into his. I loved him.

"Isn't this nice?" said Menelaus in a deep domestic voice. He did not seem a warrior or king. He was just a father, glad to be home, slouched on puffy pillows, watching his children play.

Pleis' clumsy little fingers found the magic jar. "You can't have this," I said to him. "You might put it in your mouth."

"What is it?" said Hermione, interested.

"A magic jar. Your father the king bought it for me."

Menelaus laughed. "It's just glass. A trinket from the bazaar. Helen, we will have Callisto as another daughter until she weds."

"We will not," said the queen. Her voice was bored and

final, as a mistress refusing permission to a slave. She did not bother to glance at me.

"Now, Helen," said her husband, paying just as little attention to her as to a slave. He was half-asleep against soft pillows. Hermione curled up next to him.

The slightest expression touched Helen's smooth face. I could not read it. "I am curious, Menelaus, my husband. Why do you wish to treat this unknown girl as a daughter? This girl with red hair like your own. *Is* she your daughter, Menelaus? You who sail the wide seas for months at a time? You who could have any woman from any isle and I would not be the wiser?"

I dropped my magic jar. The vendor had been right. When it fell on the tiled floor, it split into shards. Pleis was entranced by the sharp shiny pieces and wiggled to get down.

"Now, Helen," said Menelaus, as if she had disagreed with a dinner menu. "Of course not." He gestured to a slave to clean up the broken glass. He yawned and closed his eyes again.

"The isle of Siphnos is out of your way, Menelaus. From Troy, you would sail to Antissa, you would cross the Aegean Sea to Euboea, and then proceed down the coast to Gythion."

"Now, Helen. A ship doesn't control its route as easily as that. Strong wind swept us south the moment we left Troy. We weren't able to cross the Aegean Sea in the north. The winds didn't favor us until we reached Samos." He sat up a little, speaking to his daughter instead of his wife. "On the isle of Samos, they worship the goddess Hera," he told Hermione. "All Hera's statues are copper. Her sanctuary is guarded by peacocks. I brought you tail feathers from the peacock. They're as tall as you are. Green and indigo and sparkling silver."

"Oooooh, lovely," said Hermione. "Let's get them right now."

"I'm too tired. The slaves will bring them in the morning."

As a summer storm rolls over the sky and fills the air with dark anger, so Helen changed from statue to woman. "And Siphnos?" she said sharply.

I had been in her palace but a few hours, and already I knew that with her husband, the daughter of a god had to raise her voice to get attention.

The room shifted uneasily.

"Now, Helen," said Menelaus patiently. "From Samos we wove our way east. That part of the Aegean is so full of islands it's hardly even sailing, it's just paddling from one shore to another. By chance we saw a burned citadel and stopped to see. On the shore, guarding the grave she dug for Nicander, was this brave and true little princess. Naturally I brought her home with me."

Helen twitched her gown as a stalking cat flicks its tail. The great piece of wool she was embroidering fell open on the floor. I was awestruck. From her needle had spilled wild birds and cascading roses, glittering suns and trailing vines, arching lilies and proud stags. I yearned for her to be pleased with me. I wanted to sit by her, to study how she created such beauty, to hand her the wool of her choice and cut the threads with my own knife.

But Helen whirled on me. "How did it happen, girl, that you alone survived such a brutal attack? A king died, yet you lived? An entire town died, yet you escaped? Did you walk away from your destiny? Were you meant to die?"

But Menelaus had not been listening. "Helen, my dear, sing for me, won't you? I have missed your voice."

"Yes, Mother, sing!" cried Hermione. "I want Callisto to hear you. Callisto," she told me, "you have never heard a voice like my mother's."

Hermione was correct. Helen's voice rang low and ominous like distant thunder. She flicked a torrent of notes off a golden lyre while long angry syllables poured from her throat.

> They came armed, the suitors,
> > To see the daughter of the swan.
> They fought each other, the suitors,
> > In duels and to the death,
> From a stallion sired by the wind,
> > Blood poured forth.
> With their feet in the wet hot blood
> They stood, the suitors.
> And they swore, the suitors.
> For love of Helen.
> They swore.

I had expected a typical ladies' lament. Let me love the cry of the lyre; let me soothe with my lullaby; that sort of thing.

When Helen had finished the song, she folded her eyes down, as the eyes of a lion will lower when it has eaten its kill and is sated. She seemed to be within that long-ago circle of suitors, reveling in their desire for her. I knew she remembered every aching glance, every heaving chest and reaching hand.

"That was lovely, dear," said the king sleepily. "It's nice to be home. Although actually they swore for my sake, as you will recall. Since I am the husband you chose."

Helen's eyes opened very wide. She regarded Menelaus as a lion regards prey.

VII

THE CELEBRATION WELCOMING Menelaus lasted for days. But grateful as the people were to Menelaus, it was Helen they loved.

How the multitudes hoped for the privilege of her smile, the sound of her voice, the light touch of her hand in praise. She glided among her people like a swan on the Evrotas River. Her shining hair was pulled up into a cup of beaten gold, and below the gold hung one very thick braid, woven with gold threads. Her earrings were puffy gold biscuits and her necklace a gold filigree.

Her face stayed still. You could read no prophecy, understand no mystery, looking at that smooth facade. But neither could you take your eyes away.

People said there had been a contest once among goddesses to see who was the most beautiful. People said goddesses came in second. Helen was first.

I believed it.

I stayed clear of Helen, having remembered only three generations of Callisto's genealogy. Since I did end up sleeping in Hermione's room, I was afraid Helen would be all too aware of me. But Helen turned out to be aware only of herself. Every day, it took the entire morning for her maids to prepare her hair and complexion, adjust her gown and jewelry, paint her toenails and shadow her eyes. Helen kept her apartments sweet smelling, anointing the pillars with scented oils, rubbing mint against the plaster walls and lavender over her robes. The air around Helen was rich and dusty.

Hermione's room was large and four maids slept on her floor.

But the two women who had helped me on the beach at Siphnos were sold at Helen's instruction. Whatever slave woman was not busy had to fit me in. Once it was Aethra, the old crumpled queen.

I made up names for the rest of the generations. If Helen insisted I had them wrong, I would look confused and bow to her superior knowledge.

It was very hot even after the sun went down, so we slept on Hermione's high porch, hoping for a breeze from the mountains. I had lived on the tops of cliffs, but never at the bottom. I found the sight of those mountains so stirring, so profound. I could more readily imagine Helen sired by a jagged black peak than by a swan.

There were fifty-six rooms on each floor of the palace. I doubt the island of my birth had fifty-six huts. I knew now that Chrysaor's house had been three rooms on a rock; the palace of Nicander merely a pleasant house on a hill.

Wherever I turned at Amyklai were long stairs, long shadows, and bright frescoes on walls.

The royal ladies used a peculiar room, which was on a lower floor. Hermione and Aethra demonstrated several times before I was willing to use the seat.

On my birth island, we used the cliff. We had our favorite spots to sit, my brothers and I, and down our manure would drop, splashing into the sea with a satisfying plop. The peasants went in the straw as did their donkeys, sheep and goats.

Now and then they would throw the old straw into a field and bring in new. At Siphnos, I learned to use pots, which the slave women emptied in the morning and washed in the sea. But in the palace of Amyklai, a clay tunnel ran from a fountain into a tiled room and you sat on a chair while the water in the tunnel carried everything away to a distant pit.

Aethiolus and Maraphius did not simply have manservants; they had tutors whose purpose was instruction, and with these tutors, they had to repeat not only their genealogies back ten generations, but the lineage of all kings and all heroes. Then they had to learn strategies, battles, treaties, and wars.

Every day Hermione wore an amber necklace, a treasure only a princess of great wealth can enjoy. Each bead was a slightly different shade of yellow and inside each bead was frozen a wasp or bee, so Hermione was hung with yellow stinging insects.

I loathed the necklace, but Hermione's nurse, Bia, said it was magic. Hermione said only that her father had brought it when she was very little and put it around her neck himself, so every time she touched it, she thought of him.

A wasp in amber did not describe Menelaus.

It described Helen.

A few days after my arrival, just before sunset, Helen and her women and Hermione walked to the great temple of Apollo. "Here we are, Callisto!" called Hermione, although I was hoping to escape notice. "We'll wait for you."

I dreaded being with Helen and kept my eyes down. When I caught up Helen said, "Girl. Whose gown are you wearing?"

Everyone else said "my princess" or "Callisto." Helen

86

addressed me as a slave. I wondered how long before every-body followed Helen's example.

"The gown is an old one of yours, my queen," said Aethra. "I thought it fitting for a princess."

"It *is* fitting for a princess," said Helen, "so when we return to the palace, take it off that girl."

"Now, Mother," said Hermione. "Father says to be kind to Callisto."

"How like him," said Helen. "Always being kind. Is this a king? A king should stain the world with blood. Bring honor to his name and treasure to his house! A king should live for his spear."

Helen strode on ahead. She was no swan today.

"Father thinks it's funny," whispered Hermione. "He says not to worry, she'll get used to you."

I did not think Helen got used to things any more than Medusa had.

The temple of Apollo stood alone on a rocky ledge in a wide valley. Fifteen pillars by seven, the beautiful sanctuary was painted black, gold, red and blue. It shouted to the gods.

We walked right in, as if we too were gods, and I trembled to be there. It was fine for Helen, daughter of a god, and for Hermione, her child, and even for Aethra, once a queen. But for me?

Inside stood an Apollo three times the size of a man.

The god was losing his paint. In some places, bare marble glowed. Aethra went down with difficulty on her swollen knees to embrace the feet of Apollo. It was adoration that had removed his paint.

Goddess of yesterday, you are so small next to this Apollo. But you must protect me. You let me do this. In fact, you told me to. If anything goes wrong, it's your fault.

Helen went to the god as if he were nobody and fingered the tunic he was wearing. Every year the noblewomen of Amyklai wove Apollo a new tunic. They used flax grown just for that purpose, taking turns at a sacred loom on which nothing else was ever woven.

"You weave, girl, do you not?" said Helen to me.

"Yes, queen!" My heart leaped up. What joy to work on Apollo's tunic.

"The task takes many ladies," said Helen.

"I would be honored," I whispered.

"Oh?" said Helen. "And are you a lady?"

Her loathing scraped me as barnacles on a boat scrape the bare skin.

"You have captivated the king, girl. But it is only the color of your hair, you know."

I stared at the well-kissed hands of Apollo.

"One who lies to the gods brings down their wrath," said Helen. "Plague. Famine. Death. You lie about your heritage."

Aethra spoke as if she were still the equal of Helen, not the property of Helen. "I would think that a king such as Nicander is not a background to be proud of, my queen," said Aethra. "Why would Callisto make such a claim unless it's true?"

"To get an island," said Helen.

In Amyklai, the people did not enter their palace freely.

Those awaiting the king's attention sat in a reception room. There their hands and feet were bathed, that they might not bring uncleanliness into the king's presence. Every petitioner, whether peasant or noble, received a gift goblet. There were so many visitors that two slaves were needed just to stock and distribute the goblets.

Every guest at any meal kept his bowl and cup. The potters of Amyklai worked ceaselessly to create so much dinnerware.

When Menelaus rose from bed, there would already be a dozen men in the throne room awaiting the king's attention, and all day long more would arrive. They did not call it a throne room, but used a very old name for a cave. Megaron.

A watcher could sit on the balcony above the megaron protected by a carved screen, looking down through smoke and shadows, while voices echoed against the vaulted ceiling. I went once with Hermione, but she found it dull and would not go a second time.

When Helen was there, men forgot their arguments, and lost the focus of their eyes, and confused their hopes with their fears.

Around Helen the hall murmured.

In the afternoon, when his kingly chores were done, Menelaus and his sons would go hunting. More often than not they would come home with a rabbit, but the boys made their hunts sound so dangerous I would look around for the carcass of some vicious wild pig, whose tusks could rip open the chest of a man and his hunting dogs with a single slice.

"One of these days," Aethiolas would say, grinning.

The boys were their fathers' sons. They had skinned knees and torn knuckles. They sparred with wooden practice swords and got sick of it and tried to take their father's real ones. Their servants were always either dragging the boys apart to stop a fight or trying to separate them to go to bed.

It was not easy to explore a palace so filled with guards. Hermione had never thought of exploring, and her older brothers had probably finished exploring years ago. I went alone.

One day I found a bright and sunny room full of men squatting on stools and playing with wet clay squares. I was unable to figure out what the game was. Each man played by himself, and each seemed proud of his results, but I saw no dice and no game pieces.

I asked Menelaus, who loved to give answers. Sometimes when men gathered in the megaron for the king's decisions, they squirmed with boredom as the king answered and answered and answered.

"Those are my scribes. I have twelve. They sit all day making keeping-track lines. I have difficulty doing it myself, but my slaves have spent their lives mastering the art. Into wet clay they make marks for storage counts and trading records. How many amphorae of wine, how many bales of leather, how many horses or spears."

I did not understand. "Can't you keep track of spears by looking?"

"I would have to walk from room to room, from wing to wing," said Menelaus. "I would have to visit every citadel and barn and outbuilding and guardhouse."

It was true that the palace was crammed with goods. He was a king and yet he lived like a sea trader: rooms full of pottery and wine and grain and oil and nuts and linen, all awaiting exchange. Helen despised everything but the precious metals.

Helen had seen through me. And yet she was making no real effort to destroy me. Because in spite of everything, she is still a wife who must obey, I thought. Menelaus has given me his protection and she cannot void that promise.

"This way," said Menelaus, who never noticed if the people around him began thinking of other things, "the keeping-track lines are on a tablet, and my slave can tell me that so many shields are kept here and so many vats of oil are stored there. Sometimes we put rent arrangements or the sale of property on the tablets, and then when men argue about what month the payment is due, it is saved, right there on the clay. It makes it easier to be a king."

I figured out some lines right away. The mark for barley was a tilted stroke holding up one grain. Cloth was a square sagging at the top, like a sheet hanging from a line. Sheep was a line crossed twice, while goat was the same but with a ripple on top. I puzzled over these two.

"Crossing the line twice gives each figure four feet," said the slave. "The ripple is because goats dash around, while sheep just stand there."

I ran my finger over the little dents; the clay had now dried and was permanent.

Keeping-track lines were for sheep and shields. But what if you could use them for keeping track of a family lost to you? For keeping track of your heart and your sorrow?

The thought was as smoky and dark as the megaron, and I could not see it clearly enough to speak of it. It did not matter anyway.

Anaxandra had ceased to be. Only Callisto drew breath.

For a long and lovely week I played with Hermione and Pleis.

The real Callisto's pursuits had been so quiet they were motionless, but Hermione and I ran races and played tag and hopscotch. We loved ball games, hitting with bats or feet or forehead as each game required. We had dolls and dollhouses, and Hermione stole the boys' toy soldiers and when nobody was looking we played war instead of house.

We played chess and checkers, kings and pegs. Hermione

especially loved pegs. A throw of the dice told you how far you could move your pegs, and if you could get all your pegs into the circles before the other person, you won.

Pleis was still struggling with my name. He separated the word "Callisto," as if I were two people. "Calli?" he said anxiously. "Sto?" he added.

He was solemn. He laughed only when tickled or chased. His nurse, Rhodea, was tender and loving with him. How her name suited her. Rhodea was indeed a rose, pink and sweet smelling.

But it was I who crawled on tiles and rugs, in the grass and up and down stairs, making Pleis laugh, wrestling with him and wiggling under furniture.

There was a dinner party every night, for Menelaus loved company.

He always asked after a guest's family. Some men could not answer, on voyages so long that they had not seen their families in years. Others would speak of wives and children, while Menelaus would show off his own family. I loved how Menelaus loved his children.

But when parties were over, and we withdrew to our rooms, Helen would give her husband a light kiss on the forehead and waft away. They did not spend the night together as often as they should.

I had been in the palace two weeks when Menelaus' older brother Agamemnon came to hear about the voyage to Troy.

As Helen was a golden woman, Agamemnon was a golden man. He was much more king than Menelaus. The gods choose the body, and how the gods had chosen for Agamemnon! He was exceedingly handsome and as frightening as a shipload of pirates. You could feel all over him the blood he had shed, the cities he had sacked and the ships he had sunk.

"How's my Pleis?" said Menelaus, taking his little son from Rhodea and nuzzling Pleis' throat and cheeks. "How's my big boy? Snuggle with me, little son. Keep me warm."

Helen turned her face away and saw me, which only increased her annoyance. She said to Agamemnon, "That dull little sparrow, we are told, is the daughter of the king of Siphnos. You remember that fellow Nicander, who boldly cheated Apollo."

My cheeks went red with shame, as if Nicander really were my father and I really did carry his crime. I could not meet the eyes of Agamemnon, lord of lords.

"*We are told* that she is the daughter of Nicander?" repeated Agamemnon, grinning. His wide face was sliced by a long steep nose. Above his narrow lips was a thin mustache, something I had never seen, and he straightened his beard with oil. "You mean, my dear Helen, that we do not quite believe?"

"Nicander and Petra had dark hair. Look. Hers is red."

"Oh," said Agamemnon. "I thought you had interesting gossip. If hair color meant anything, then you, my daughter of a swan, would have white feathers, would you not?"

The day Agamemnon left, we children went on a picnic. Rhodea took Pleis to wade in a shallow brook, where he splashed joyfully. Squires carried baskets of food and jugs of water while the huntsmen prepared to flush out birds and small game for the boys to shoot. The nurse Bia paid no attention to Hermione at all, but lay on her back on a blanket, dozing in the shade.

Aethiolas and Maraphius set up clay targets and

contested each other with their slingshots. "I can do better than that," I said contemptuously when they consistently missed their mark.

"Girls can't use slings," said Aethiolas irritably.

"Get out of here," added Maraphius.

I took Aethiolas' sling in my hand and swung it to get its feel. It was a little long for me, Aethiolas' arm being bigger. But it would do. I chose a stone, fingered it to know its shape, and swung. My stone split an old clay goblet in half. I took another stone and smashed the second target.

When I stepped back, pleased with myself, fixed upon me were the astonished eyes of two princes, two squires, two tutors and Hermione.

"You *are* good, Callisto," said Maraphius respectfully. "But what kind of princess knows how to use a slingshot?"

No kind. Ever. I had made a mistake. But I shrugged, as if it were nothing. "My parents buried five sons. I became the son they never had."

Aethiolas was fascinated. "They raised you as a boy? Can you use a javelin too? A sword? Darts?"

I have heard that you can protect yourself from your own lies by crossing your fingers. I did not do it. I must not think of this as lying. I must think of it as truth I had not told before. "Father was planning to teach me to use a javelin this year," I said breezily, "now that I am tall enough."

Maraphius nodded. "Father brought me a baby-sized javelin from Troy. I'm too old for toys. He should have—"

His squire had had enough. "She's nothing but a girl, no matter how tall. Come, my prince, the huntsmen are ready. Leave the girls here to spin and stare at clouds."

Hermione waited till they had gone. Then she said to

me, "I've never stared at a cloud in my life. But you are worth staring at. No wonder you try not to talk about being a princess. You are actually a prince in disguise! Show me how to use the slingshot."

"Mother," said Maraphius after dinner.

I found it strange that anybody could call Helen Mother. She never embraced or kissed any of her four children. She seemed mystified that they existed. But they, like their father, treated their goddess mother quite routinely.

"Guess what Callisto can do," said Maraphius. "She can use a slingshot. She's good. And she taught Hermione. We saw. Hermione, show Mother what you can do."

"I'm not very good yet," said Hermione. "And Callisto and I are out of stones. Do you have any, Maraphius?"

"Sure." He handed her a full purse.

"Callisto was brought up as a prince," said Aethiolas, "because her brothers died when they were babies and so her father trained Callisto in weapons."

"Callisto always wanted to be a pirate when she grew up," Hermione added. "She drove off a hundred ships of pirates in one day all by herself."

Helen turned her long, slow look upon me.

"It wasn't really a hundred ships," I said. "But it was a lot."

"Hermione," said Helen, "return the stones to your brother. Aethra, take the slingshot away from the girl. Girl, sleep in the weaving room from now on. Do not go near my daughter again."

"Now, Mother," said Hermione, in exactly the voice Menelaus used. "Father said to treat Callisto as our sister."

"I hated my sister," said Helen.

She fixed her eyes upon me and I could not stay in the room with those eyes, but fled into the corridor, and then had to run down the hall until there were safe thick solid walls between me and the stare of that Medusa called Helen.

There did Aethra find me. Gently her twisted fingers took mine. Eighty years of lanolin from spinning sheep's wool into yarn had made her skin so soft that even Helen's was not its equal. I had always thought of my goddess as slender and strong, like the slim whip of a willow branch, but there in Aethra's wrinkles and washed-out eyes stood my goddess.

"I was once a queen," she said. "My son was the great and famous Theseus, who saved the children from the Minotaur in Crete. A warrior finer than Menelaus or Agamemnon could hope to be. And *still* my fate is slavery. My child, to stay a princess, stay away from Helen."

"How?" I whispered.

But she was not listening to me. She was speaking as an oracle speaks, the words coming out of her mouth from the gods. "Helen has drawn her breath from many fathers. From Madness, Hate, red Death and every rotting poison of the sky."

I stumbled back from her. The words were too strong. I could not listen.

Neither her good eye nor her blind eye saw that I had moved. "Your goddess of yesterday touched you with magic, my child, but Helen's magic is as a cup of death. Beware."

VIII

THE FIRST, FOURTH AND SEVENTH days of every month are holy, but fifth days are harsh and angry. On the fifth day of the last month of summer, the Trojans arrived: Prince Paris, killer of that innocent little boy, his cousin Aeneas and a dozen companions apiece.

The three older royal children were permitted to come to the formal welcome, Hermione led in by her nurse, the boys by their squires. I knew I should obey Aethra and stay away. But I could not bear to miss anything. Never before had a Trojan been under the roof of Amyklai.

Trojans are armed to the teeth: sword in hand, spear hanging from the shoulder, dagger clenched in the jaws. But guests disarm in the forecourt, their weapons stored by the host. "It's exciting, isn't it?" Hermione whispered. "I wish we could see Paris and Aeneas with knives in their teeth."

Paris was as beautiful a man as Helen was a woman. Bare from the waist up, Paris wore a panther skin over his shoulders. His muscles glistened and slid over strong bones. His body was perfect, without a single scar; his hair the same honey and spice as Helen's, every curl tight, as if just wound around some woman's fingers. His lips were as rosy as a child's, full of movement, as if every time he saw a man he thought of speaking, and every time he saw a woman he thought of love.

The court furniture that had been brought out in honor of Agamemnon was brought out for Paris of Troy. Paris and Aeneas were seated on ebony chairs inlaid with gold palm trees, which Menelaus had found in Egypt. Menelaus sat on his throne, and Helen beside him on her chair.

The companions gazed openmouthed at Helen, like young boys. Menelaus might sit on the throne, but when Helen chose to glitter, he was in shadow. Her tiara that evening was wisps of gold, flying gold wasps among gold-hammered flowers. I thought it perfect for Helen. Spun with a sting.

King and prince exchanged greetings, ingots of bronze and tin, bales of brocaded cloth and boxes of gems and ivory. Each side praised the other, and honor was paid to the gods. Then Paris stepped back from Menelaus and turned toward the queen.

I never saw a person who did not want to touch Helen. Strangers yearned to drape her cloak. Servants ached for the privilege of combing her hair or washing her feet. All who lived in this kingdom wanted Helen's praise.

And now a Trojan.

Yet the prince of Troy did not speak.

The room seemed oddly still and very hot, as the sky heats before thunder. When Paris knelt, he sank so slowly I did not see how he could keep his balance, and when he clasped her knees, as men do when pleading for mercy, she looked at his hands as if they were the hands of Zeus.

"I heard you were a white swan, my queen," said Paris. "A crown of glory. A star fallen from heaven. I was told that in your presence I would stumble. Those who have had the privilege of resting their eyes upon you discover that never again are they able to rest, for their trembling hearts forever think of none but you. O Helen. Aphrodite, blessed goddess of love, has led me to your feet."

Breathes a woman who would not like to hear such things?

Breathes a woman who would not enjoy having the goddess of love invoked at the sight of her?

But breathes there a husband who would permit it?

Menelaus, however, had heard this kind of thing from dozens of princes when they were all begging Helen to marry one of them. He seemed bored by Paris' speech.

Aeneas, the cousin, broke the spell. He was not handsome like Paris, but he was more important, for Aeneas, like Helen, was half god. His mother had been that same Aphrodite, goddess of love. We did not worship Aphrodite on Siphnos, so I did not know her. I had heard that she was as cruel as Apollo, and that frightened me, for how could love be cruel?

"Actually, my lord Menelaus," said Aeneas, "Aphrodite did escort us. She is the figurehead on Paris' ship. The goddess went first through the waves, bringing us a speedy and blessed arrival."

I did not think that was respectful. A goddess forced to break the waves day after day? Splashed in salt spray and plastered with seaweed? A figurehead should be a fish, not an immortal.

Hermione whispered to me, "Aeneas doesn't talk as if Aphrodite really is his mother, does he?"

Many claim to be the children of gods. In this room, both Aeneas and Helen. Is it true? Is any man or woman actually son or daughter of a god?

Paris stood reluctantly, as one who would have liked to

spend his life looking up at Helen. "O queen, you are not simply a swan and you are far greater than a dove. I see in you also the eagle."

Helen's eyes were very bright. "I do not have wings, Paris of Troy."

"Yet you fly into the heart of every man who sees you."

She had to smile then. I had not previously seen her true smile. It lit the room. It warmed every heart. It stayed so short a time on her lovely face that every one of us in the megaron yearned to do or say something to make that smile return.

Paris snapped his fingers. Forward came servants struggling under the weight of two extraordinary gifts for Helen: larger-than-life hounds of polished red marble, with collars of gold and obsidian eyes that glittered black in the smoke.

"May they guard your doors, O queen," said Paris.

The husband responsible for guarding Helen's doors sat right there. But Menelaus seemed not to be insulted. He just laughed. "It's more appropriate than you know, Paris. Helen doesn't care for real dogs. They shed fur and nip ankles. Our sons' puppies have to be kept at some distance from my wife's room."

Paris had brows like shelves above his deep dark eyes and he raised them high and regarded Menelaus with amusement. The king of Amyklai had just admitted publicly that he and his lovely queen did not share a room. "How wise of you, Helen," said Paris. "A queen must have perfection. Thus, I bring you perfect pets of stone."

"And what form of perfection must you have, my prince?" asked Helen. "A good fertile farm? A gentle life at home? A host of fair children?"

Paris shouted with laughter. "Those are not to my taste,

my queen. I revel in long ships with oars. I love the heft of a polished lance and the slice of arrows in the skirmish."

His body, however, was notably free of blemishes. A warrior's flesh tells a tale, for it is scarred and pitted from attack and defense. Even a youth learning to use his father's weapons ends up scabbed for life. But Paris was as smooth and beautiful as a newborn babe.

"What a king you will be one day, Paris," said Helen, although the whole room knew that forty-nine brothers stood between Paris and the throne of Troy. "A king should stain the world with blood. A king should live for his spear. Some warriors," she said, "go soft the moment they return home."

I and all the court knew that Helen was accusing Menelaus of such softness. I prayed Paris would not understand. I prayed Menelaus would not.

"Such a man," said the prince of Troy, his eyes as fastened to Helen's as the suction cups of an octopus had once been fastened to my arm, "cannot be called a warrior."

Squires entered, bearing cups for wine, while Paris and Helen stared at each other. When everyone had a cup, the squires poured each man a few drops, and Paris and Helen still stared at each other. Menelaus stood to lead the guests as they tipped out wine for the deathless gods. Then was each cup filled and then did each man drink.

Paris lifted his cup to Helen.

Helen lifted her cup to him.

"Men have all the adventures," whispered Hermione. "But now at least we will hear about them. And from the lips of a Trojan warrior."

The first story Paris told was how he himself had caught the panther whose skin now covered his back. It had been a huge beast and the room shuddered to think of combat with such a creature.

But his cousin Aeneas studied the fire on the hearth during the story, pushing ashes around with the tip of his boot, drawing circles of soot.

Aeneas does not believe it, I thought. Possibly Aeneas is the one who really slew the panther.

When the story had ended, and Helen was stroking the fine soft panther hide, her long white arm brushing the bare gleaming chest of Paris, Aeneas turned to the royal children. "You must be Hermione, for you look like a child goddess, dusted in gold. And these two fine young men must be Aethiolas and Maraphius. Lord Menelaus, how envious I am of such sons. And who is this little princess?"

Paris turned his back on Helen to see what princess Aeneas meant.

Me.

Helen turned to ice. The princess who was no princess had drawn Paris' gaze away from *her*? I felt the obsidian eyes of her two hounds. They would rise up and bite me if Helen had such a command in her power.

"I am Callisto, sir, from Siphnos," I said to Aeneas.

Paris laughed. "So you are the daughter of that king with the gold mine, who broke his word to the gods. Your background is lead, not gold." He turned again to Helen.

I burned to defend Nicander. But he had no defense.

"In more than one way she is lead and not gold," Helen told Paris. "I believe the girl is an imposter. I believe she comes from some other isle altogether."

"Fascinating," said the prince, and a second time he turned his back on Helen to examine me.

"Now, Helen," said Menelaus. "Nicander, along with all

his people, was slain by pirates," he told the Trojans. "Only this brave and sturdy daughter survived. I have taken her into my household, of course. When an island or a prince or a princess is born, Zeus shakes his two jars and pours out the future. Both a person and an island will have some good fortune and some dread."

The court prepared to be bored by lengthy stories they had all heard too many times. "Poor Nicander," said Menelaus, "drank deeply from the cup of sorrow."

"I, however," said Paris, "drink only from the cup of joy. For I look upon this face. This queen. This Helen." Taking Helen's gold cup from her hands, stroking her long slim fingers, very slowly he brought the queen's cup to his own face and ran his lips around the rim where hers had touched.

Something came over Helen and shook her, like wind falling on mountain oaks. Her ivory cheeks pinked and her hand trembled.

Aeneas joined his prince. Nervously, I thought. Certainly the rest of the court was a bit nervous. "What evidence have you, Helen," asked Aeneas, "that the little princess is not in fact from Siphnos?"

"Who cares what island some urchin comes from?" said Paris. "One rock in the sea looks like another. Let us discuss something worthy of you, O queen. You will visit Troy one day, I promise you, Helen of the sun and the moon and the stars. We are glory and gold. We are wide skies and a great plain. Brilliant warriors and splendid horses."

"Strong princes," said Helen, "and swift ships."

I drifted out of the megaron, keeping the wide shoulders of Trojans and Spartans between me and Helen. I need not have troubled. Helen never took her eyes from Paris.

Tiptoeing down the wide dark hall, I climbed up the long stair that clung to the whitewashed walls, around the landing, up the next stair, and from there to the fretwork of the balcony. It was packed with women who made room for me.

Menelaus was eager to learn of every city and shore, every adventure and storm at sea. The companions of Paris obliged. The wine was passed continually, for nothing pleases men more than another sip. Paris laughed steadily. There was something discomfiting about a man so easily amused. Especially one whose reason for coming was that he had murdered a little boy.

Maraphius fell asleep, sagging in his father's arms. Aethiolas drooped. Bia had long since escorted Hermione out of the room.

"I have a request," said Paris languidly, "from my father, Priam, the great king of Troy."

Aeneas studied his cup. He had drunk very little and Paris had drunk a great deal. Aeneas did not seem happy with this new subject.

"Perhaps, my dear king Menelaus," said Paris, "you recall that my father, Priam, had a sister, Hesione by name. Many years ago, Hesione was kidnapped by one of your kings, Telamon by name. He made our beloved Trojan princess his slave."

Menelaus was very angry. I was not prepared for his anger and I do not think Paris was either. When Menelaus stiffened, you could see the great breadth of his barrel chest, the width of his shoulders, the fury in the huge hands that now gripped his own knees, as if he were preventing himself from knocking the visitor down. "When you refer to

Hesione, young man, do not make up your own version. The great Hercules, the hero and warrior of Greece, went to Troy. Hercules found your gates open and your people slack. He attacked Troy and won handily. Am I correct?"

I had never known that. I had never heard anybody refer to any defeat of Troy, let alone within living memory. We in the balcony held our breath. The Trojan companions who had been tired and a little drunk were now flushed and humiliated. Their muscles shifted as they considered reaching and gripping weapons. But they had none, not even studded leather to bind their knuckles, a weapon that permits one strike of the fist to kill.

Aeneas, graceful and calm, said quietly, "It happened as you say, lord."

Menelaus did not stand. It was his throne room. He had power just sitting there. But at a glance from him, his men too shifted position. Their spears were not leaning against a distant wall. They had not had too much to drink. "When Hercules had beaten Troy," said Menelaus, relishing the words, "the great hero took his due. His soldier Telamon, having slaughtered many, was awarded the princess Hesione as his prize. All this was just and proper."

The stories of Hesione were many. She had been raped by Hercules or saved from sea monsters by Hercules. She was now a pitiful drudge slaving in the house of Telamon or she was Telamon's honored wife. Every year she bribed traders to take her home to Troy or every year she laughed in their faces and spit on Troy.

"Wise King Priam knows all this," said Menelaus, "for he and I discussed it at length during my recent visit. Telamon *married* Hesione. Hesione is his *queen,* not his servant."

There was no need for any man to wed his captive. Telamon must have loved her to do that.

"Hesione is not only Telamon's queen in Salamis," said Menelaus, and no man in the court was bored by the story he told now, "she is also the mother of his beloved son Teucer—your cousin, Paris. Your age, in fact. But unlike you, Teucer will become a king. The son of Hesione has a future. You on the contrary are the youngest son. You will do nothing in your life except obey your brothers."

In the balcony we cringed. What a slap in a guest's face to remind him how lowly his position really was. But Paris just smiled.

"We acknowledge," said Aeneas carefully, "that there is much truth in what you say, Lord Menelaus. But our king Priam nevertheless yearns for his sister. We will of course report to him how happy she is as queen of Salamis and how proud of her son Teucer."

Paris found this as amusing as he had found the entire evening. "My father's request having been made and refused," he said, "I am free of obligation." And then he shouted, as if he and not Menelaus were the host, "Let us have dancing now, and song, for these are the crown of a feast."

And Paris it was who led the dancing and Helen who watched with a feverish flush.

The next day Menelaus took Paris and Aeneas on a boar hunt. Aethiolas and Maraphius got to go along. Hermione and I spun. Helen spent the day on her balcony.

"Isn't that odd?" said Hermione. "Usually Mother detests sun on her skin."

I did not think it odd. She would see Paris return. She expected that he would get the boar.

But Menelaus got the boar. The peasants had feared the boar, for a boar has no fear of man and will rip apart a shepherd or a sheep, a woman in the field or a child on the path. How they sang the hunter king's praises.

Helen sang nothing. Paris smiled.

The following day, Helen escorted Paris to the temple of Apollo in preparation for the ceremonies in which the prince would shed his blood debt. In the megaron, Menelaus listened to petitions. Maraphius and Aethiolas memorized history with their tutors. Pleis napped. Hermione spun. I made my way to the keeping-track room.

I hoped the scribes would let me try. If I could whirl a slingshot, surely I could wield a marker thorn. I had been working on my thoughts and they were less smoky.

I kept thinking of that Trojan princess Hesione, who must be quite old now. As old as Aethra. At this moment Hesione sat in a palace in Salamis on the western rim of the Aegean Sea, while Priam her brother sat in the palace of Troy on the eastern rim.

Could there be a keeping-track line which spoke not of objects on shelves but of thoughts in hearts?

Could there be a way for people who would never see each other again to talk to each other?

Yet if there were such a thing, what good would it do? If I could keep track with that marking thorn that I hoped my parents still loved me, all I would have was a dried square of clay telling *me*. It wouldn't tell *them*.

And yet . . .

Clomping boots down the dark hall startled me. Still

107

thick with thought, I stepped into a side room and slipped behind the door curtains. The steps were loud and many, but there were only two speakers, and I recognized their voices.

"Lord king," said the captain Kinados intensely, "Paris and Aeneas have warriors on their ships."

"Now, Kinados. I would hardly expect a prince to travel unescorted," said Menelaus.

With ferocity, as if Kinados would gladly shove the king against a wall to make him listen, the captain said, "Menelaus! These are not escorts. These are troops! We need to know what Paris is really planning. He does not care about blood debt."

"Now, Kinados. Paris is my guest. He has gone hunting with me. Bounced my little son on his lap and played with my hounds."

"Paris just wants to get to know his enemy before he attacks," said Kinados. "Lord, at table you came close to mortal insult."

"And yet he laughed, didn't he?" said Menelaus patiently. "Is that the mark of a dangerous man?"

"Didn't you hear him tell the queen what a fine warrior he is? That he lives for the joy of throwing the lance?"

"He's no warrior, Kinados. We all bathed together after the hunt. You and I have seen every inch of his body. If Paris loves battle, he loves it from a distance. No spear tip, no arrow, not even a fist has ever touched that skin. Paris just wants a good hunt followed by a good party."

"Amyklai is what he wants!" snapped Kinados. "And after that, Sparta. And then all your kingdom. And when he has gotten us, he goes to Salamis to get his aunt Hesione."

"Send a messenger to Salamis, then. Let King Telamon

know that an overgrown playboy named Paris frightens you. But bother me no more." Menelaus walked away.

His soldiers were so angry they could not at first follow him.

"The king is a good man," said one, trying to find an excuse.

"In a king," said Kinados grimly, "that is a flaw."

I did not go to the keeping-track room after all. I had so many thoughts in my head I could not keep track of anything.

"I don't trust Paris," said Hermione.

The hour was very late. Most of the palace was asleep. Hermione's nurse Bia and the maids were snoring on the porch. Hermione and I were sitting on her bed whispering. I had first pulled back the window curtains and then opened the hall door in hopes of a cool draft. None came. "Why not?" I asked.

"Father taunted Paris," she said. "I think that was a mistake. I think Paris has a plan and Father does not."

I was impressed. Hermione thought like a seasoned captain. I, however, agreed with Menelaus, not Kinados. Paris was just watching himself shine. He had no plans. He had only parties and laughter.

"If I were a general or an admiral," said Hermione, "Father would listen to me. But when I told him that Paris is a danger to the kingdom, Father just patted my head."

I loved Menelaus. His captain criticized, his wife scolded, and now his daughter was correcting him. I changed the subject. "Did you see the tusks from that boar?" I said.

"Aethiolas and Maraphius were bragging about that old boar. I don't think Father really let them anywhere near it. I bet Paris didn't get near it either. Everyone is joking about his smooth skin."

"How old do you think Paris is?"

"Twenty-five?" she guessed.

"How old is your mother?"

"Twenty-eight. Last year was a very sacred year for her, because twenty-seven is nine threes. She was sure something important would happen, but it didn't."

I thought of that ninth day when I returned to the sacred olive tree. It was only weeks ago, yet Siphnos seemed as distant as the mountains from the sea. Hermione and I leaned close, and the night wore on, and still we whispered.

And so when all the household slept except the guards at the gate, we were awake when Paris of Troy walked barefoot down the hall and Helen met him at her door.

I was too shocked to breathe. If a queen is with a man not her husband, it is treason, for if she should bear a child, it will not be the king's. A stranger's blood and history will step into the royal family and defile it.

Hermione and I climbed off the bed and stepped out into the hall and looked down toward Helen's room. The two red marble dogs stared back, their black eyes glittering.

"I will kill them," said Hermione.

The days passed.

The number of people who knew what Hermione and I knew grew larger. The secret filled the palace like the stench of rotting meat, stinking in our hearts.

But Menelaus arranged competitions for the pleasure of our guests, not knowing that one guest was enjoying a different sort of pleasure.

We rooted for runners in quarter-mile and half-mile

footraces; we screamed as chariots tipped over on the turn; we cheered for sweating wrestlers and long-throwing ball players. Harpists vied for a prize and bards sang new songs.

On the eighth day of Paris' visit, I woke to the soft clink of stones. From Hermione's window, I watched two men and a boy as they laid a new slate roof on the low granary beyond the women's garden. How neatly each stone slice lay, like fish scales.

How well men put together a roof. How poorly they put together their lives.

I was exactly what Helen accused me of: a girl of lead, not a princess of gold.

What was I to do about this life I had stolen? For among such cruel gods, such stern kings, I felt a dread fate before me.

That morning, a messenger brought news from Crete, largest island in the Sea. It has ninety cities. I tried and failed to imagine ninety places like Gythion and Amyklai all on one isle. While visiting the king of Crete, the messenger told us, the grandfather of Menelaus had died in his sleep. Crete was holding off the funeral games until Menelaus arrived.

Suddenly Amyklai was buzzing and active, Menelaus' closest companions assembling to escort him to the funeral. Helen's much older brothers, Castor and Pollux, came from Sparta. They would attend in honor of the old king. It was decided that Aethiolas and Maraphius would go, too.

"Boys always get adventure," said Hermione. "Girls always stay home. You are so lucky, Callisto. You have had adventure."

Priests arrived and choirs sang songs of mourning for the grandfather. Captain Kinados put together the honor guard. The treasury was opened and Helen and Menelaus chose the funeral offerings. Menelaus decided to bring two of his best smiths as his gift to the king of Crete. These men forged bronze, but one of them had worked the new metal, iron. The smiths were obedient and prepared to live forever in a strange land, but their wives were heartbroken and full of fear.

Menelaus turned suddenly to the queen. "Helen, you must honor my grandfather. Cut off your hair. I will place it on the fire of his bones."

Helen was aghast. Cut off her beautiful hair like a common woman? How could Menelaus ask such a thing of Helen, daughter of a god?

Menelaus pulled his dagger out of its sheath, flipped it in his hand, and passed it to her handle-first. For a moment, the blade lay in his palm. So sharp. So stained by blood. Into how many hearts had that been plunged?

Helen wore her hair that day in an intricate pile of braids and curls. One by one she pulled out the pins. How long and thick was her honey gold braid. She tossed her head so that the braid swung and she caught the braid in her left hand. In her right, she held the knife as if she would rather slit her throat.

Her eyes moved around the room, summoning affection. The room loved her. The room resented Menelaus for such an untoward demand.

A handmaiden held a silver salver to catch the falling braid.

Helen swung the knife.

From the curling tip at the bottom of the braid, she cut half an inch of hair. Half an inch is contempt. *You are nothing to me.*

Menelaus said not a word. The high color in his face said

it for him. The queen returned the knife blade-first and for a moment the knife balanced between them, aimed at her husband's heart.

Paris smiled at the ceiling.

"Don't go to Crete!" cried Hermione suddenly, her child's voice as piercing as the flute that guides the ship. "Father, I don't think you should go. Please stay here."

He patted her head. "I'll bring you a present," he said. "Paris, my priests will proceed with the ceremony to release your blood debt. Feast and hunt until my return. The weather is perfect and the sail to Crete should not take more than two or three days. I expect to be back in a week or two."

Paris smiled at the ceiling.

At dawn the slim ships of Menelaus would sail the wine-dark sea, and still the king had no idea why Paris smiled.

Hermione almost told him. But she could not do it. Nor could any man or woman at Amyklai. They loved Helen and Menelaus both.

"My goddess of yesterday travels with you," I said to my king, and Menelaus patted my head too. "I'll bring you another magic jar, Callisto."

It is you who need magic, my king, I thought sadly.

Aeneas accompanied Menelaus all the way from Amyklai to the shore. I felt a little better. No one can ensure a safe journey better than a guest-friend. Aethiolas and Maraphius twittered like sparrows in their joy. I spotted Tenedos carrying the little princes' baggage and I was glad for him. Funeral games on the great rich isle of Crete would be exciting.

The soldiers and servants of Menelaus raised a cloud of

dust under their sandals as they marched to Gythion. Even when we could no longer make them out, we could see their dust. Finally they vanished into the darkness called forest.

Bia her nurse told Hermione they would weave together, as it was high time the princess acquired more skill.

Rhodea his nurse told Pleis that he would nap.

"Perhaps you and I will also nap, my swan," said Paris to Helen.

I saw now what had made Helen's hands flutter in the megaron. What had gone through that beautiful body like mountain wind. What had pierced a heart as bleached as marble.

It was love.

The heat of the day passed and the sun went down.

The dusk turned to dark and the moon rose, dropping silver light on the great walls.

My thoughts were too sad for sleep.

I climbed a long stone stair to the battlements and sought answers in the first stars. Not only did the people of Sparta name their stars, they were planning keeping-track lines for each star.

From the parapet I looked down upon the snarling lions over the gate. The gate was open. Menelaus had left open the gate of his marriage, too.

The air stood still, thinking its own thoughts. Every distant mountain peak, every deep ravine, seemed as infinite and dangerous as the gods.

Far away and very low in the sky traveled an unusual row of flickering stars. Hundreds were colliding and flaring, then vanishing like wicks of oil lamps being blown out. I knew of no such stars in the sky.

Time passed.

No guard walked by me.

No night watch closed the Lion Gate.

One by one, much nearer now, the strange stars appeared again.

I stood alone at the battlements, a child in the dark, and said to myself, "Surely not."

But yet I knew the truth. Not stars—but torches in the hands of men.

Briefly I had seen them. Then they had entered the black forest and disappeared and now were out of it, and fast approaching Amyklai. It is risky to walk at night—wild beasts, bad footing and evil spirits. But with hundreds of torches, these men were safe from robbers and wolves.

Aeneas the cousin of Paris had not spent the night in Gythion. As soon as Menelaus and Kinados had sailed away, Aeneas had gathered the very warriors Kinados had feared and the Trojan army was marching upon Amyklai by night.

Aeneas' men *were* the robbers and wolves.

I ran to warn the queen. Clattering down stone steps, racing across courtyards, throwing open one door after another, to the women's wing I sped. I flung myself toward the barred wooden door of her bedroom, to beat my fists against it until she came.

But the door was open and in her fragrant well-lit room, Helen admired herself in a silver mirror.

"O queen! They have broken their guest-friendship," I cried. "The Trojans come armed with Aeneas as their general. You must protect yourself. Paris is your enemy, not your friend. In your husband's stead, you must call out your soldiers. I have seen what pirates can do. You must—"

"Paris is not my enemy."

"He is, O queen. I know you do not trust me. I beg you to trust me now. For the sake of your children. For your own dear sake. The Trojans have come for Amyklai."

"No," said Helen, angling the mirror and smiling at what she saw. "The Trojans have come for me."

IX

SIX DOORS STOOD BETWEEN Helen and the treasure of a kingdom.

She unlocked them herself, sliding the narrow curved arms of the key tree into the slot, and turning it carefully to catch the edge of the bar within. Paris stood beside her, breathing deeply, his laughter waiting inside his chest until he heard the bar scrape upward.

"How dare she!" breathed Hermione. The little princess was trembling with fury.

I was not sure which of the many things Helen should not dare to do that Hermione was thinking of. I was stunned at how easily Helen dealt with her own soldiers, the soldiers of Menelaus. She spoke not one word. White arms bare, her hair bound up with a golden veil, Helen dismissed her own men from their posts. With her fingertips, she touched the lips of a guard about to argue, and he hung his head and said nothing. She took the hand of the soldier trying to block a door and gently guided him and he let her. Sweetly she shook her head when another guard stepped forward, and she waited until he had stepped back.

It was treason.

Helen was the wife of Menelaus, king of Sparta.

Sister-in-law of Agamemnon, lord of lords. Mother of three princes, heirs to Amyklai.

Yet, just as she might toss grain to a singing bird in a cage, Helen tossed the wealth of her kingdom to the enemy.

The nobles of Amyklai were in their own homes, asleep behind their own barred doors, and they did not emerge. A dozen soldiers of Menelaus allowed themselves to be tied up. The Trojans barely knotted the ropes, as if Menelaus' men were a joke. A dozen more allowed the Trojans to herd them into a room and lock them there. A dozen more surrendered weapons without using them.

Paris and his companions swaggered, as pirates do when they capture beautiful women. But the tips of the spears with which they saluted one another were unblooded.

Hermione was a phantom, all staring eyes and white shocked face. "Mother," she whispered, "the Trojans will take you as slave. Just the way Castor and Pollux so long ago took Aethra. The way Telamon of old took Hesione. The way Callisto's mother Petra was taken."

Helen neither saw nor heard her daughter. She swung the final door and held it open for Paris, guest-friend of her husband.

"My men have commandeered every cart and donkey," Paris said, waving his troops into the glittering storeroom. "Aeneas, meanwhile, is removing the temple gold."

"The temple gold!" cried Hermione. "Mother! Prevent this! Apollo attacked our kingdom with plague for two years! Father has only just rescued us from disease! What will Apollo do when we let foreigners carry off his honors?"

"We are not foreigners, little princess," said Paris, smiling. "We are Apollo's own children. We are taking his gold back where it belongs. Troy." Standing on the threshold of

Menelaus' storeroom, Paris kissed Helen. "We'll be in Gythion by tomorrow night, my swan, and the following day, we will sail for Troy."

Hermione bunched up her muscles to hurl herself against Paris, but in the end, she did nothing either. The Trojans would laugh at her and her own mother would not bother to look. I dragged Hermione into the shadows.

"The gold veil on her hair?" said Hermione, jabbing a finger toward Helen. "It was a wedding gift. My mother is wearing her wedding veil to loot her own palace."

I felt weak and hopeless. How Helen hated Menelaus.

"I will kill her," said Hermione.

I could think of only one thing worse than a queen handing her kingdom over to the enemy. The murder of that queen by her daughter.

"No, Hermione," I said, although I understood. I had wanted to kill a pirate once and Helen deserved to die as much as that backstabber. In fact, she was a backstabber, kicking Menelaus as that pirate had kicked my king. O my kings, my kings. "I cannot let you commit that crime, Hermione. Come, return to the women's wing. Something will set these men off, ours or theirs, and fighting will begin. We must be sure your baby brother is safe."

I knew that little Pleis was safe. Rhodea and Bia were no fools; they would bar the doors. It was Hermione I had to keep safe.

We emerged in the largest courtyard. The moon still crossed a black sky. It may take years to build a palace and fill a treasury, but in one small part of a night, it may all be destroyed.

Hermione wanted to storm across the wide space but I held her back. We would work our way from shadow to shadow. In the end, the Trojans were nothing but pirates after loot, and in the end, a princess is the best loot of all.

By the flickering light of torches, we saw Pyros storming up to a squadron of the enemy. I had not seen the overseer since we arrived in Amyklai. He carried only his mule whip. "Stop this, you Trojans!" the overseer shouted. "I demand that you cease!"

My heart found room for Pyros, whom I disliked. He alone on that black night placed his loyalty with his king. But an overseer is not himself free. Pyros might be feared by other slaves, but he evoked no fear in the soldiers of Troy.

"You have been welcome guests in the palace of Menelaus!" yelled Pyros, lifting his mule whip. "You have broken his bread and drunk his wine. Behave yourselves!"

The Trojans laughed and shoved a spear through his belly. When the spear was yanked back out so the soldier could use it again, the guts came with it, spooling onto the grass. Pyros tried to stuff his intestines back in, but the dogs got there first and ate eagerly.

I put my hand over Hermione's mouth, to stifle her scream. We must not let these Trojans see her next. They had tasted blood. Hermione tried to bite me.

Fifty steps away, Helen and Paris reached the doorway we had come out of.

From the ground, the dying Pyros raised up on one elbow. "Helen of Sparta!" he shouted. "I curse you! *You* ordered the gates to be left open! *You* are a traitor to the king your husband! May the gods eat *your* belly! May you—"

Paris left Helen's side and jogged forward. Snatching a spear from one of his men, the prince finished Pyros off. Then he thrust his spear tip skyward in the jagged fist action of victory, as if he had risked his life; as if this had been a well-armed hero, a man on his feet, not a slave three quarters dead on the ground.

Helen swiftly crossed the pavement and stood beside him in the moonlight.

"There is no Helen of Sparta!" called Paris, adjusting the gold veil over the queen's hair. "There is Helen of Troy, and she is mine."

Thus did the guts of a slave shame the men of Amyklai. The battle began. The Spartans were raging and the Trojans were glad.

Where is the joy of strolling in and taking? You want to fight, burn and slash. You want to hear groans and screams, see terror and submission.

You want to earn that gold you rip from the treasury; earn the pretty girls you pull from their beds. No longer could the Trojans pretend this was a dinner party.

They killed many as the day dawned and the morning brightened. They slashed the throats of men they would have left quietly tied up; raped the women they would have ignored; threw over the battlements tiny children they would have forgotten.

And Helen smiled.

Two armies were fighting over her. Shouting her name in love or in hatred. Dying for her.

She was everywhere, like weather, passing through the chaos as a goddess, untouched. She wore a white gown, and it was never sprayed with blood.

Hermione and I stumbled up the long stairs to the women's wing. "I know you keep a knife in your fleece," said

Hermione. "Give it to me, Callisto. I have seen that blade. Long and thin and sharp. Even I am strong enough to shove it through soft flesh and into the softer heart."

"Helen's heart is not soft," I said. "It is stone. She cannot be killed. And if you did kill your own mother, the gods would never forgive you. They would go like wind through your ears and make a wild gale of your thoughts. The gods would destroy you."

"First I will destroy her," said Hermione.

Bia stood at the top of the stair. "Thank the gods!" cried Bia. "You are all right!" She was bulky in a comforting way, all bosom and waist. The thickness of women can be so warm and safe.

"I am not all right," said Hermione. "I will never be all right. Not even after I kill Helen. Get out of the way, Bia." The nurse didn't move fast enough, so Hermione shoved her. "Apollo has not struck down one Trojan! Not even the ones who attack his own temple! I believe that Apollo himself is on the side of these Trojans. When I think of the sacrifices my father has made to him! Callisto, pray to your goddess of yesterday. I shall need her with me to accomplish the death of Helen of Troy."

I tasted the smoke of torches meeting the damp of stones. I saw the shadows lifting in the first light of dawn.

Helen of Troy.

That her own daughter, princess of Sparta, child of Menelaus, could call her that! And yet it was true. In heart and word and deed, Helen had already left Sparta.

I obeyed Hermione in part. "Goddess of yesterday!" I called. "Still the heart of Hermione. Quiet her rage."

I thought Hermione would spit on me but she had already left. As a hawk plunges from the sky, with such speed did she enter her room and fling my fleece into the air and shake out what I kept there. My Medusa fell safely onto a rug. My knife clattered on the floor and spun away from the princess.

I leaped toward the knife, slamming my foot down upon it. Hermione dropped to her knees to peel it out from under my sandal.

Bia dragged the princess away. "Hermione!" she scolded. "Behave yourself." Bia was too strong for a nine-year-old. Hermione could go nowhere. I retrieved the knife and wondered what to do with it.

"Why don't you tell my mother to behave herself?" Hermione's voice shook, but not as a little girl's trembles. Her voice shook as the earth shakes when it throws mountaintops or palaces to the ground. "My mother intends to travel with that Trojan. My mother intends to go to Troy."

"Well, then," said Bia sensibly, "let us enter the queen's chamber and discuss it with her. Perhaps we can present arguments that oppose her decision."

I thought perhaps we could present a hundred arguments, but Helen would ignore them and Paris would laugh.

Bia coaxed, her voice humming, her arms rocking, and soon she had Hermione calmed down, and they went together down the corridor to the queen's room. I kicked the knife under the bed and followed.

Helen might have been supervising the transfer from summer palace to winter palace, mulling over which cloaks ought to go in which basket. She was singing softly to herself. Every now and then she glanced out the window and smiled. The low sobs of despair that came from her serving women bothered her not at all.

Hermione stood as tall as a nine-year-old can. Half the

123

height of a soldier. "Mother, think of Father and the boys. This is your kingdom. Think of your honored parents, only three miles away in Sparta town. Think of your famous brothers, Castor and Pollux, who have brought honor and glory to our name. Who stood in this house only yesterday. You have a trust to pass on to your sons."

Helen held up a lacy shawl, admired it, and handed it to Aethra to fold and place in a chest. "Menelaus will still have his kingdom," Helen pointed out. "I am not taking the land, just a few important things and my women."

Vials of perfume and jars of powder were being arranged in a shallow wicker box. Inside a large chest, Helen's fluffy slippers, soft sheets and fragrant pillows had been packed in and around the silver yarn basket to keep it safe. She will sail away with Paris, I thought, but not without her finest clothing and jewels. Not without a hairdresser.

"Mother, you are looting your own home."

"Hush now," said Helen gently, as if they were talking about whether Hermione could stay up late. "Love dictates this. You have never felt love. Until now I have never felt love either. Now at last I possess it. Paris is the finest, strongest, most wonderful man in the world."

"No! Father is!"

Helen shook her head. "Paris is my destiny. I was not conceived by a god to waste my years with so dull a man as Menelaus. It was the red hair, you know, that made me choose him. I thought a man with a flaming mane would himself be fire. No. Menelaus is merely an ember on the hearth."

Helen left her packing and went to her window. Her housewifely demeanor vanished. She feasted her eyes upon battle and plunder. It brought color to her face and glitter to her eyes. "I have met fire at last. Paris flames. Paris is mine and I am his." She turned her back on the chaos below and faced us all, but she saw none of us. I think she saw her destiny. "I," she whispered, "am Helen of Troy."

Paris entered as she said these words, and he repeated the sentence with her and embraced her. They kissed in front of us: in front of the children and their nurses, her maids and his soldiers. And smiled as if none of the burning and killing mattered.

And it didn't. Not to them.

I uttered a silent curse upon Paris. May you freeze to death, starve to death and be frightened to death all at one time.

But the curse did not take.

"To Gythion, my bride," he said. "My warships await. Soon you will have the city you deserve, with high walls and shining towers. You are a goddess. Troy will treat you as one."

Aethra, who had nothing to risk, took up the argument. "You cannot leave your baby son, Helen. Think of little Pleis. Only two years old. He will have no memory of his dear and beautiful mother. Nor can you abandon sweet Hermione, image of her lovely mother. Think of your children, Helen."

Helen was stealing from her husband, her sons, her town and her temple. She didn't care what people or gods thought of that. But she did not want to be thought a bad mother. She hesitated.

Aethra pressed her advantage. "They need you."

This was untrue. Pleis and Hermione were brought up by their nurses and their father. I was confident that once on board ship with Paris, Helen would never think of her children again.

"I shall take them with me, of course," said Helen. "Rhodea, pack everything the little prince needs. Bia, supervise packing for Hermione."

Paris had not expected this. It gave him pause. To steal a man's wife was part of the fun. All the better to filch a queen. And how delightful to take a little princess, for her father would know exactly what would be done to her.

But to take a king's *son*.

Never.

Nobody needs another man's prince. The usual thing to do with another king's son is to kill him.

In Aethra's old eyes I saw horror. Had she not spoken up, Pleis would have been forgotten. If the little boy went with Paris, he was dead. Accidents are easy to arrange for two-year-olds.

Paris had thought quickly. "The children will sail on the ship of Zanthus," he said. "Zanthus' ship is called *Ophion,*" Paris told Helen. "My ship is *Paphus*. Aphrodite the goddess of love on our prow, leading us to Troy."

Ophion. The moon snake. *Paphus*. Sea Foam.

Paris would let Helen have her children, but he would not let them interrupt his honeymoon.

"I will kill both of you before I take such a journey," said Hermione.

Paris did not glance at her. Hermione's pale cheeks stained red with helpless rage. Bia held her tight enough to break bones.

The captain Zanthus stepped forward. This man had been in all the fights that Paris had stayed out of. He had no front teeth. He had no left eye. A slice had been taken out of his left ear. A scar ran from the empty eye socket into his hair, and the hair around the scar was white. The rest was braided into a single heavily oiled plait, like a slimy snake. His beard was a bush in which small birds might have hid.

O my princess. O my little prince. Entrusted to such a pirate? Surely even Helen would not allow it.

"You are taking the *son*?" Zanthus demanded of Paris.

Paris did not bother to answer. "Come, my shining bride." He kissed the tip of Helen's nose and her earlobes and her throat. "You will ride a white mule and I a white horse."

This is long planned, I thought. Aeneas' men and Paris' men were on the shore, ready and waiting. Had Menelaus not so handily left for Crete, they would have attacked in battle.

I wondered suddenly about that messenger bearing news of a grandfather's death. Had he, in fact, come from Crete? Had a grandfather, in fact, died? Whose messenger had he really been? Had he actually been in the pay of the Trojans?

Zanthus called after Paris. "Where am I supposed to put all these passengers?"

Paris shrugged.

The Trojans had come in warships, not cargo ships. There would be no cabin. A warship has a tiny foredeck and a tiny afterdeck. Zanthus the captain would need one, his rowing master and the cook the other. Hermione and Pleis would sit in bilge water, bruised by the tips of oars, crushed by sacks of loot. I could think of no place where Bia and Rhodea could sit.

Zanthus shrugged. "Get moving," he said to Rhodea, so roughly she almost dropped Pleis. The baby stared, his rose-bud mouth open in confusion. "Pack!"

Bundles of clothing and bedding, sacks of toys—these were thrown together and slung around by the Trojans.

Rhodea had no time to get her own things. She would trot to Gythion in bedroom slippers—twenty miles—she who rarely walked farther than from one end of the nursery to another. She would be aboard a ship for days with not a single piece of clothing or a blanket.

"You! Girl!" said Zanthus to Hermione. "Pack."

Here at last was someone Hermione could scream at. "I am a princess and you will address me as your superior."

"Get moving, girl, or I will strap you to a mule like a sack of oats. I am not treating the spawn of Menelaus with honor. Your father, may he rot, insulted my prince."

Bia and I dragged Hermione to her room. Bia closed the heavy door behind us and threw the bolt.

Hermione grinned, a smile wholly her father's. The smile of a warrior. From the sheath at Zanthus' side, she had lifted his dagger. "I shall kill Helen. There is time and I am armed. You saw that pirate. His knife has killed before. It is a better choice than yours, which has only peeled fruit. When Helen is dead, no matter what else he carries away, Paris of Troy will have lost. My father's honor will not be wholly destroyed."

Bia tried to take the knife, but Hermione slashed the air with it and the nurse jumped out of range.

Greece is a violent land, with violent weather and violent men. Always the sea churns, the heroes clash and the passion burns.

But I had not thought the violence extended to a sheltered princess in the quiet of her palace.

From the corridor came the voice of Zanthus. "Girl! Nurse! Now!" He was not quite ready to barge into the private room of a princess, but he would. He would break the door down, and perhaps break us as well.

"She comes, my captain," called Bia, who had not yet begun packing. She looked around wildly. What to choose for a lifetime in another land?

"Hermione," I said, "kill Paris instead. The gods will not mind that at all. He deserves death. He has broken his guest-friendship. I think you can get to him more easily, anyway. His men don't actually guard him, they just stand around. And he doesn't fear you. He'll be laughing when the knife goes in."

Hermione puzzled about this and in the brief instant that her body sagged and the knife drooped, I shoved her into her dressing room and slammed the door shut.

Bia dragged a heavy trunk up against the door. The door was so thick we could hardly hear the pounding of her fists nor could we make out her screams. This was good, because she must have been bringing dreadful curses upon us.

"Callisto, you go in Hermione's place," said Bia. "As soon as you have gone, I will take the princess over the mountains and place her in the care of her uncle, King Agamemnon." Bia flung together a great bundle of clothing, plucking at anything she could reach, and thrust it into my arms.

"Now!" yelled Zanthus, banging at the door.

"Coming!" shouted Bia. She looped Hermione's amber necklace around my throat and put Hermione's blue cape around my shoulders, tugging the hood up to cover my red hair. Into the bundle she thrust my Medusa.

"But Bia," I whispered. "Helen will kill me."

"Yes," agreed Bia. "Delay that as long as possible."

X

I STOOD LIKE BONES inside two princesses I had never been.

The sun rose in the sky and the heat beat down and I hid beneath a felt hood that scratched and clung.

Far ahead rode Paris on his white horse and Helen on her white mule. He wore a parade helmet whose great plumes stood high above anything else. Her gold veil fluttered in the breeze.

Aeneas' men kept the rear of the baggage train safe from attack, while Paris' men led the way. Helen's five women and Rhodea were the only slaves. A warship carries no servants other than a cook. Rowers are warriors and must care for themselves away from home.

Aethra was one of the five. She seemed an extraordinary choice, even for Helen. There was so little a woman of such great age could contribute. Aethra could never walk to Gythion and had been given a tiny gray donkey. In all this chaos, she had her bag of wool and was sitting sideways on the donkey, spinning. Her mind would be occupied by the pleasant rhythm of the twist climbing into the wool. My mind had to twist over death, awaiting me in Gythion, or whenever Helen looked back.

Poor Rhodea was whimpering in pain before we were out of sight of Amyklai. The heat and her unprotected feet were hard on her. If she had been a rose, she'd have had a short bloom.

A Trojan soldier held Pleis gently, though, and the little prince seemed not to be afraid. I remembered sitting on the shoulders of Lykos, the wolf who had carried me away from my birth island. I had enjoyed it. It is good to be too young to understand that your family is ruined.

Zanthus strode up to me. "Where is your maid, girl?"

I did not let him see my face. "I am the Princess Hermione, captain. I will answer your question when you have phrased it respectfully."

Zanthus snorted and walked on.

What defines a princess is that everyone cares about her. Noble children are half in the hands of gods and the other half must be protected by humans. No Trojan cared about a princess called Hermione. She—I—was baggage.

Most likely, I would be dead by nightfall. There was no need to rush into such a finish, however, and who knew what information I might glean that would postpone my doom or even lead to escape? I kept my ears open.

I was astonished to find that the Trojans regarded the Lord God Apollo as their own property. They were confident that Apollo cared not one twig about Amyklai, Sparta or Menelaus. They had not, in their own eyes, looted a temple; they were reverent men returning Apollo's treasure to its rightful place. Troy.

When they were not boasting that they had sole rights to a god, they boasted of Helen. She was a pool of light, they told each other, a halo from heaven. Proof that Paris was first among princes. They told vicious jokes about Menelaus' manhood, or the lack of it.

Yet we were not making a leisurely and proud return. The pace was swift. We were taking flight.

131

You may have stolen his wife, Paris, I thought, but you are afraid of Menelaus. You are afraid of his great brother, King Agamemnon. *You are afraid.*

I stared into his spine, using the eyes of Medusa to pierce his back like a dagger, but nothing happened.

For me, the twenty miles were not difficult. It had been only a month or so since I had last dashed over the hills and vales of Siphnos. This time, when we entered the forest, I saw only beauty: how each green leaf filtered the light, and butterflies threaded like embroidery among splashes of sun.

When we emerged, it seemed that the same slaves were working in the same row of the same field under the same sky, singing the same song.

I needed a good explanation for Helen concerning my presence. If I said that Hermione would have put a knife through her, it would simply inspire Helen to put a knife through me.

I will tell her my true name, I thought. I will die as Anaxandra.

Far ahead of us, like a war belt of purple and blue, I glimpsed the noble sea, flecked with the ships of Troy.

And in the rushing salt wind came my goddess. I lifted my face to let her kiss me and held the hood off my hair that she might ruffle it.

O goddess of yesterday, thank you for coming.

It was as if Menelaus had never existed; as if Helen were not married; as if this were the normal betrothal of a normal prince and princess. The royal couple rode through Gythion, never dismounting, the surefooted horse and mule managing the wide stone steps down to the harbor.

The people of Gythion wisely stayed indoors, but the army of Troy cheered in the streets and the sun went down into the sea and the world turned lavender and silver.

The two children of Menelaus were put up in the house of Axon, where not long ago a princess named Callisto had been sheltered. Axon himself had been thrown out. The princess Hermione was placed in the very same bedroom in which Callisto had slept.

From the balcony of that room, I looked down into the harbor. Helen and Paris were crossing a slender isthmus to an islet so small it made my birth island look substantial. Nothing stood there but a small summer house and a delicate airy temple. Paris held Helen's hand and they gamboled like lambs in spring. His men—Trojans! armed to the teeth!—flung bright flowers over the happy couple.

The soldier who had carried Pleis the whole twenty miles entered the bedroom and set him down gently enough and walked away.

Rhodea was in terrible shape. Her feet were torn and bleeding, her cheek bruised from slaps every time she tried to rest. I nearly gathered her in my arms, but I dared not let her see who I was. If I were discovered now, Paris would have time to send men back for Hermione. Bia might be killed. And since the slaves of Axon might recognize me as Callisto, I could not explain the situation to Rhodea while they bustled around us.

There were two beds, one for a prince and one for a princess. I wrapped myself from head to toe in the cloak of Hermione and lay down with my back to the others. If Pleis came over to cuddle, he would crow happily, "Calli! Sto!"

The little prince was exhausted from a long day under a hot, hot sun. He was cranky and anxious. He was not willing to lie down on a strange bed under a strange blanket without his usual toys and songs and kisses. "Princess, help me with your brother," begged Rhodea.

"No."

"May we bathe you before you sleep, Princess?" the slaves asked politely.

"No."

"May we tempt you with a hot barley casserole? Yellow cheese and honey. Easy to swallow."

I said nothing.

They had done their duty. Taking him from Rhodea, they comforted and fed and rocked Pleis. I loved them for that.

Pleis would not sleep without Rhodea, so at least she had a soft mattress, and she and Pleis were asleep in moments. The slave women slept like a litter of puppies, using each other's stomachs and backs for pillows.

Sleep was a waste of being alive. I tiptoed onto the balcony. Gythion was like a hive of bees when the keeper thrusts in his hand to take the honey. All through the night, the Trojans loaded loot into their ships and pillaged the town for supplies. Crews counted off amphorae of water and oil; checked for bread and bedding; argued whether the bronze weapons on this side of the hold would properly balance the ingots on that side.

Clever escape plans came to mind. Happy futures.

But it was my destiny to guard the future of Hermione. For in the end, she was a princess, and I had to take up my duty toward her. I prayed to my goddess. *Do not let me weaken.*

I wondered if my sacrifice for Hermione would soften some angry god against me for pretending to be Callisto. But

I did not need to worry how much was left in the jar of unhappiness. I would not be alive long enough to taste it.

When dawn came, I was still leaning on the railing of the balcony. In the first light, I counted ships. No wonder Kinados had feared Paris. Nobody ever needed thirty-three ships for a friendly visit. I wondered what Kinados had thought, sailing past all those ships as he took Menelaus to Crete.

But no—Paris would have used the strategy I had once thought of. Most of these ships would have been moored elsewhere. Even thirty ships could have been easily hidden among the jutting peninsulas and curling inlets. As soon as Kinados and Menelaus were out to sea, Aeneas would have sent some signal, by fire or by foot, and summoned the ships here.

Paris led Helen off the tiny isle. She clasped his neck. He carried her in his arms aboard his flagship. *Paphus* was the only ship with a true cabin. The rest were hollow. The stone anchor of *Paphus* was raised and the oars taken up.

And Helen, a queen abandoning her country, sailed away on a ship of Troy.

I let the cloak slip down my shoulders and puddle on the floor.

If only I had known it would play out like this! I had not wasted time on sleep, but I had certainly wasted time. At any time during the long night I could have slipped out of Axon's house with Pleis asleep on my shoulder. This town had not one wall and not one gate to stop me. In the to-ing and fro-ing of thieving Trojans, who would have noticed? The little prince and I could have been halfway back to Amyklai by now!

Helen, the only person who cared whether Pleis and

Hermione sailed for Troy, did not in fact care. Had not even looked.

O, Helen, if you do not care whether your little son is safe, no one will care. And therefore he is not safe. I must not let the Trojans take him. I must—

The slave women were stirring. I would need Rhodea's cooperation. Could I count on Axon himself, if I could find him? I would promise to marry him after all. I would give him Siphnos. I would give him sons.

It was time to stop worrying about little things like bloodlines and falsehoods in marriage vows.

But the movement in the bedroom had not been the slave women's. Zanthus stood there with two of his men. The bundle of Hermione's things was scooped up and my fallen cloak added to the pack. For good measure, the sailors took the bedding and some artwork and then snapped the bronze finial off the railing and took that, too.

Zanthus thought I was the daughter of Helen.

Helen thought I was the daughter of Helen.

In fact, everybody except the slave women and Pleis would think I was the daughter of Helen. I prayed Pleis would stay asleep for hours to come. I lifted him gently, singing as I shifted him, and he dozed on, as babies do, his little body melting into my thin shoulder and unrewarding bosom.

Zanthus kicked Rhodea to get her moving.

"Captain, you will treat my woman with respect," I said sharply.

It would have taken an oar to prop up the jaw of Rhodea. "Princess? But—you are—you are—"

"You have my permission to call me Hermione, Rhodea, for you and I are in this together. You need not stand on ceremony during our long voyage. In return I shall help you with the care of my little brother, the prince Pleisthenes."

"I'll treat your woman any way I feel like, girl," said Zanthus. "It's an insult to have the whelps of Menelaus on my ship." He frowned. "Where's your slave? I'm not nursing you. She has to carry this load. My men aren't your servants."

"The princess's nurse ran away," Rhodea said. "And I wouldn't let you touch the children of Menelaus if the other choice were drowning. I will care for the prince and princess. You stay away from them, you dog tick."

I could not have said it better.

Zanthus' eyes lit up. There is nothing a pirate likes more than spirit in a woman, because it gives him the opportunity to crush it.

Ophion was long and slim. Her eyes were painted exceptionally large and looked very far ahead. The bow had a deep inward curve, making a tiny platform where men could piss, catch fish or wash clothing. Denting the platform were tiny boarding steps so that when given a hand, a passenger could embark gracefully. I was not given a hand.

"This is a warship," said the helmsman to Zanthus. He was furious. "Do you expect me to steer with children crawling around?"

"I expect you to throw them overboard if they get in your way. Go down the gangway," Zanthus told me, pointing toward the stern.

Rhodea made it on board. Her right foot had split from toe to heel and the sailors swore at her for bloodying their just-scrubbed ship. Pleis woke up. "Calli," he said happily. "Sto."

"Baby talk," Rhodea said to Zanthus, but the captain was

paying no attention. He had a ship to sail and the helmsman was calling out the check. "Water?" bellowed the man.

"Sixteen amphorae!" came the response.

The gangway was only two planks wide. It was difficult to balance with Pleis on my hip. The mast, half as long as the ship, lay right where I had to walk. I inched sixty careful steps, a foot-length at a time, and counted twenty-four benches. There would be forty-eight rowers.

"Wine!"

"Eighteen two-handled jugs."

"Barley meal!"

"Twenty bushels in leather bags."

The afterdeck was a triangle, seven feet across, as was the *Ophion,* but quickly tapering to a narrow point. Rhodea, Pleis and I perched on the gunwales. Pleis snuggled in my lap and said his two words over and over. "Calli," he comforted himself. "Sto." He was getting better at it; the "s" lasted longer and the baby talk sounded more like a girl's name: Calliss-ssto.

I could not guess how long we would be at sea.

Men who went to trade for grain beyond Troy left in early summer and were home by fall. I was not sure what they were doing all that time, because in a good wind, Troy is only a week away. Three days to Cyprus; five or six to Egypt. But no captain could count on the wind, even one who has lately roofed a temple or sacrificed a white calf. For all I knew, Paris might plan to ravage the kingdom of Salamis as well, and get his aunt Hesione. He might stop off at every city of every ally of Troy, and display Helen in Lydia and Phrygia, in Caria and Mysia.

Even one night would be a long time at the mercy of Zanthus. I had to establish myself as a royal personage due royal respect or I could not protect Pleis. "The little prince my brother will need milk and yogurt, Captain," I called out. "Bring a ewe on board."

Zanthus grinned. "Sheep!" he shouted.

"None!" yelled the men, and they slapped their knees and howled with laughter.

I glanced back at the shore. Not one citizen of Gythion was visible. There would be no rescue. No potter dared approach his workshop and no fisherman came near his dory. A single brown pelican swooped past.

I looked out to sea. It was utterly still, the ships just toys on a pond, the distant islands like paintings on a vase. The colors were stiff and bright.

The flagship *Paphus* had nearly reached the horizon and yet half of Paris' ships had not raised anchor. The most important rule in commanding a fleet is that ships not separate. It would be difficult to keep together thirty-three ships buffeted by wind and current. But a single ship is an easy target for pirates, and every sea captain *is* a pirate, should the opportunity arise.

The men fastened leather strips around their palms, to help with the grip, and the pipes skirled, and the rhythm began, and *Ophion* headed after *Paphus*.

The Main Land grew smaller and smaller. Rhodea wept. I had no words to comfort her. Twice I had been lucky with kings: Nicander and Menelaus. I would not be lucky with Prince Paris of Troy.

All day the crew rowed.

No man can row without rest. In turn, a half dozen men would climb off the benches to rest on the two center planks, while those finished with rest would take over their oars.

Our yellow sails would not fill with wind. The sun shone through the patches, some gold, some lemon or flax, depending on their dye lots. The glassy sea and silent sky gave us no help.

Nicander's ships had every one been black hulled and red sailed, but the scattered ships of Paris came in many colors—blue and sea green and bloodred. Some sails were white, others black or yellow or red, and one was striped.

As a courtyard is spattered with mud after a child has jumped into a puddle, so the Aegean is spattered with islands. Rhodea and I had to occupy Pleis only for the day. When dusk came, I thought, the ships would pull up on some shore, the cook would produce a hot meal and we would set our fleeces on the sand. Perhaps I would know the shore. I would slip away with Pleis. I would have to abandon Rhodea, who could not walk.

But after leaving the bay, the fleet of Paris did not take the northern course along the edge of the Main Land, which was the safe and usual direction. The ships headed due east into the open sea and the water began to churn. I had felt safe on a smooth sea. But now we sailed at a god-sent speed and the waves churned around us, and the ship was nothing but a tiny cup in a frothing ocean.

Dolphins swam alongside. Now and then they would leap out of the water and spin themselves like yarn. Pleis waved and called and they seemed to wave back with their powerful tails.

The wooden cross beams of the ship groaned and sang as they lifted and sank with the waves. The song of a ship's beams is called threnody, sorrow for all that has been and all that is to be. A ship is constructed of the strongest wood; I

140

did not know how well I was constructed. I feared that I might collapse. I had to think of something to do.

I opened the bundle of Hermione's things.

Cloth is more valuable than gold, for it takes so much time and effort to go from shearing fleece, through spinning and dying and weaving and seaming, until at last there is a gown. Hundreds of hours might exist in the fine cloth of a princess's gown. I sorted through the choices Bia had made. I who had lately owned an island now owned one yellow shawl, a Medusa and four gowns. All were too beautiful to rip up, but I chose one and tore it into bandages for Rhodea's feet.

Zanthus watched.

The cook had prepared rations for the crew before sailing. Two benches at a time, the men got cold oatmeal with a bit of honey, cold flat bread and cold clear water. Rhodea, Pleis and I were fed last. The cook squatted beside us, sitting on his heels, and held out a bowl for Pleis. Good white bread was soaking in goat's milk and honey. It was the little prince's favorite meal and he put his face into the bowl and drank and chewed.

"Thank you," I said.

By nightfall we were far from any shore. We could see other ships in a soft foggy way but we certainly could not see thirty-three of them. Zanthus cut back on the number of rowers, letting as many as possible rest, but kept his ship going through the night.

The cook, to my horror, started a fire on the ship. He insisted that it was perfectly safe to have a fire on top of the ballast stones. He broiled the fish he had been catching, flipping them one by one to rowers.

A warship is not built for sleeping. The crew curled up on benches and on top of one another. Our tiny deck pitched back and forth. The gunwales were not three handspans out of the water. Rhodea was terrified. "When I fall asleep," she cried, "I'll fall into the sea."

"You fall on me when I'm asleep, woman," said a rower, "and I'll see that you fall overboard."

I lashed Rhodea to the rail, using a coil of papyrus rope and the knots taught me by the shepherds. Then I tied Pleis to my waist. He molded himself to me and slept. Zanthus examined the knots. I met his eyes and he was the first to look away.

The dark descended utterly.

The word for sea along the coast is *kolpos,* a smooth and motherly word. The word for sea far from the coast is *pelagos,* open and uncertain. But the word for deep sea is *laitma,* grim and terrible. A word to drown in.

We floated on *laitma.*

And then the men who were awake but not rowing began to sing. Every ship sang: drinking songs and long sweet ballads, rowing chants and tunes of war. Their voices were deep and rich. The threnody of the creaking ships had made me weep but the song of the sailors gave me rest. I slept, waking now and then when the sea tossed enough that the rope choked my breathing.

Dawn brought a white sky, as if the sun had gone mad. The heat was brutal. The men drank far more than their rations. The leather water bags shrank and folded. The hardened paws of the men blistered where they gripped the oars and then their blisters broke and bled.

Rhodea and I could no longer distract Pleis. Trapped in his tiny space, unable to play or run or even get out of the sun, he cried on and on. The men glared and Zanthus stooped over us. "I'll tell you a story," he said.

"No, thank you, Captain."

"When the sun hangs high in the heaven, the sea god slips into his dark and slimy caverns. There he plays with his brine children."

Seals. Pretty things until you watch them eat.

"Later in the day, his brine children rise up from the waves, shiny with foam, exhaling the stench of their last meal. Do not let the boy whine. Or the stench you will breathe from the guts of seals will be the son of Menelaus."

"Captain," I said, "you need not tell more stories."

"As long as you understand this one."

Hanging Hermione's cloak over my stretched rope, I made a tent for Pleis to sit beneath so his skin would not burn. To protect my own skin, I put the yellow linen shawl over my hair, draping it over my forehead and my cheeks. We did not know what had become of the bundle of clothing and toys for Pleis. Pleis played with my Medusa and Zanthus stayed away from us.

That second night we stopped on an unknown island with a bare and bony aspect. The men were so stiff they had to lift one another out of the benches. The cook made a fire and broiled fish, which he laced with onions and cheese. The seamen slept the moment they had finished eating.

The watchmen stumbled back and forth, never varying their pattern. Their yawns were as loud as their footsteps. They let the fire go out. The moon also went out, covered by clouds. On such an island, there would be neither wolf nor bear.

"Are you going to slip away?" breathed Rhodea.

"Of course not," I said, although my heart was already running in the hills.

"Only you can protect the little prince. I worship such as you, Lady Callisto. Do not leave us to face the Trojans alone."

"I am not worthy of worship, Rhodea." I told her how Bia had told me to take Hermione's place; how I expected Helen to kill me when at last we landed on the same shore.

Rhodea dismissed that. "Your death would not amuse Helen. She will treat you as she does Aethra. She loves a queen laid low. Do you know what Aethra did for years, until she could no longer lift anything heavier than a fleece? She drew every bucket of water for Helen's bath herself, hand over hand from the well, the rope tearing her palm. And when it had been heated, she alone carried the hot water up the stairs, two buckets at a time. Ten for a bath. Helen enjoyed saying the water wasn't warm enough. Aethra would have to bail it out, carry it down, heat it again and carry it back. That's why her shoulders are knotted and her spine twisted."

"Maybe I should just roll into the sea and breathe salt water."

"Helen would want to watch," said Rhodea.

On the third day, the weather changed so quickly that the men could not get the sail down in time. The bow plunged in great gusts and without warning the sail split. A great strip of it lashed out like a flag. The men fought to get the rest of the sail down. The mast was lowered with difficulty as the ship thrashed in a wild sea.

Ophion rose high and fell hard. Time and again our bodies were smacked against the deck and twice I bit my tongue. Pleis found it a joyful game to be hurled skyward and fall with a thud.

Rhodea became seasick.

I used the rope to bind Pleis to my chest and that was not enough, so the cook lashed us to the rail.

The sea climbed into the ship with us. Every resting rower bailed, leather bucket after leather bucket. Water gathered in the hold and the ship became unstable. The loot from Apollo's temple and Menelaus' palace shifted. *Ophion* would be swamped.

Again and again, Rhodea threw up. The sailors would give her nothing to drink. They were low on water.

Zanthus offered his best wine to the sea, but the weather did not change.

A wave as high as the walls of Amyklai came upon us like the hand of a god shoveling sand. It singled us out. The impact of that wave was like a great wet stone.

A steering oar snapped.

The helmsman needed two to control the boat. One steering oar merely makes a ship go in circles.

Men sprang toward our tiny deck. The cook yanked on the slipknot of my rope, dropping Pleis and me onto a bench whose rower had climbed out to bail. Rhodea he flung into protruding handles of oars. The rowers cursed her and shoved her away so violently that she was thrown into the oars on the other side.

From the now empty afterdeck, the men ripped up a plank for a splint, attaching the old steering handle to a spare oar to replace their rudder.

We were riding so low in the water that every wave felt like a mountain. Then I saw real mountains: Sheer cliffs loomed in front of us like the legs of Zeus. In a moment we would smash on those rock and be driftwood.

Rhodea screamed in terror.

The wet fingers of the sea held *Ophion* up in the air and then dropped her beneath a wave. We came back up, ship and men sputtering.

Rhodea vomited into the lap of a rower. The man tossed her overboard, as if she had been the pit of an olive, and continued rowing.

As swiftly as the gale had come, it ended.

The wind settled and the sea lay down. The men stitched a quick repair to the sail and stepped the mast, and we were spinning east.

"The woman was our problem," said Zanthus confidently. He thanked the rower. "The seals will eat her now. It is good."

XI

NOT ONE SHIP HAD BEEN lost in the gale. In a few hours, Zanthus caught up with the fleet. Thirty-three ships sped beneath the blazing sky.

Yet the crew was uneasy. The wind was pushing us southeast when we wanted to go northeast. We were not in danger, but neither were we in control. There was much calling back and forth between ships. "If this keeps up," said Zanthus glumly, "we shall be visiting Egypt."

"It wasn't enough to give that slave woman to the sea god," said a rower. "We are never going to get home." He jutted his chin toward Pleis and me, which is how they point in the East, with their sharp beards instead of their fingers. "Give the god of the sea a prince and princess, my captain, and we'll have a chance."

I yelled loud enough for three ships to hear. "You touch my prince, you dog of a Trojan, and the gods will rip your *Ophion* apart board by board and pierce your heart with its splinters."

Zanthus laughed and saluted me.

I had spoken like a servant or a guest, referring to Pleis as "my prince." Hermione would have said "my brother." I did not think any of them had noticed. After all, a boy and a prince is far more important than a girl and a princess. It was

147

not actually wrong for me to call my brother "my prince." Still, I must not slip again.

Once or twice we were close to the flagship *Paphus*. I stared at the tiny cabin in which Paris and Helen sheltered. I hoped Helen had been as sick as Rhodea. I hoped she had gotten sick all over Paris. I hoped the Trojan prince despised Helen now and regretted his stupidity in taking her.

But I knew better.

The half-god part of Helen would not be humiliated. That beautiful body would not vomit, not cling in terror. In fact, I found it amazing that such a woman had had four childbirths. Had Helen suffered the usual pain? The fear? The after difficulties?

Pleis played next to me, accustomed now to the fact that he could move only a few inches in any direction. He climbed over and around me, marching his only toy, my Medusa, up and down my spine. "Calli," he said to me contentedly. "Ssssto."

The crew had not noticed that Pleis did not call me "Hermione" or "sister." They thought him backward, because he spoke nonsense.

Isle after isle tilted in the shining sea. Had I been captain of the fleet, I would have put in at some safe harbor and waited for the wind to change in my favor. But Paris did not.

Ophion was always the straggler. Continually we arrived on a shore as the others were departing. And yet Zanthus to me seemed a fine captain. I did not understand why we failed to keep up.

The wind flung us where it chose until on the sixth day we arrived at the end of the sea. We were hundreds and hundreds of miles south of Troy. The Main Land here in the Far East had no cliffs and no mountains. It hardly rose above the water at all and its beaches were without end. The city whose harbor we entered was called Sidon.

Ophion was the last Trojan ship to reach port.

Not content with the shape of the land, Sidon had increased her bay with immense stone bulwarks, reaching hundreds of feet out into the water. What labor it had taken to load so many huge stones on rafts and lower them into place! Yet the walls were as smooth as if the masons had been standing in a field, not in dories tossed by waves.

Children and dogs raced along these great stone piers. Women sat dangling their feet toward the water, making fishnets. Slaves were washing salt and seaweed out of old nets and patching the tears. The Trojan fleet had largely beached, their bright sails already spread on the shore to dry. Excited vendors were trotting around, shouting for customers.

The flagship *Paphus* had been moored at the outermost end of the longest wharf, facing out toward the sea. Zanthus tied up closer to shore, *Ophion* bumping against the hulls of other Trojan ships. Fat reed mats were hung over the edges of each boat to keep them from scraping each other.

We too moored facing out. I felt oddly frightened by those thirty-three bows. The ships were not moored for easy loading but for swift departure.

But we were not here to loot. Sidon was treating Paris as a friend. I could see where flowers had been strewn, that Helen might walk on rose petals. Inside the walls, the flag of Paris was already flying next to the flag of Sidon. The king of Sidon was doubtless even now calling Helen a star in the sky, thanking the immortal gods that he had the privilege of sheltering her.

Paris could rest here only a few days, to restore the supply of food and water, and then we would have to set off. We were in danger from the changing season. Summer was nearly past. The autumn sea was too wild for ships. *Ophion,* at least, had already experienced some heavy sea.

I tidied Pleis as much as possible, given that our clothing was stained and ruined by salt water. I arranged the yellow shawl over my red hair, letting the hem dip down to shade my eyes.

Zanthus stepped off *Ophion* and onto the stone dock, where he took a long deep breath and then another one. He was braced for something. The crew stayed on board, the only crew to do so, Zanthus standing as if to protect them. He was worried.

He could not have been as worried as I was. With Pleis in my arms, I too stepped onto the wharf. Pleis wiggled to get down and I let him. He hopped up and down on the solid rocks, his chubby fingers exploring the rough edges of stone. Joyfully he tugged at the loose end of a great coil of hemp rope.

Zanthus grunted, and Pleis, who knew enough to be afraid, stood very still.

But Zanthus was watching the approach of Paris.

Paris! I would have expected him to be with the king of Sidon or with Helen. Why was he not inside the city, enjoying the admiration of his host, and good rich food and warm bathwater? Surely when Pleisthenes and Hermione were sent for, a slave would run such an errand.

Paris was wearing his parade armor, but carried no weapons and wore no helmet. His chest plates glittered in the sun. I stared at my feet, my features hidden by the scarf. My heart could not decide whether to beat faster or give up altogether. Pleis waved the frizzy end of the rope.

Twenty paces away from us, Paris came to a halt. He put his hands on his waist and stood with his legs spread. Zanthus saluted. The crew saluted. Nobody spoke.

"Rope," said Pleis, holding it out to Paris.

"They survived," said Paris.

Zanthus said nothing.

O my captain, O Zanthus! You were told to see that the children of Menelaus died. You sailed at the rear of the fleet, using your great skill to be slow instead of swift, that we would not cross paths with your prince. That you would not have to do such a shivery thing as take the lives of two royal children. You did protect us, Zanthus. You had orders from your commander and you did not obey them.

O goddess of yesterday. Thank you for your unexpected messenger. Thank you for your protection.

Paris turned on his heel and walked away.

The wind tugged like fingers and my scarf came loose and blew into the water, where it curled wetly as if over a drowned face.

A little parade of servants scurried toward us. "Your mother awaits you in the palace of the king of Sidon, princess," said a fussy little man. He was beaming and excited.

"If you mean Queen Helen," I said, "she is not my mother."

"We heard that you are very angry, princess," said the man. He bowed twice and gestured toward a carry chair. "But you must no longer speak in such a manner. The queen your mother is a goddess. No one in Sidon has ever seen her like."

That I could believe.

I pried Pleis' fingers off the rope coil, stuck the Medusa in them instead, and got into the carry chair with him in my lap. Four men lifted the chair. The slaves had been branded like cattle, which I had never seen before.

"Princess, how you have suffered!" cried the little man, trotting beside us. "Soon you will be bathed and comfortable, and your hair braided and perfumed. Jewels befitting your station will be pinned to a fresh and flattering gown. Then you shall be reunited with your lovely mother, who even now graces the finest suite we have. Tonight you and your brother sleep safe in a king's palace."

Yes. Tonight Pleis would be safe. In that fine suite of guest rooms, Helen would cuddle her little son for a moment or two. But from the look of the ships, Troy would sail in the morning. Helen would have handed me over for execution, and for Pleis, Paris would choose a different captain, to whom a prince's life was nothing.

Sun hit pavement with a ferocity that even my homeland could not equal. It blazed through my eyes and under my skin and into my thoughts. I was broiled like a fish on coals.

Sidon was lumpy and low, buildings spread like seed scattered by a careless hand. The palace walls were not painted, but left the color of sand, and its floors were plain stone, buffed smooth. Wherever sun could get in, heat came also, a seething blast, so there were few windows and the dark ceilings were high to let the heat rise. There were few statues or embroidered cushions or even flowers. The palace was decorated only by coolness and dark, and it was enough.

My bath was joy.

Six servants, all for me.

Soft oils and lotions. A comb gently taking out snarls, fingers cajoling curls back into place, a file to shape my broken nails. Perfume and ribbons. A gown of soft warm blue like a bird's egg. A shining sash, tied high and wide.

The servants found Hermione's amber necklace in my little bag of possessions, but I could not wear that noose of dead wasps. "Is there other jewelry I might borrow for the evening?" I asked.

"Of course, princess," said the women, delighted. They opened an ivory box, and from its piles of gems chose ornaments for my throat and ears and hair, for my wrists and fingers and even ankles. It was far more than a girl from Siphnos or Amyklai would wear, but in the shadowy rooms, it gleamed like treasure in a cave.

I tucked my Medusa into my gown, where she rested in the safety of the sash, and at the last moment, I wore the amber necklace after all. Perhaps the sight of her daughter's necklace would soften Helen toward me.

Pleis had won the hearts of all six servants. They fed him sweets and cooed over his smile, while he ran back and forth, exploring every corner and showing me everything. He was out of breath with excitement. He had not been able to run around like this in days.

Who would calm him tonight, when he was cranky and afraid? Would Helen rock him and sing him a lullaby?

I spoke firmly to my goddess, instructing her to stay with Pleis as long as he should live. It would not be easy to speak so firmly to Helen, goddess of another sort.

"Your daughter wanted to murder you, O queen, so be grateful. I have saved you and her from such a fate."

What mother could believe that?

"Bia, slave of your daughter, forced me to do this."

A slave could not force a princess to do anything.

"I took Hermione's place for Menelaus' sake, because he was kind to me and what you have done will destroy him."

I would merely hasten my death by mentioning Menelaus.

"I was afraid for your son Pleisthenes. And how right I was, for Paris gave orders that your son should die at sea. You do not owe me death. Helen, you owe Zanthus the life of your son."

But Helen would simply have Zanthus killed as well, for telling such lies about his commander.

I walked slowly to Helen's room. The servants chatted excitedly about the great feast to come. It would not come for me.

Who was ever prepared for the pale gold phantom of Helen?

I had forgotten how people drew back, stunned by her, and slightly afraid. The six servants lined the wall like paintings.

I had forgotten that Pleis loved her. "Mama!" he cried, running forward joyfully. "Mama!"

Helen swung him into the air, kissing his little throat and cheeks, hugging him and laughing into his eyes.

She does love Pleis, I thought. Thank you, all gods, that I was wrong about her. Thank you that Pleis is safe now.

I had forgotten that even I yearned for Helen's smile. She was so beautiful it hurt the eyes, as looking into the noonday sun hurts the eyes.

"Calli," Pleis told his mother happily, "sto."

Helen glanced my way, surprised but not yet angry. "Girl, tell my daughter I am here."

I swallowed. "Your daughter the princess Hermione remained at Amyklai, my queen."

Helen stared at me.

I felt very thin, as if the queen could see through me, as I had seen through the magic jar.

"Impossible," hissed Helen. She set down Pleisthenes, who immediately began whimpering and pulling on her dress. "Up," said Pleis, tugging. "Up, up."

Helen hated her gown to be in disarray. She looked at the toddler with dislike and the six slave women, like a flock of hens, flapped forward to get Pleis. He opened his mouth to complain, but they popped a cake onto his tongue, whisked him into a corner and kept him busy eating.

"I have just received a report from Zanthus," said Helen. Her voice was very cold, as if sleet were falling. "The captain of the *Ophion* told me my daughter behaved well. Did he mean you, girl? Am I to understand that you dared pretend to be my daughter?"

"I had to, my queen. The servant Bia kept Hermione by force and ordered me to take her place."

"Why did you not run after me and tell me? The soldiers of Paris would have dealt with such a slave woman."

I had nothing to say.

Her voice hung like snakes in a tree. "A little nobody from some rock in the sea. You deny me my own daughter in a foreign land!"

"I have cared for your son, my queen. He had no one else. His nurse was thrown overboard when she provoked the rowers. I—"

"Liar!" Her voice was a thin whip against my skin. "Zanthus told me how gladly Rhodea sacrificed herself to the sea god."

The door filled with men. Soldiers and sailors and Paris. Paris would not mind that Hermione was still at Amyklai. One less child of Menelaus to get rid of.

Helen was trembling with fury. "Dispose of the girl," she told Paris, who smiled.

But Pleis broke free from the flock of slave women. He ran to me, arms out to be held. "Calli," he demanded, tugging on my borrowed blue gown. "Sto. Up, up."

I obeyed, and he hugged me in the strangling way of babies, and from the safe and well-known seat on my hip, surveyed the room.

Zanthus' voice came from the doorway. He had told an untruth about Rhodea, but he did not tell one about me. "The girl did care for the little boy. She tied him to her during storms. She fed him and rocked him and kept him safe. She did at all times behave like a princess."

"She is not one," snapped Helen.

"I regret that I have not pleased you, O queen," I said. "I beg for the privilege of continuing to serve the prince."

Paris turned Helen toward him, kissing her diadem and hair and forehead. He stroked her cheeks and shocked everyone in the room by reaching into her gown to take out and stroke what should be kept hidden. The slaves blushed and dropped their eyes. The sailors gaped.

"Let her be a slave, Helen," he said, "and care for your dear son. He is happy enough with her and we have much travel before we are safely in Troy. Before I show off the most beautiful woman in the world to the most beautiful city." He stepped back to admire her. "Come, my goddess queen. Let us show the world how the gods have smiled upon us."

They walked out together, two stars in the night sky. But Helen paused in the door and turned to look back. "I do not like the girl's red hair," she said. "The color reminds me of someone I would prefer to forget. Shave off the hair. Do not permit her to have hair again."

Aethra held Pleis as they removed my hair. Pleis had never had a haircut himself and I suppose had never seen one. He was upset by the auburn curls and braids that piled on the floor as the sharp knife cut them away. He screamed when the knife pared close to my scalp. The king of Sidon's barber shaved my head smooth.

Many people gathered to watch.

Hair is the glory of man and woman. Even a slave may have fine hair. A warrior always prepares his hair before battle. Now I stood like an old man, comic and bald.

When it was done and people had finished laughing at me, Aethra oiled my bare scalp as one oils the feet. "Listen to me, princess. I have wept much over the years, and I am wise, for when they have dried, tears are the source of wisdom. Helen will do no more to you."

I was a slave and bald. What was left?

At least Aethra looked well. Perhaps for her, the sea air had been a tonic. I thought of Rhodea, whose last breath of sea air had been mixed with seawater. "Aethra, I am glad you are all right. We had a terrible voyage on the *Ophion*. They threw Rhodea overboard. Aethra, she was trying so hard to take good care of her little prince. Why didn't the gods help her?"

"Gods move only in the best of society," said Aethra. "No god yet has cared what happens to a slave. Therefore, my Callisto, never forget that you are a princess."

But I was weak without my hair. They had sliced away my courage. I could not keep from crying.

Aethra pressed her thumb against my forehead, exactly

where the bloody print of Queen Petra had blessed me six years before. She raised her voice so all could hear. "Now, my princess, I give you a turban. See how finely this scarf is woven, eight feet of scarlet and purple lace. I twist it around your head like so; tuck it here; pin it there. And now, my princess, look into this mirror of silver held by your slave. See how dramatic and striking you are in such a turban."

Every person in the room had heard Paris refer to me as a slave. But Aethra was not going to let it stand.

She is an island in the sea, I thought. She is my goddess of yesterday, or sent by my goddess.

How unexpected were the messengers of gods. *Angelos* is the word. I had met two of them that day, Zanthus and Aethra.

A squire poked his head into the room. "Are the prince and princess ready?" he asked. "The king has sent me to escort them to the banquet."

I could understand that the king of Sidon was confused. Was the girl from *Ophion* a princess or slave, daughter of Helen or child from a rock? Certainly Aethra was not going to make it clear. "They come," Aethra told him.

I could not appear in the king of Sidon's court as if I really were Hermione. Helen would rip the turban off my head. Then she would rip my head off my shoulders.

"When you bring them into the dining hall," said Aethra to the squire, "you will announce first the prince Pleisthenes, son of Menelaus, and you will announce second the princess Callisto, daughter of Nicander."

The squire bowed, as if Aethra were still a queen.

And she was.

———

A corps of musicians stood between us and the banquet. As one, they lifted their rams' horns and blew hard. Each sounded a different note. In the great room all of stone, the music echoed and trembled, hanging in the air after the horns were lowered.

Hundreds of citizens had to look. They were pressed against each other, against immense plastered pillars painted with battle scenes, against high walls flaring with torches. Many were the seated nobles and many were the slaves moving through the crowd, serving food.

Nobody was being announced. Aethra had not known, or, knowing, had been giving me status in front of the slaves and placing courage in my heart.

Aeneas, the cousin of Paris, beckoned. We were brought to his table, which I thought oddly placed for so important a prince. Deeply shadowed, half hidden by a column of stone, Aeneas sat with his back to Paris, facing the crowd.

Aeneas, you dog tick, I thought. You walked Menelaus to Gythion, pretending to be his guest-friend, and you waved him off to Crete, and then you turned around to attack his city. "My prince," I said politely.

"A lovely arrangement, Hermione," said Aeneas, smiling at my turban. "You are so tall and elegant in that."

No one had had time to explain the situation to Aeneas! And no doubt I did look familiar to him. He half recognized me from that dinner party at Amyklai, when there had been more discussion of Callisto than of Hermione.

He would learn soon enough. Helen, however, would not bare my skull or my secrets in this packed room. It would take attention away from her. In a crowd, I was safe.

Aeneas took Pleis on his lap and the little boy found a

cup on the table and began banging happily. I was glad to have Aeneas baby-sit, since it took all my attention to keep my head level. I thought the worst thing that could happen was that the turban would shift.

I was slow to realize that something was very wrong. A stillness had come over the great hall. Aeneas put his hand on the cup so Pleis could make no sound.

It seemed that the king of Sidon had not understood that his beautiful guest Helen was wife to Menelaus. He had not understood that the prince of Troy had in fact snatched a queen away from a living king. He had certainly not understood that this had happened when Paris was guest-friend to that very king.

A king wants every other king shown the respect that the gods handed him at birth.

"Helen is my bride now," said Paris. "Be easy in your mind, my host. Our wedding will take place as soon as we reach Troy."

At least Paris intended to wed Helen. A woman taken by force is generally made concubine, an ugly word for a woman who matters less than a wife. Helen was too fine for any title except bride, even though she had already been one, and to another man. The fact of Helen's husband did not bother Paris at all.

It bothered the king of Sidon. "Scoundrel!" he said, smashing his cup down upon the table. It was real gold, I saw, because the force of the slam dented it badly. "You had hospitality at Menelaus' hands, Paris, and yet you did the unholiest thing! You came at your host's wife."

"Now, now," said Paris easily. "Such is the habit of great warriors. Many before me have done the same. The men of Crete stole the Lady Europa from the Phoenicians. Jason and his Argonauts stole Princess Medea from Colchis."

Trojan men were nodding. It was a mark of good health if you could entice another man's wife, and Helen was not just another man's wife.

Paris went on and on, extending his list of queens taken in battle. "Of course there's Io," he said, "and Ariadne and Hesione." The same lost princess over whose fate Menelaus and Paris had argued.

The king of Sidon had yet another version of her story. "Hesione was not taken in battle, which would have been just and proper!" he shouted. "Hesione had to be sacrificed to stop a plague!"

This is one of the purposes of royal children, since they have more value than ordinary children. If a hundred white calves will not please the gods, a king's daughter will.

"The oracle ordered the sacrifice, but the king—your grandfather!—wanted to cheat, didn't he? Didn't want to kill his own daughter, did he? Wanted to kill the daughter of some lesser noble, didn't he? As if any god ever wanted lesser things." The king's voice was as loud as his trumpets. His Greek slumped and hobbled like an old donkey, but we understood every word. "But the wise nobles of Troy had already sent their children abroad for safety. Did not my own family shelter half a dozen princesses of Troy? So the old king—your grandfather!—had no choice. He bound Hesione naked to a rock in the sea. And there she was rescued by the hero Hercules. A greater warrior than you, Paris."

I thought any warrior would be greater than Paris, but his own men did not see it that way. They sucked in their breath, a unison sound, like a chorus warming up.

The king held out his dented cup for more and drank deeply. A good servant would have watered his wine to nothing. This was no time for a king to get drunk.

Aeneas transferred Pleis to my lap and freed his long hard legs from the prison of the table. He caught the eyes of other Trojans. Every man would have left his weapons in the forecourt, spear point up against the wall, until all the weapons of all the visitors had made a glittering bronze fence. To reach his weapon, Aeneas would have to get past several hundred Sidonians and many doors and halls.

And yet I thought Aeneas was actually considering it. It would be suicide. There were barely fifty Trojans in a room with hundreds of Sidonians.

The king of Sidon did not back off. This time when he slapped his cup down, the wine flecked everyone near him with purple, even Helen. "You, Paris, pretend to valor?" he bellowed. "Pig of a Trojan! You are no warrior, but a thief. I give you three days to quit your anchorage. After that you will be treated as enemies."

Paris leaped to his feet, wrenched a spear from the un-ready hand of a Sidon guard, and plunged it through the chest of the king. As blood erupted from that noble heart, so did battle erupt in that hall.

The walls and ceilings seemed to fall in. Men fought with fists and feet and fingers. They fought with chairs and tables.

Aeneas did not have to run to the forecourt for weapons. Trojan soldiers burst through every door. Thirty-three ships of men had been armed and waiting for a signal. Paris had faced his ships out for the worst possible reason: He had planned to kill and loot.

162

The body of the king of Sidon lay like rags over the royal table. Poor king! He had been told, in detail, that Paris was a guest who would rob and rape. Yet still the poor king had believed in the power of guest-friendship and had left his gates open.

In another life, I had worried because Callisto cut her bread with a knife. Truly I had been as simple as a peasant.

What you must worry about is the perfidy of man and woman.

Pleis and I survived because Aeneas did not leave us. Pushing us under the table, he drove a spear through many chests. The men of Sidon had nowhere to run. When the slaughter was complete, Paris and two score of his men surrounded Helen and headed for the ships. Aeneas held Pleis in his arms and me by the hand, while his men swarmed around us.

Outside, we found that the battle had spread into the town and across the wharves.

As on Siphnos, so here. Old women mending nets and children playing with toys were killed, soldiers and servants cut down, boats torched and roofs fired.

The Trojans cut a swathe for us. Pleis and I were handed over to Zanthus while Helen and Paris were safely taken aboard *Paphus*.

Helen stood on the prow, but that was not high enough, and she had them lift her to the roof of the little cabin for a better view.

They die, and she rejoices, I thought. She wanted them to fight over her. Just as at Amyklai. And there will be more of these battles. Menelaus will go to his brother, the Lord Agamemnon, and those two kings together will attack Troy, and again men will die for her. At Troy she will have the greatest excitement of all: husband and lover on the same battlefield.

When the battle for Sidon ended, Troy had lost two ships in the harbor and thirty-eight men in the palace. On his flagship, Paris stood hardly sweating, the only marks upon him the stains of blood and wine from the king of Sidon.

The corpses of Trojan soldiers were laid out on the sand. Helen walked among them, speaking as if they could hear, praising them for dying to protect her holy name.

She bandaged the wounded. I thought she did not touch those grisly wounds to heal them, but to have blood upon her hands.

And the living Trojans did not spit upon her nor revile her. They were proud of the risks they had taken and the damage they suffered and the pain they endured. They too would die to have the honor of her touch.

The dead were piled and set afire. Usually a dead warrior's weapons and armor are divided among his companions, but this was different. A man who died for Helen was too fine for his gear to be handed about like a used pottery bowl. Eagerly the Trojans flung every single possession of the dead into the flames.

Regally, proudly, Helen walked out the stone jetty toward *Paphus,* pausing to survey the harbor. You would have thought she had built the breakwaters, constructed the ships, trained the rowers. "We will have sons, Paris," she told him, the finest boast a woman can make.

The men burst into a great cheer.

"Our sons will be as strong and valiant as you, Paris. Our sons will bring back spoils stained with the blood of men they have slain, and make our hearts rejoice."

A great stomping of Trojan feet applauded this, feet against decks and docks, against stone and wood. The noise almost drowned out the next words of Paris to Helen. "Our sons," he promised her, "shall rule by might over Troy."

O Paris. It is you they should drown on the voyage home.

Poor Troy. You too have left your gates open.

Paris will destroy you.

XII

THE LAND OF TROY was dull and smooth like a sheet spread on a riverbank to dry.

Fields stretched for miles and miles. Only a few ancient tombs bothered the grass. Far to the south lay a low strip of mountains, dark and sullen, shifting like uneasy shoulders.

But O, the city of Troy!

Amyklai had been dwarfed by the upthrust mountains. Gythion had skittered on the edge of a great sea. Siphnos had perched on a cliff.

But Troy simply stood there, a warrior alone on the field. It did not cringe inside its walls.

Troy *was* the wall.

The hill it covered was barely a hundred feet high, but the immense walls were half again that high. They crushed the hill beneath their weight, as they would crush an enemy daring to advance. Towers, thick and muscular, squatted at each corner.

The sky was deep straight-to-god blue. Wind yanked white clouds out of the north and threw them violently.

On the battlements appeared hundreds of soldiers. Every one held a spear longer than an oar, and in unison they thrust up and out. A thousand bronze tips pierced the sky.

As from one throat came the shouts of victory: Men and women and children poured out of that great city while trumpets and ram horns and flutes and pipes wailed.

Paris!

Helen!

Troy!

"I am here, my people!" called Paris. "You have back your bright and shining son. I bring a bride. Welcome my Helen, your daughter."

Helen accepted bouquets of roses and sheaves of wheat.

Paris accepted the roars of the troops. He had adorned himself beautifully, wiring his pale hair in silver and gold. His armor bore the royal insignia of the king of Sidon. Helen's braids fell like gold tassels and she was dressed all in white, like a swan.

Only yesterday had we sailed past the island of Tenedos, whose son had warned me about swans.

The parade moved slowly over a vast flat meadow.

On an earthen bridge, we crossed a very deep man-made ditch. No enemy chariot or horse would get past that. Through wooden palisades we went, entering a lower city of workshops and potteries, sheepfolds and bakeries, crowded houses and tiny huts, stacked cords of wood and the gardens of the poor.

Aethra used me for a cane. Pleis sat on my hip, holding tight as he stared.

Every soldier, pirate and thug of Troy stomped his feet to drum a welcome for Paris.

The magnificent walls started with boulders at the bottom and rose in layers, each of slightly smaller stone, but even the smallest was more than I could ever have lifted. I was surprised to see that the walls raked slightly. If I had still been on Siphnos, still half shepherd boy, I would have scrambled right up them.

Truly there was no end to the number of kings who were sure they could not be beaten. But perhaps Troy really was different.

The road became a steep ramp. Fastened to the great gate before us, on a door thicker than an ox and taller than an oak, was a great carved horse head, snarling like a wolf.

Troy put her history in my hands. I could feel her ancient battles and hatreds. The ground seemed stained by blood.

A hideous shriek came right out of the sky. In this god-swept land, I would have believed anything. I held Pleis even tighter and pulled Aethra against me and found the courage to look up.

Jutting from the heavy watchtower that bulked out above us was another, more slender tower, built of wood. Against the great stones, it almost seemed built of splinters. Standing on a ledge so narrow it seemed safe only for birds was a girl. Dark hair swirled around her head. Her gown was flung in the wind like the white wings of many doves. Stretching her arms straight to heaven, she screamed, *"Nooooooooooooooo!"*

The people ceased their welcome. The parade halted. The sun closed its eye. The wind turned cold, as if a thread of ice connected the girl on the tower to the gods.

The girl's voice cut like a curved blade across the throat of a lamb. *"Do not take Helen in!"*

Paris gritted his teeth, snarling like the wooden horse on the gate.

"The noise of her name will shatter our gates!" screamed the girl. *"That woman is loathed of God."*

168

The girl was not looking down. High as she was, sixty or possibly eighty feet, she stared directly out. I balanced myself on the slope and looked to where her eyes went, north beyond the bay, out into the sea, past distant bright islands. Her eyes were fastened on the mountain peak of Fengari, where the blue-haired god of the sea rests when he comes out of the waves.

"It's my sister Cassandra," said Paris irritably. "Pay no attention to her, Helen, she has to be locked up for her own safety. She thinks she can see the future. She's just insane. Fifty brothers, twelve sisters, I suppose it is to be expected that one of them would go mad."

As if she had been dropped into a glass jar, Cassandra remained visible and yet disappeared. She was just there, thin and wavering against the sky. The crowd went back to celebrating and shouting.

Dozens of young men trotted forward to greet Paris and to admire Helen at close range. Helen looked slowly at each man. Each quivered and flushed, dropped his eyes and caught his breath and stared again. Her beauty was impossible. Even for me, it was impossible. They could not talk to Helen. She was overpowering. They could only talk around her.

"You missed Menelaus and his embassy by only two days, Paris."

"The king of Sparta was demanding Helen's return and the return of his treasure. We told him we didn't know a thing about it."

"Paris, did you really scrape the palace of Menelaus dry?"

"Did you actually dare empty out the temple of Apollo?"

Paris embraced one man, calling him brother, and then

did so again, and again, and it dawned on me that *all* these young men were his brothers! Priam really had fifty sons.

"We laughed at Menelaus behind his back," said another, "but we were cordial in public. Any embassy deserves honor."

"*I* wasn't cordial," said the next brother, embracing Paris. "I voted to kill Menelaus. The man will just come back a second time and be even more trouble."

They vote? I thought. How curious. Is there an assembly of princes? How could that work?

"Deiphobus," cried Paris, leaving Helen's side to move to this brother. They embraced and studied each other gladly. He had a very strange name. It had the word "fear" in it, but also the word "loot."

"Menelaus brought criminal charges against you," Deiphobus told him. "Our father beseeched him to go more slowly. Priam said he could not charge a man who was absent and unable to defend himself."

"I'm here now," said Paris, touching the hilt of his dress sword. "Let Menelaus come. I'll defend myself."

Helen smiled and took Paris' arm and together they moved forward into the city of Troy.

On the tower above, the dark-haired girl leaned into the wind, as if hopeful of being taken to heaven.

Aeneas wanted to know more about this embassy of Menelaus and questioned Deiphobus closely. Aethra and I were stuck behind him and could not move on. The old queen was shaking with exhaustion. I did not know how much longer she could stay on her feet.

Deiphobus listed the men who had accompanied Menelaus on his embassy. I knew a few of the names from song, but the name I had expected was Agamemnon, and he had not come.

"And two young boys," said Deiphobus. "The sons of the great hero Theseus. It turns out that when their father was murdered, Elpenor took the boys in. They hadn't known that their grandmother Queen Aethra was alive and servant to Helen, and Menelaus hadn't known the boys had been spared. The youngsters came hoping to ransom their grandmother."

Aethra and Pleis and I stood for a long time while the crowd flowed around us. Aethra was as wooden as the horse on the gate.

If only we had gotten to Troy a few days earlier.

But Aethra was not grieving. Her face was set in anger. "Cassandra, sad sister of Paris, was gifted with prophecy by Apollo," said Aethra. "On the same day, Apollo also cursed her. Cassandra always tells the truth, because she always knows the truth. *But no one ever believes her.*" Aethra twisted painfully so that she could look all the way up to the little tower, but the ledge was empty.

"You and I are different, Callisto. We believe. The noise of Helen's name will shatter these gates."

And Aethra smiled grimly.

King Priam was very old. His beard was entirely white, soft as lamb's wool, while the hair of his head was sparse from great age. Hands which had clenched the shaft of many a spear had stiffened, and his knuckles and fingers were twisted like knots in a sailing rig. He could get up from his throne without help, but staggered a few steps until he had his balance back.

His sons loved him.

You would think every one of those fifty sons would be waiting for him to finish up and die. You would expect them

171

to have formed alliances and hatreds among themselves, fifty little cities reaching out for power. Yet every son regarded the tottering father with affection.

Priam looked past all those sons and all their wives. He looked past all his daughters and all their husbands. His eyes fixed on Helen.

The hall of Priam was perhaps a hundred strides north to south and only about twenty east to west. Its high balconies, jammed with spectators, nearly met in the middle. Narrow slot windows high above their heads let in a chilly breeze and little light.

I could no more keep my eyes off Helen than could the shivering strangers on the balcony. Could this be the same woman who had turned her cheek half an inch to receive the lukewarm kiss of Menelaus? She was a cloud of gold and a storm of beauty.

As a swan upon the water, she glided from Paris to the king of Troy. The court was entirely silent, drinking in the sight of her. She knelt before Priam and grasped his knees, as if she were an ordinary woman with an ordinary request.

"I beg of you, dear king," she said in a new voice, an intoxicating compelling voice like a nightingale, "to accept me as your daughter. Permit me to love you and serve you. Forgive whatever trouble I may have caused. Bless my adoration for your fine son Paris. Give us a wedding, Father, and your blessing, and assure us the blessings of your people."

Helen shone in the dark megaron as a sapphire on a ring.

A sigh of pleasure came from the throat of the whole crowd.

"Daughter," said the king of Troy, "you are bride to us all. There can be no trouble. Beauty such as yours will bring only joy. You are welcome indeed." He motioned his son Paris forward, and as a groom kisses his virgin bride at the altar of the gods, so Paris kissed Helen in front of the whole court, the kiss long and slow, and every one of us in the room kissed with them, lips aching and hearts full of envy.

And Helen turned to those hundreds of strangers, and smiled upon them, and they were no longer strangers. They were hers.

For some time Helen and Paris conferred with the king, and when they left, there was still more business to transact. Aeneas revealed details of the army and navy of Menelaus. An officer described the precise geography of the kingdom of Sparta, listing towns and temples still to be looted. Still another had investigated half a dozen ports while Paris had distracted Menelaus and Kinados.

If Menelaus did not attack Troy, Troy would certainly attack Sparta. It had been so easy for Paris; so clear to the Trojans that Menelaus was weak. They hadn't murdered him only because they didn't fear him.

O my king. Did you realize that?

Which of my kings had had the worst of it? Nicander—buried in the sand? Or Menelaus—palace, family, temple, kingdom and dignity stripped by his wife?

Aethra had left the room in Helen's wake. Perhaps I would drift away with Pleis, meld into the city, find a hut, some little corner. A son of Menelaus in the city that had declared him an enemy . . .

But the next order of business *was* Pleis.

I set him down, praying that he would neither whine nor

cling, and took him by the hand to the throne of Troy. I knelt to the king while Pleis, in his sober openmouthed way, stared around. "I am Callisto, O king. Daughter of Nicander and Petra of Siphnos. I beg your permission to serve this child."

I did not repeat out loud the lineage of Pleis. I would have had to begin with Menelaus.

"My dear princess, slaves will nurse the boy. You will share a room with the princess Andromache, who is betrothed to my dear son Hector." The king smiled proudly at Hector.

Hector was the largest man I had ever seen. I didn't like looking at him. He was too big, as if he were partly bear. His hands were too large, as if they broke oxen instead of bread. His black eyes were shadowed by a forehead too jutting and his beard was not trimmed, let alone braided, but left furry like wild goat hide.

Pleis hid behind my legs at the sight of Hector. How the court laughed at fear in the son of Menelaus. He's only two years old! I thought, picking him up and comforting him. "My king, the little prince loves me. I have been his nurse for many days in many desperate moments. I beg you—"

"No," said Priam, still smiling. "Helen made these arrangements." He leaned into the word "Helen," caressing it. She had asked for this; she would have it. She would have anything Priam could give her. "Set the boy down," said the king of Troy.

With Menelaus I would have argued. Perhaps even with Agamemnon.

But the power of this trembling old man was drawn in the smoky shadows to the fine point of a knife. I set Pleis down.

"I am so glad that you and I will live together!" cried Andromache.

Her name was complex. "Andro" means "man," but "mache" means "battle." An *drom* ah kee. I puzzled about it. A girl over whom men fought battles? But that was surely Helen.

"There will be four of us princesses in one chamber," said Andromache. "Troy is very crowded. Well, what did King Priam think would happen when he had fifty sons? But someday I will finally be old enough to marry Hector and then we'll have our own house. Actually Hector already has a house; it's a fine palace, but I can't live with him yet. King Priam wants me to wait another three years. They say you're fifteen, Callisto. I am fifteen also. Waiting is boring, don't you think? I want to get married and I want to get married now."

She was small and dark and soft, with no sharp lines. She was as cuddly as Pleis. I could not imagine her with Hector.

Her chamber appalled me. Anywhere else, it would have been called a wide place in the hall, not the boudoir of a princess. And this space was to hold four of us? Each girl had a trunk, but to save room, bedding and fleeces had been rolled up and stacked on top of them. It was just as well I possessed nothing.

"You have nothing, Callisto!" said Andromache. "This is dreadful. But that's what happens when you travel on the water. The storm blows your fine things into the waves and the rest rots from the salt. How you must have suffered! In my experience, sailing is merely another word for suffering. I came here by ship and I was sick the whole way. I hope never to stand on the deck of a ship again. You will find Troy a very healthy place, though. We are high above the marshes and the wet poison of their air. The wind that comes steadily from the north? You can hear it now, banging every shutter? If you look out that window, you'll see every flowerbed protected by a fence. The only plant that wants to grow here is grass. But the same wind blows every illness out to sea. Now, do not worry for a moment about your wardrobe. Queen Hecuba loves me; you have not met the queen yet, she is quite old and rests a good deal, but Hecuba will do anything for me. I'll see that you have all the gowns you need and lots of jewelry. I love jewelry. And perfume. I love perfume."

Andromache and every other Trojan woman I had seen wore exceptionally long gowns whose hems trailed on the stones. It was a sign of great wealth, for the cloth would quickly wear out, and few households could support that luxury.

"Now let me see your hair," said Andromache. "I love how you have twisted that scarf into a turban, but it isn't fashionable, Callisto, and we must have my hairdresser come. Hector's hair is very black and he doesn't bother to braid it. He doesn't even comb it. He doesn't like Paris' hair; he says only girls spend that much time on their hair. Your hair is—" She broke off, alarmed by the sight of my scalp, just beginning to bristle with hair. "What a fever you must have had, Callisto," she said very softly. "But do not refer to it. In this city, it would be trouble."

She seemed to have trouble herself, thinking of a bald head, and I understood. It was kind of her to say I had suffered a fever and been shaved to let the heat out. She certainly knew it was more likely that I had been prepared for some great shame, like slavery.

I wondered how long I would be treated as a princess.

Why had Helen not given King Priam instructions to enslave me right away?

I rewound the turban.

Once my head was covered, Andromache became cheerful again. "Now I will show you Troy. We will run on the battlements and visit Cassandra and stop by the weaving room and of course—" A dimple poked in one cheek and she shot me a marvelous smile. "And of course, we'll end up wherever Hector is. I'm not allowed to visit Hector that often. The king says it's forward. But you're with me. You'll be my chaperone. Now, don't be afraid of Hector. He's easy to be afraid of; he's sort of like the handle of an ax, don't you think, or maybe the blade, but actually he's just a puppy."

I collapsed in giggles. "I have never seen anybody in love before," I said. "I love love. Another princess and I, long ago, used to talk about falling in love. And you've done it."

Her laugh spilled around me like water from a fountain. "Helen fell in love," she pointed out. "Paris fell in love. You watched them, Callisto."

In my heart, I introduced myself properly. My name is Anaxandra, I wanted to tell Andromache. No, not *Alex*andra. *Anax*andra. Most people get it wrong the first time.

I did not think Andromache would get it wrong. I was dizzy with the desire to tell her the truth. But truth of another sort leaped out of me. "Helen loves only herself," I said. "I agree with that princess on the tower. Helen inside your gates is danger inside your gates."

The sparkle went out of her dark eyes and she looked away.

I had torn the fragile fabric of a new friendship. Helen was their bride—their new sister—their new daughter. I should not have said a word against her.

177

It dawned on me why Helen had not destroyed me today. She entered Troy as beauty: all beauty, wholly beauty. To whip or enslave a princess, while common in war, is not an act of beauty. Helen did not want Priam to witness her as a hard woman. Not yet.

"Show me what you embroidered on your voyage, Callisto!" cried Andromache. "Is *this* what you were working on during the long days at sea? Oh, Callisto, it's simply beautiful! You are *so* good with a needle. You *must* show me how to make this stitch. It looks like a star."

I was not holding anything. I had not had needlework on the long voyage, only a lap full of salt water or Pleis. Andromache put her own needlework into my hands.

"This," said Andromache, folding the needlework over so it could not be seen, and lifting her eyes and chin in a gesture toward the door, "is one of our serving women, Kora. Kora, this is the new princess, Callisto, who comes to us from Siphnos."

Kora was a bear of a woman with pocked skin and fingers like sausages. She could have been twin sister to Hector, she was that big. Her nose was squashed and her lips puckered inward. She had lost her teeth.

"Kora often has the honor," said Andromache brightly, "of tending Prince Paris. No doubt she will now assist the Lady Helen."

I could imagine Kora in the slaughterhouse, cutting up a lamb. I could not imagine her tending a prince or a princess in the bath.

Andromache held my eyes until I grasped the manner in which Kora tended Paris.

Much as a prince might wish for it, walls do not have ears. If a prince—Paris, say—needs to listen in on the conversations of others, he must send someone. Kora would take up as much space in a hall as three pillars. Yet I thought this ugly pudding of a woman would arouse no more notice than that, either.

"You were about to tell me about Cassandra," I said to Andromache.

"Oh, poor Cassandra. She and I used to weave together, but the gods blew breezes through her mind. Now she swears at the people and screams at the gods and beats her head against the wall. Cassandra isn't supposed to have visitors and she isn't supposed to leave the tower. Of course, nobody pays any attention, especially me. I go up to gossip and bring her more embroidery floss, and sometimes we play ball on the parapet and now and then we go to the temple together. I will take you to the temple in the morning, Callisto. The Palladium is very dear to my heart."

I was not sure I really wanted to see the Palladium.

Andromache nodded. "It is frightening," she agreed. "Hector's grandmother was one of the women who saw it come down from the heavens. She thought it was a shooting star, but it got brighter and closer. Do you know it actually screamed with pain when it entered the world? It was Athena herself, and she left us her image. The image is attended by many priestesses and acolytes. The temple is the highest place in Troy. Beneath it are the treasuries, connected by tunnels, and far, far below are springs of cold water, and even deeper are the shelves where the acolytes sleep. They're never allowed out in the sun, you know, once they have given themselves to the goddess. They'd be killed if they were seen."

Andromache took my hand. She moved like a spindle whorl, twisting faster than the eye could see, and I whirled after her, and we toured Troy like two little gusts of wind.

The city was almost entirely roofed. Polished pillars and long colonnades lined streets as narrow as threads. Houses were stacked haphazardly upon and against one another. The stairs were not long fine stretches, but steep uneven steps thrown against a wall here, spouting up inside a room there. Floors followed the tilt of the hill, some floors as steep as a goat path and others with a step in the middle.

We came suddenly upon the main avenue. Its cobblestones were shiny brown in the sun. It was a dramatic road, stretching from the Gate of the Horse up to the palace, swinging right and then stepping up to the Palladium. I shuddered, thinking of acolytes in the cold wet dark, kneeling before a goddess who had thrown herself out of heaven.

"The palace has enough bedrooms for all fifty sons," said Andromache, "and on an upper floor, for the twelve daughters. But of course some sons have gotten married and they have children of their own and their wives insisted on moving out. People sleep in every corner of the palace by night, and by day they explode into the halls like the seeds of a flower when you shake it in the wind. Now this palace in front of us belongs to Deiphobus. He's everybody's favorite brother."

She pulled me down a narrow lane paved in beach pebbles to another house. Its walls were whitewashed, shutters painted blue and yellow. From behind a wall a sycamore spread its branches. "Hector's mansion," she whispered, as if it were a secret. We admired her future home. A huge tangled stork's nest covered the roof. It is a good thing to be greeted every year by a stork. She would have a good marriage.

We whirled on until we came to the house of Paris. "It isn't ready yet," Andromache told me. "The paint's still wet."

It looked very small. "How many rooms does it have?"

"A fine hall, an inner chamber and a courtyard full of flowers."

Helen had given up the great palace of Amyklai for two rooms and a bit of sun on stone. I wondered where Pleis would sleep.

"Now, *this* mansion belongs to a general who is *not* a son of Priam. He has to introduce himself that way. 'I'm not one,' he says. Here, dash up these stairs with me. Cassandra will be so glad to have company. She'll be desperate for everything we can tell her."

I was puzzled. "I thought she knew everything already."

"She can see the future," explained Andromache, "but the present confuses her. And she's so lonely, it doesn't matter if you talk about things she already knows. She just wants you to come. She likes me because I talk so much. I try not to. Hector is already a little cranky with how much I talk. He has discussed with me the beauty of silence. But Cassandra never discusses the beauty of silence."

I thought Hector was a fortunate man. I thought perhaps the battle and the man of Andromache's name were both Hector, and I expected that she would be the victor. I said, "Does Cassandra know the past as well?"

"I don't know. How interesting. You must question her."

Up on the highest battlement, Helen walked with a bent and silvery old lady. "Queen Hecuba," said Andromache affectionately.

So this was the queen who had had to put up with all those other wives. I pressed against the wall to keep from being seen by Helen. Pleis must be alone somewhere, I thought suddenly. It will be safe for me to go comfort him.

Andromache hid from Helen too. "I think Helen will insist that the rules about Cassandra are kept. No visitors. No getting out of the tower. If you were Helen, would you want Cassandra shrieking from the top of every wall that you pollute the city?"

"If I were the city," I said, "I would not want Helen."

Andromache told me a real secret. "Hector says," she whispered, "that Paris should have been stoned. And Helen with him."

I thought more highly of Hector. "Andromache, may we find Pleis?"

She regarded me thoughtfully. "You love the little one?"

"Yes."

"Then we'll find him."

The rooms in which Paris and Helen would live until the paint dried in their tiny house were in the same wing as Andromache's little space. The door was open. I stepped in.

Pleis sat on the floor between two long-legged pale gray hounds. Their muzzles were sharp and graceful, and they were neither barking nor growling. They seemed willing to have Pleis lean all over them.

Pleis was playing with a sword.

Not a parade sword, not a toy sword, but a great hacking instrument of death. It was too heavy for him to lift. He did not yet know which end was the handle and which the killing tool. He was pulling it by the blade, his little face intent upon the task.

A few feet away, Paris leaned on the wall, bright-eyed as a snake looking into a nest of baby birds. "Pick it up, son of Menelaus," he said to the baby.

"He might cut off his own hand!" I exclaimed. "Take your sword away from him."

"Well, well," said Paris, straightening out of his slouch.

"The island princess. Daughter of one who does not keep promises."

"You don't keep them either. By dining with Menelaus, you were promising him guest-friendship. You broke that promise."

"The last person who accused me of that," Paris said, "is dead, isn't he? The king of Sidon, wasn't he? I left him a corpse, didn't I?"

"Calli," said Pleis happily, "sto." The blade slipped out of his grasp and fell hard against his plump little leg. I cried out, but it fell flat side down. I moved to take the sword away from him, but Paris twisted my wrist behind my back. "Leave these rooms and don't ever come back. Or you will discover that I have a friend in need of a pretty little slave girl."

Andromache lifted the sword out of Pleis' reach and pushed the dogs away with her slippered foot. "So you are Pleisthenes," she said, scooping him up and kissing his little face.

Even though he was only two years old, this was a boy who would rather have the sword. He squirmed to get away from her.

"Why, Andromache," said Paris. He had not cared about me, but he was shocked to see her. "My dear future sister," he said uncertainly. He released me. "What an unexpected pleasure. I'm so sorry Helen is not here to meet you."

It came to me that Andromache would outrank Helen. Andromache would marry Hector, the first son, the man who would be king when Priam died. Andromache would be queen of Troy! Helen would be merely another princess at the very end of a long, long row.

"We will be sisters, Helen and I," said Andromache, as if

183

this pleased her; as if she and Hector had never discussed the stoning of Helen and Paris. "How proud Helen must be of her dear little son. Someday Hector and I will have a little boy as strong and sweet. There are so many good things happening, Paris. I see that you know my new princess friend, Callisto. We're going up to visit Cassandra now and we'll ask her what Callisto's future is." She held Pleis high in the air so his tunic exposed his fat little tummy. She nibbled his belly button and tickled his ribs to distract him from the sword on the floor. He arched his back and giggled happily. "We're going to climb a tower, Pleis," she told him. "A high tower with steps. Up up up up up. And Callisto is coming, too."

Pleis beamed at her. "Up up up up up," he agreed.

"That's very kind of you, Andromache," said Paris courteously, "but his mother wants him to stay here." Paris lifted Pleis out of Andromache's arms. I was relieved to see that Pleis didn't seem afraid of Paris. Just squirmy.

Paris dropped him to the floor, inches from the sword blade. The dogs were startled but glad. They licked his face and Pleis collapsed in giggles. He had forgotten the sword. As soon as the dogs went back to sleep, he would find it again.

Andromache spoke into the dust motes that shivered gold in the sunlight. "Do put the sword out of reach, my brother. You never were cleansed of blood guilt for the last little boy who died from your weapons. How awful were it to happen again."

Andromache was short and Paris was not. She had to stare up into his eyes, a small chubby girl ordering around a prince who had just ruined one king and slaughtered another.

Eventually, Paris obeyed her.

184

The stairs that went up inside the dark tower were narrow and without a rail. We climbed in single file. A flickering torch shot our shadows up the white plaster wall. At the top we came out onto that very slender wooden walkway. That ledge. I felt as if I were standing again on the cliffs of Siphnos. Certainly I was once again surrounded by pirates.

Around us, the fertile land of Troy lay like a blanket neatly folded and then in the distance became a blanket shoved into a pile instead. Distant forests and deep glens went all the way to the long low escarpment I had seen when we had arrived. A sluggish mountain mother with her hill children crawling toward her.

"That's Mount Ida," said Andromache. "Very holy. There are many temples and shrines there, and every forest between is thick with oak and fir—"

"Andromache! Oh, I'm so lonely, I'm so glad to hear your voice, they've locked me up again."

"Yes, Cassandra," said Andromache through the door. "It's your own fault; you shouldn't have cursed Helen. Now I've brought new threads for you to weave. Glorious colors. Hector got them from his friend Euneus, the king of Lemnos. Poppy red and dark pine green and marine blue."

"Thank you," said Cassandra gloomily.

"And I've brought a new friend. A lovely princess."

"I saw her while you were exploring the city," said Cassandra. "Girl whose past reaches out of the sea like the hands of a skeleton."

"Cassandra, try to be pleasant," said Andromache. "Callisto is from the island of Siphnos, chosen by Helen to take care of her little son on the voyage."

"Lies," said Cassandra.

185

She was right. I wasn't Callisto, wasn't from Siphnos, hadn't been chosen by Helen and never would be. But one lie Cassandra the all-knowing had missed: I wasn't a princess either.

"Even now, girl from a bony isle, your parents search for you," said Cassandra.

"My parents search for me?" I was stunned. Could Iris and Chrysaor have forgiven me? Could my father be following me over the trackless sea? Or could I have misunderstood the past, as children do, blaming sorrow on myself when nobody else thought of it as anything but war?

"They will not find you," she said. Her voice was like spun wool, soft and thick.

I thought of that lost life, on that lost isle. "Yes, they will, they must!" I cried. I pounded on the wooden door that kept the mad princess apart. "Cassandra, tell me this. If they cannot find me, can I find them?"

A puffing soldier clomped up the narrow stairs. He was short and heavy, his leather cuirass badly worn and his buckles unpolished. His uniform had no medals, no ribbons. It did not appear that guarding Cassandra went to the best and the finest.

"I'm sorry, Princess Andromache," he said. "The princess Cassandra can have no visitors. You must leave." He pointed to the stairs.

Cassandra began sobbing.

"Please let us stay," begged Andromache. "Cassandra needs me. All she has is one window to see out of."

"The problem is not that I can see out," said Cassandra. "The problem is that I can see in. Into people's hearts and futures."

"Go," said the guard, nudging us toward the stairs. It was

a very narrow ledge for nudging. We backed up. "Hector will throw me off this tower if I let that madwoman breathe on you," added the guard.

Andromache was furious. "That is not so! Hector is delighted that his future wife is friends with his dearest sister. Who said that to you?"

The guard flushed. He stepped forward, and we had to step back or fall. But when Andromache had her foot on the stair, she refused to go farther.

Finally the guard said, "Paris did. Maybe I misunderstood him, princess, but I didn't misunderstand about visitors. The king gave the order. You can't visit."

Andromache muttered something about Paris and went down the steep steps double speed. I paused on the second step. "Cassandra? Is Pleisthenes safe?"

"Ah, my new friend," said the princess of Troy, "you know the answer to that."

XIII

IT WAS JUST BEFORE DAWN when Andromache shook me awake.

We stepped over the other two sleeping princesses and their maids.

The torches in the palace halls had burned down. The scent of lamp oil and old smoke filled the corridors. We stepped around deep-breathing slave boys and over tired soldiers whose watch had ended. Some were wrapped in fleeces, some in wool blankets, some in ox hide. Some just curled on the floor like dogs.

Andromache wound down one hall and up a stair and along another hall. "Since the Palladium must not be hidden from the sky," she whispered, "the temple cannot be roofed and we who worship there cannot be covered. No one may wear scarf or veil, hood or turban."

I shrank in horror.

Andromache patted my shoulder. She slipped into a side room, was gone several minutes, and emerged with the strangest thing I had ever seen. I was a head without hair— and this was hair without a head.

She held it out to me, but I stepped back.

"It's called a wig," she breathed. "It's woven from the braids of slave girls. It was made for the mother-in-law of one of the princes. The poor thing is bald, which usually happens to old men. The shame is great, especially in this city, so her daughter had wigs made for her. Don't worry, she has another wig, and I'll get this one back before she misses it."

I stuffed my turban scarf inside my gown, where it rested in the pocket made by my sash, keeping Medusa company. The wig hair was shiny and black, and I felt safe inside the hair. My bristles poked upward and tried to unsettle the wig.

We left the palace and went out into the pink half-light that comes before sunrise. We climbed to the north promontory on stairs cut very high; each step was an effort that strained the heart. When we arrived at the temple of Athena, we were panting.

It was a slender graceful building, pillars as slim as the arms of a goddess. The endless wind of Troy sang between each pillar and around each beam, and the temple murmured to itself.

We entered a sacristy, where a sleepy priestess gave each of us a pyxis. How often had Petra carried such a delicate vase, her right hand extending it toward the goddess, her left fingers blocking the hole at the bottom. With measured step and reverent head, Petra would have approached her altar. Her maids would have been carrying the flowers and her squire the flame.

And yet the gods had not protected Petra when pirates attacked.

How dare you? I said to those gods. How dare you accept her holy oil and reverence? How dare you accept any gifts of life—fruit and flowers, blood and flame—and not return the gift when it is needed? *How dare you?*

The cold wind leaned down, murmuring a message from those gods: *You will never understand us. Do not even try.*

I held my pyxis as far out in front of me as I could, mumbling my prayers. Then I slid my finger away from the tiny hole, letting the sacred oil fall drop by drop.

As once a little girl had been horror-struck by a frozen boy in a strange courtyard, so was I horror-struck by this goddess. Her rock prison had saucers of gleaming black, ridges of black scar tissue and pockmarks of black disease. I could see where the head strained to be free, where the arms fought against the grip of the stone.

An attempt had been made to pacify the trapped goddess. A spear was bound where its right hand might someday emerge from the rock, for Athena is a warrior. Laced where three stone fingers had gotten halfway out was a gold distaff, for Athena is a spinner.

"Don't get closer," breathed Andromache.

I would never have gotten closer.

The priestess took back each empty pyxis and we lifted our hands outward, as if to embrace the knees that were not there, and then we backed away.

I knew then that Cassandra was wrong. Even the noise of Helen's name could not shatter the gates of Troy. No enemy could take Troy. This goddess was so much stronger than my goddess of yesterday. No man could desecrate this holy hill.

The stables were vast affairs, with barns for hay and oats, corrals for foals and mares, training rings for the colts, and shelters for chariots, where the wheels were carefully laid against one wall and the folded cars on the other. The horses of King Priam lived better than most peasants.

"Hector's horses are Golden, Whitefoot, Blaze and Silver

Flash," said Andromache. "I visit most days and feed them out of my hand."

I too would have eaten out of Andromache's hand. The moment we were out of that temple, she pulled me into a corner not yet lit by the sunrise, whipped out a scarf of her own and tied it over my wig and under my chin, so the wind could not pull off my stolen hair. I probably looked quite ordinary, although with dark hair instead of red.

We were below the citadel now, far beyond both the first and second palisades. Dry pasture stretched for a mile until the ground became soggy and green, filled with reed and sedge and horses. Hundreds of horses wandered in marsh grass up to their bellies, around willows and young elms, thorn thickets and tamarisk.

I had thought the plains were dull. Now I wept at the beauty of wild horses and tall grass.

A silver river poured toward the sea, like an echo caught between stones.

"The Scamander," Andromache told me. "When we have our first son, Hector will name him for the holy river. Scamandrios."

I was so envious of her. She knew she was loved, that she would have a palace and sons, that she would be first among women in Troy.

I too will be a woman soon, I thought. I believe I have turned thirteen years. I was born at the end of a summer, and summer is over. In fact, autumn is nearly over.

"Oh, look!" cried Andromache. "Hector's riding Silver Flash."

I have seen chariot races, those wonderful displays of speed and power and daring, the driver in his race colors, the stallion with his mane braided. But now for the first time I saw a man on a horse's back.

Riding a donkey or mule is merely a slow and bumpy way to get somewhere without using your legs. But riding a horse is an act of grace.

"No stallion bred Hector's horses," Andromache told me. "His horses were sired by the wind."

It shivered me. A mare alone in a meadow—and the breath of a god gives her a foal. But then, all Troy was god-swept.

Hector was not alone. A friend was riding with him, and I found it astonishing that such a rare and handsome skill as riding a horse was just play for Hector—like a ball game! He had invited a friend along.

Hector's hair was hanging in loose untended curls and his black beard was even shaggier than before because of the high wind. He looked like a piece of a forested mountain, thrown down by a god.

His friend, too young for a beard, had threaded his curls through the gold rings of a cap. The rings bounced against his back. Both men wore heavy capes against the chilly dawn and divided tunics, a piece for each leg.

When Hector and his friend removed themselves from their horses by vaulting down, I could not contain myself. "Oh, sir, please, I beg of you. Will you take me riding? May I do what you are doing? May I sit on your broad-backed horse and speed like the wind? Oh, sir—"

"Girls don't ride, Callisto," said Andromache, giggling. "Most men don't either. Hector and Euneus are just showing off."

"We certainly impressed our newest princess," said Hector, grinning. His grin was largely hidden by the overlap of beard. "I am Hector, Callisto, and this is my friend the king of Lemnos."

Lemnos is a large island in the Aegean Sea, west and north of Troy. We had not sailed near it. I knew nothing about its noble families. I bowed to the young king.

"His name is Euneus," said Hector. "He is the son of Jason of the *Argo*."

We were in the company of the son of Jason?

I no longer cared about Hector. I didn't even care about horses sired by gods. "And do you have it still?" I cried. "The Golden Fleece? And do you have the ship? Is that what you came to Troy in? The *Argo*? And have you explored as far east as your father did? Have you traveled over the Second Sea and into the Third Sea, the one they call Black?"

Euneus was laughing. "Which would you rather do, my princess? Ask questions or ride?"

"We can do both," I said quickly. "Your horse is beautiful," I told the son of Jason. "What is her name? Is she really strong enough to bear you? Is she one of Hector's god-sent horses? I thought a king would ride a stallion."

"Her name is Dove," said the king of Lemnos, "because she is white and gray. Stallions can be difficult to manage. For pleasure, a mare is best."

"Do you still have the Golden Fleece?"

"We never did have the Golden Fleece," said Euneus. "My father had to give it to King Peleas."

Hector put a finger on my lips to keep them closed. "I see, Andromache, why you and Callisto became friends," he said. "You are both quicksilver."

Quicksilver is a metal I have seen only a few times. It is liquid, like honey, and comes from the ugliest rock that lives, the cinnabar. Cinnabar is used to make vermilion, the beautiful dark red dye, but quicksilver is just a curiosity. Spill it onto a plate and it pours like water, but whip it with a stick and it separates into shiny beads. You cannot pick these beads up, but if you roll them against each other, they become solid again.

"I'm not sure I want to be called quicksilver," said Andromache. "It is a poison, after all. You can put it out in grain and the rats eat it and die."

"I didn't mean it that way," said Hector. "I meant that you and your new friend are all dance and motion. Shining like silver. Beautiful." He touched her cheek as if she were the most precious thing in the world, and my heart ached with wishing I could have such a love one day.

"Come, Callisto," said Euneus, giving Hector a chance to be alone with Andromache. "I will show you riding."

I checked the knot of the kerchief under my chin. It would not do to have the wig fly off as we sped over the Trojan plain.

Hector bent down and made a cup of his two linked hands. Euneus put one foot on this step of fingers, thrust himself up as Hector lifted, and was aboard the horse. I prepared to place my foot there too, but Hector put his great hands around my waist and lifted me as easily as a doll, setting me down sideways in Euneus' lap. I wanted to sit frontward like Euneus, but I had no divided tunic.

Euneus wrapped his cape around both of us and I sat in the cozy tent of his chest and cloak. He tucked my fingers into the soft white mane of the mare while he gripped the leather leash that ran through the horse's mouth.

"Can't the mare chew right through that leather?" I asked.

"Yes," he said, "so it isn't leather in her mouth. There's a cylinder of bronze for her to bite down on."

"I don't think I would want to bite on that. What does it feel like on the tongue?" I asked, making a face.

I felt his laughter underneath me. "I don't know. I suppose the way the tip of the knife feels when you put a bite of meat in your mouth. Perhaps when we return to the stable, we'll try it."

We rode gently for a time, and then picked up speed and galloped down the wide plain. The four hooves of the horse pounded in a wonderful rhythm. It was remarkably loud. The whole world would know that we were coming.

But there was no one to hear. The world was three: a king, a girl and a horse.

The wind flowed through the mare's mane as a river flows downhill. I had to breathe carefully so I would not choke on all that quick air hurled into my lungs. The earth passed beneath us at a terrifying speed. Euneus was hanging on by the muscles of his thighs, tightening them against the horse's great flanks. I could have sat forever in his lap, tasting speed.

But at last he pulled Dove down to a slow pace and circled her in a long gentle walking curve, and we looked back at the city of Troy. Her flags and banners stood straight out in the wind, scarlet and gold embroidery on the blue cloth of sky.

"Thank you, my king," I whispered. "Thank you so much."

I have been lucky in my kings. Nicander. Menelaus. And now Euneus, who had let me ride a horse.

Euneus slid off the mare, leaving me alone on her back.

He led her for a bit and I swung my leg over and sat astride, tugging the gown to cover myself. It didn't quite cover. Euneus looked at my legs, bare from the thigh down. He did not look away.

Then he stopped walking and the mare stopped with him. I put out my arms and he lifted me but he did not set me down. Still holding me at the waist, he swung me in a circle and kissed me.

I had never been kissed.

I had not known that a kiss could sweep you away as fast as a racehorse.

I gasped and swallowed and wet my lips where his had been, and he kissed me again and set me down. "I didn't think I was old enough for anybody to want to kiss me," I said shakily.

"You're old enough." He wrapped the mare's reins around his wrist. We walked toward the city on soft earth, and my hand was soft in his, and my heart was at sea.

He said, "Tell me of Siphnos, princess. I know only that it is a rich island, an island of gold."

I told him of cliffs that bled stone and crescent moon beaches. I told him of Petra's flowers and Nicander's mining engineers. Of Seaweed, the puppy I had had so short a time, although in this version, I lost Seaweed at Siphnos. I told him of my goddess, and my room at Amyklai, and the decision Bia and I made when Zanthus knocked on the door and I put on the cloak and hood of Hermione.

"You had such courage," he said. "To defy Helen? To impersonate the princess Hermione? No wonder she dislikes you." He turned my hand up and traced the lines. "Look what is written in your palm. You are strong in the magic, Callisto," he said softly.

We were both talking gently, as if sharing secrets. Or hearts.

"Petra said that," I whispered. "That I am strong in the magic."

He looked at me strangely. "You refer to your mother the queen by her first name?"

My hand in his went cold. My cheeks turned hot red and my mouth dry. I had lied to so many people. How I wished I could tell the truth to fine people like Euneus, Andromache, Hector. "I have had many mothers, my king," I said finally. "I have been lucky in my mothers."

"I envy you," he said. "I have not been lucky in mine."

He told me about the queen his mother, a terrifying woman, beside whom Helen was weak and yielding. His stories made me giddy with that helpless horror and we could not help laughing, and the horse whickered, as if she too caught the joke.

But no matter how slowly we walked, the walk came to an end. We reached Hector and Andromache once more.

"You have given me much to think about, my dear," said Hector, letting go Andromache's hand. "But return now to the palace. The day grows colder. Winter comes very soon, I think. You two are not wearing warm enough clothing." He gave me a worried look. "You did not ride as much as I thought you would. Was it unpleasant?"

My smile covered my whole face. Hector raised his eyebrows at Euneus, and Andromache giggled. "It was pleasant," I said, and my cheeks turned red once more, but not from fear.

The real Callisto and I, playing with her dolls, used to pretend that one day we would fall in love. We talked of boys, of whom we knew very little. I would tell the princess what I knew from watching shepherds, none of which was very promising, and she would say hopefully, "But a prince would be different."

And she was right.

A prince was different.

But I had another prince to think about.

Morning in the palace of Troy meant rolling up hundreds of fleeces and blankets and sliding them beneath benches, onto shelves and under beds. The morning after my ride in the lap of Euneus, I dawdled until the three princesses and their servants moved on.

Winter shutters were being fastened over most windows. The first few days of a completely dark hall is rather fun, everyone a child again, playing hide-and-seek or blind men. Those halls that would not have torches had to be memorized, and where torches would be necessary, they would not be used so early in the lighting season. It was a waste of good lamp oil.

Ladders and step stools were dragged down the halls as men got to work on the shutters. These were beautifully painted, gauzy flowers in every shade of pink and rose, but the moment they were shut, it would be too dark to tell.

I had but moments before the workers came into our hall. I rummaged among the possessions of the squires until I found a divided tunic. In Andromache's room, I tore off my gown and pulled the short tunic up my legs. It was strange to have a skirt on each leg. I knew from the eyes of Euneus that I was fast becoming womanly, but the tunic covered my thighs. If I laced my sandals all the way up to my knees, it would cover any shapely ankle I might have developed.

It took longer than I expected to find enough courage for the next step.

I am strong in the magic, I told myself.

But it was not true. No magic makes hair grow back. Only time will serve.

I unwound my turban and tucked it carefully into my rolled fleece.

Hair this short was peculiar, for boys generally wore their hair quite a bit longer, but not strange enough for questions. I was now dressed and shorn as a boy.

From my fleece I removed my only treasure other than Medusa: the amber necklace of Hermione. I unstrung the necklace, removed a single bead with a single dead wasp, and tied the necklace back up. I found I was not quite brave enough to go bareheaded, even in such dark. I rummaged in the shadows and took the unknown boy's old woolen cap. It was moth-eaten and smelly. It was perfect.

Twice I bumped into someone, but we apologized as one does when the halls first go dark, and I felt my way onward. In the streets, I was just another servant boy, huddled against the wind. There had been frost. I pitied the field hands grubbing for the fallen olives.

Somewhere in my heart, I must have known that my fate was to be as harsh as that, for I thought so much about the slaves now, and about their hard lives.

If I saved Pleis, would some god forgive me for stealing the life and name of a princess? Probably not. Once a god is angry, there is no end to it.

I left by the Scaean Gate. "Scaean" means "on the left." I wondered what it was on the left of, so when I had found my way to the market in the lower city, I looked back.

It's to the left of an attack, I thought. If I were Menelaus, and assembled my troops on the plains . . .

I wanted to run to King Priam. *You opened your gate!* I would shout. *Don't you know what happens when a king leaves his gate open? You let Helen in—Helen! She who opened the gate to destroy her own kingdom! How can you so blithely say that any trouble she brings is fine with you, you are so honored by her presence? Do you know what it will be when Menelaus and Agamemnon go through your city with a net?*

But he would not listen to his own daughter Cassandra and he would not listen to me. And although I was falling in love with Troy, with Andromache and Hector, with the lovely city and broad plains, with the horses in the marsh and the river of silver, and yes, with Euneus . . . still, I was no Trojan. Still, it was Menelaus to whom I was loyal.

And Pleis.

The citadel of Troy was paved, but not the lower city. It had rained a little in the night, and everything was muddy and skimmed with ice. The worst thing about winter is the filth.

I worked my way through the market. Only staples were for sale. Oil and vinegar, dried peas and lentils, flour and honey. No fresh vegetables except onions and leeks. No flowers or fruit. Cheese, of course. Sheep's yogurt, my favorite.

I had a sudden sharp memory of my birth island. We had berries there, dark and juicy and sweet. My mother would mash them and stir them into the thick soft yogurt and spoon the sweet cream into my mouth as if I were still too young to feed myself. We would laugh and my brothers would roll their eyes. I would let Seaweed lick my mouth clean and my mother would shriek in disgust and the game would end.

It took only a minute to find a dealer in weapons.

The day was gloomy and I could hardly see. I tugged off the cap. It was the first time I had been in public with my bristle hair.

No one looked at me. They were busy with their own lives and I was just another peasant boy slipping in the mud.

The flinging cord of a slingshot must be the exact right length for your arm. I measured myself against several until I found a fine sling.

"Good choice," said the dealer.

I was aware of being watched. I did not turn to meet the eyes. I am an ordinary boy doing an ordinary thing, I told myself. Getting a new slingshot. I have rather short hair, but my father is careless when he trims it. He took too much, that's all.

I handed the dealer my amber bead.

He shook his head.

It isn't enough? I thought anxiously. But surely—

"Look, boy, this is a fine piece of jewelry. See the hole drilled in it? Put it on a gold thread and give it to your girl-friend for a necklace. I can't take this. Come back with a bowl of mutton stew or a jug of beer and the sling is yours."

Why could I not find a greedy arms dealer? Now the man would remember me. I did not want to be remembered. But that also meant I couldn't argue and force him to take the bead. How was I supposed to take a bowl of stew away from the great hall, where Priam and his fifty sons and twelve daughters and all their spouses and children and friends took their meals, and slither back to Andromache's room in the dark, and dress once more in the split tunic . . .

"I trust you," said the dealer. "Take the sling, bring me the price later."

I had no choice. "Thank you," I said glumly.

I turned to leave and felt eyes all over me. I felt very bare. I opened the cap to put it on and tripped over a trembling yellow puppy at my feet. She was all alone, quivering in the mud, yipping little half-barks. I picked her up and kissed her sweet little wrinkled forehead. Her big brown eyes fixed on mine and she snuggled against me the way only a puppy can, warm and soft and glad to be held. She had long yellow fur and a white belly and soft floppy ears. "Ohhh," I said, in love with her already. She licked me, but she was very young and very tired and she sighed in my arms and went to sleep.

And the voice of Euneus, king of Lemnos, said at my side, "That's a happy puppy. I believe you are the mistress she was hoping for."

I stared up. I nearly dropped the dog. Tears sprang to my eyes. He had seen me without hair. He, of all people.

"And the black hair of yesterday?" asked Euneus. He was laughing at me.

"I . . . had a fever. My hair . . . had to be shaved off. Andromache found something called a wig for me yesterday. I don't actually have black hair."

"I see that," said Euneus. He put his palm on my bristles and smoothed them down. They sprang right back up. "I'd call that red hair, Callisto."

I could not bear it. Just when I had been preening myself that I was becoming a woman, soft and curved and desirable, here I was—bald and bristling and comic. "I have to go now," I said desperately.

"Without trying out the sling?" Euneus could not contain his amusement. "Why don't you and I go down to the shore and get some good stones? I've got a pouch you can use. In fact, why don't I supply the jar of beer for the dealer? That'll save you coming back."

I could not think. Perhaps Cassandra felt like this: only wind in her mind. "The puppy . . . ," I said.

"Is yours. When you described Seaweed, I knew right away what my first present to you would be. Prince Deiphobus has a wonderful hound, beautiful and smart. She had a litter of puppies a couple of months ago and the prince was grateful to find a home for this one."

Euneus was giving me a puppy to replace Seaweed.

The tears overflowed and I could not wipe them away because I was holding the puppy. I gave up and sobbed.

"Please don't cry," said Euneus, horrified. "I'm sorry. I saw you sneaking out of the palace in a stable boy's clothing. I thought you were going to try riding a horse by yourself and I couldn't let you do that because it's rather dangerous until you know how, so I followed you and then you yanked that cap off and you had short hair! Callisto, please don't cry."

"I didn't expect to be noticed. I thought an ordinary boy would just be part of the crowd and—"

He laughed. "You are not an ordinary boy, Callisto. You are a beautiful girl in an extraordinary costume. The short hair is surprising, but it sets off your lovely profile and your royal lineage."

I buried that profile in the puppy's yellow fur and dried my tears there. "I'm not sure I can have a puppy," I told him. "I should see if Andromache and the other princesses don't mind."

"All right. I'll keep her until I leave Troy."

"Leave Troy!"

He nodded. "I've stayed too late in the season as it is. But Lemnos is only a half day's sail. I'll wait for a perfect day, and autumn will give us plenty more of those, and then I'll ship out."

"You'll be gone all winter?" I whispered.

He opened the old woolen cap with his spread fingers, shaking his head at the moth holes and the raveling ends of yarn. Then, smoothing my hair as if it mattered, he set the cap carefully on my head. "All winter," he agreed. "Come. It's only half a mile to the shore. We'll find a stone or two, and you can show off your sling skills for me. You are a remarkable princess, Callisto."

"Please don't tell about my short hair."

"No. I wouldn't do that. Especially in Troy. And your turban is most attractive, although I have not thought of a compliment for the cap. When I see you in the spring, your hair will be long again."

Again we walked slowly. We took turns carrying the puppy, who slept on.

Euneus said carefully, "I do believe there will be war, Callisto. Menelaus will return to his brother Agamemnon, lord of the far-flung lands. Menelaus will call upon every prince who swore in the Blood of the Horse to be loyal to him. In the spring, they will attack. Hector and I spent much time discussing it. But tell me, little princess. Why are you preparing? What's the slingshot for?"

I could not tell him what the slingshot was for, because I didn't know. I wasn't going to take aim between Paris' eyes, or Helen's. I wasn't going to herd Pleis in front of me like a wayward sheep.

But I wanted to have the ability.

I mumbled the same ridiculous story I'd given Aethiolas and Maraphius, about how my father the king had raised me as a boy, having had to bury five infant sons in the walls. And then I burst out, "Will you be loyal to Troy, Euneus? Tell me, for I don't know what to do. Everyone here is so good to me. But Menelaus rescued me. He trusted me, even though I am unworthy. And I love his son, the little prince."

"It's difficult," admitted Euneus. "Hector wants me to commit to Troy. I want to be neutral. He says there is no such thing as neutral in war."

I had seen my king stabbed in the back. I had seen a queen made to walk over her husband's body. I had seen Pyros die with his bowels spilled on the earth for the dogs to eat. I had seen the king of Sidon just a pile of rags on a table. And that was not even war, just pirating. I dreaded war. "Aethra says that Helen's father was Madness, Hate, red Death and every rotting poison of the sky."

Euneus actually laughed. "I don't think she's that bad."

But he was wrong.

I opened my mouth to beseech Euneus, when he left Troy, to take Pleis with him. With Euneus neutral, Menelaus would pause in his harbor. Euneus could—

But if Euneus took the son of Helen, he would not be neutral. He might as well forge a treaty with Menelaus. Hector would hate Euneus. Not only would their friendship be over, but war might begin between Euneus and Troy, instead of Menelaus and Troy.

"What is wrong, little princess?" said the king of Lemnos gravely.

"Helen hates dogs. They shed and get fleas and make a mess. Euneus, I love this puppy already. I want to have her this winter to keep my heart and feet warm, but I cannot. Will you keep her for me? When you sail back in spring, will you bring her with you?"

He stared at the cold gray water of the bay. "From here we cannot see my island," he said, "but Cassandra can, from the height of her prison. Yes, I'll take the puppy, Callisto. But you name her for me."

I had the name ready. "Anthas."

"Flower," he repeated. "It's perfect."

We never did try out the sling. He showed me other things that were perfect and when we said goodbye, I put the amber bead in his hand and tucked his fingers around it and we both knew that he might not come in the spring, for war might come first.

As it happened, the next morning dawned clear and sunny and warm. Euneus would leave this day, for it was sailing weather. Hector summoned Andromache and me to bid the king of Lemnos goodbye. Euneus was surrounded by a dozen sons of Priam, princes trying to convince Euneus not to be neutral, but to commit his army to Troy.

It was a parting of soldiers, full of offers and anger. There was no room for first love. I could only wave goodbye, for not even Andromache knew what had sprung up between us.

I wished I had thought to tell Euneus about keeping-track lines. I wished there were a line to keep track of the heart. But even if such a thing could be designed, ships did not sail in the winter, and I could send no clay tablet to testify.

A week later there was snow.

The mountains of Ida were shrouded like great corpses

awaiting burial. Drifts covered the gray salt surf, and the breakers moaned under heavy slush. To ease a city worried about a harsh winter, King Priam held a banquet.

Cassandra was permitted to join the feast.

"Priam hates locking her up," Andromache confided. "Hector hates it even more, for he loves his sister."

I had not yet laid eyes on Cassandra and somehow expected crooked teeth like a hungry animal, greasy hair and starved eyes. But Cassandra was beautiful, as lovely as Helen, though not honey and spice. Beautiful like the snow in the dark.

Cassandra sat next to her father and mother, who saw that she had everything she could want. Bribing her, I thought, with tasty morsels. Cassandra looked at the other guests as a little girl looks to her nurse, aching to be picked up and cuddled.

But no one touched Cassandra. No one spoke to her. Most people even looked around her, as if she were just a space.

"I'll go keep her company," I said. "I'll speak with her."

"No, don't, Callisto," said Hector. "She'll answer."

Into the great fires, maids tossed chips of wood heavy with dry sap so the fire sparkled and hissed. There was a trained bear and a tame leopard. There were jugglers of carved purple balls. Atop a great stone table, tiny girls danced, arching their backs as if they had no spines.

A bard carelessly set down his lyre within reach of Cassandra's fingers and the god-swept princess picked it up. Hector drew in his breath and went quickly to take the lyre away. "My holy sister," he said softly, "give me the strings."

She never looked at him. He did not want to take it by force, so he just stood helplessly.

I have heard lovely voices, but none to match Cassandra's. The notes flew from her fingers. Her voice twined like ivy around fifty princes and their wives, binding the hands of guards and freezing the step of a king.

> The sound of joy has gone from the earth.
> The altar loses the flame.
> The wreath falls from the door.
> Moonlight is broken like bones.
> The bride of wrath slits every throat.
> The storm of her coming is ten years of pain.
> Sing of the curse of Helen.

Helen blazed. She snatched the lyre from Cassandra's fingers, flung it to the floor and stomped on it, breaking the song forever.

Cassandra sang on, the terrifying song spilling like water from her lips.

Helen slapped Cassandra's ivory cheek.

The song stopped.

When she had her rage under control, Helen turned herself back into a swan. Gliding, she went to Priam and took the king's hands in hers. "Dear father, I ask as a new bride, still a stranger. I ask that this creature in her holy terror be removed from me. Lock this croaking gull in solitude. For the sound of joy is *not* broken. In fact, today, joy begins. For I bring glad tidings. I bear the child of Paris. In the spring I will honor your house with our son."

The room burst into laughter and delight. Cups of wine were lifted and congratulations shouted. It was as if Helen had not just slapped a princess. Not just broken a cherished instrument as a jealous child breaks the toy of someone getting more attention.

Helen sailed on the sea of Troy's adoration.

The king made a sign to his guards to remove Cassandra.

His men were edgy and did not want to touch the mad princess. They wanted her to walk out of the hall by herself. They muttered at her, but Cassandra gave no sign that she heard.

Hector sighed. "Stay here, Andromache," he said softly. "You also, Callisto."

He moved through the crowd to take his sister's hand. He was so massive that the mountain of his heavy beard and the spread of his shoulders were visible even in this crowd of soldiers. He would not need a sword and spear to kill. He could crush a skull in his hands as I would crush the empty shell of a bird's egg.

And yet it was Cassandra the people feared.

Not I.

I was afraid of Helen.

XIV

As DURING THE STORM the ship is wrecked and the surf tosses its broken wood onto the sand, so Pleis was a reminder of a ship that had sunk: the marriage of Helen to Menelaus.

I went in search of Pleis, but could not find him, so I went up thin stairs along a thick wall to see Cassandra instead.

There was no guard and the door of her tower swung open, banging in the wind. Perhaps this was her summer prison, and they had a winter prison for her elsewhere. Did she spin and weave like the rest of us? Dream of love? Hope for children?

I peeked in.

Like an ice princess under mounds of snow white fleece, Cassandra sat in the middle of a large carved bed. "I knew you would come. But I thought you would be here earlier."

"Nobody wanted me to come."

"I thought you did not worry about what everybody else wants."

"I do worry. I worry mostly about Pleis."

"He is safe today. He will be safe tomorrow."

"How do you know these things?"

"Get under the fleece with me. It is too cold for you to stand there."

"Where is your guard?"

"It was too cold for him to stand there either. I promised him I would not go anywhere."

"If I were you, I would go."

Cassandra regarded me thoughtfully. "Where?" she asked.

It was a good question. I could think of no place Cassandra could go.

"There is nowhere for you to go either," she said. "Tell me your name, since I know it isn't Callisto."

"Anaxandra. Most people get it wrong the first time."

Cassandra raised her eyebrows.

"I'm sorry," I said. "You don't get things wrong, do you?"

"I have everything wrong," she said. "The gods in their supreme cruelty arranged my life so that those who love me do not trust me. Hector, the brother I adore, does not trust me. My honored father Priam does not, nor my dear mother Hecuba. But that is for me to bear. Let us talk of you. Anaxandra is a beautiful name. It suits you. Your father taught you to swim underwater," said Cassandra.

I turned as cold as sleet. I could not bear being close to her. I wanted to fling off the covers and leap out of her reach, slam the door behind me and call the guard.

"You may do that," said Cassandra. "Everyone else does."

She is without friends, I thought. Truly the gods have cursed her.

"Truly the gods have cursed you," Cassandra said to me.

"Me?"

"It is a shivery thing to steal the birthright of a princess. Do you think the gods will let you go unpunished? They are laughing even now. The gods will take away your greatest glory just when you think you are safe."

211

I had no glory for a god to take. I thought it was mean of her to talk like that when I had come to be her friend. "Try to be pleasant," I said, exactly like Andromache.

"Instead of truthful?" she said. "Why is it that we are so fearful of the truth? Why is it we always wish to talk of sewing and weaving instead?"

"I do think the tapestry you have on your loom is very beautiful," I said.

"I was weaving a gift for my future husband, should such a person exist and dare make an offer to the king for a lunatic like me. But then I received knowledge of that man and I cannot bear it. I no longer weave."

We sat for a long time. "Who will the husband be?" I whispered.

"Agamemnon. He will take me as loot, not as wife."

I held her hand, which was very cold. "I met Agamemnon," I told her. "He is frightening, but I thought he was just and kingly. Perhaps it won't be so bad."

And then the earthquake came.

I have felt them several times in my life but one does not grow accustomed to the wrath of that god. When he stands beneath you and shoves up with his hands, throwing aside your tall columns and wide roofs as if they are nothing more than broken pottery—no, you do not get used to that.

A tiny table in Cassandra's cell danced across the floor. The poles of her hanging loom split. The roof fell in, opening her prison to the sky. The hand of the god even wrenched the bottom of her tower, trying to tear it off and fling it to the earth. I screamed but Cassandra was unmoved.

The quake ceased.

The city struggled for breath.

"No one has died," said Cassandra. "But they will count heads and you do not want to be missing. You must not make Helen think of you."

I got out of Cassandra's bed. I did not see how she could survive in this frigid place. "Why does Helen hate me?"

"How do you suppose it feels to be the most beautiful woman on earth, and your husband doesn't see or care? How do you suppose it feels when a little girl, filthy with sand and dried gore, gets more attention than you, his holy wife?"

Helen? Jealous of me? "You are wrong, Cassandra."

The god kicked the world once more and the floor quivered. From nowhere came great clouds of dust. Some stones toppled. A baby wailed.

"Oh, Cassandra, I must find Pleis! I have to be sure he is all right! Where will I find him? Is that the kind of thing you know?"

"He is with the children of the princes. He is laughing. He thought the earthquake was a grand game. He loved how everything fell off the walls and splashed on the floor. Do not go near him. All that keeps you safe is that Helen and Paris have for a moment forgotten you."

"He is my prince, Cassandra. How can I be neutral when my prince is unsafe?"

"You are not neutral," said Cassandra. "It is not your nature."

I almost asked about somebody else who wanted to be neutral. I almost asked whether the king of Lemnos would come back in the spring, and whether he would love me. But if Cassandra were to say that I should never see him again, I could not get through the winter.

Zeus sent a howling gale of snow and gloom. At night when the sun went down, the ice turned purple, like frozen wine. Our toes and fingers felt the same.

We did not see much of the men. They were shoveling away snow and rebuilding the roofs of Troy.

We girls spun donkey loads of wool. Hour after hour, day after day, we twirled the clay cups. To keep our minds off blue toes and chapped fingers, we went in circles telling stories. One day I described the keeping-track lines.

The princesses laughed so hard they dropped their spindles. Twisted threads of unplied yarn tangled over each other. "That's why you have clerks, Callisto," said one of Priam's daughters. "It is not the work of a king to call out how many barrels of salted fish have been sold. Slaves exist to remember such things."

The princesses were always happy to make ugly remarks about Menelaus and how poor a king he was. I listened for some time. "Keeping-track lines are very useful," I said stiffly.

"How?" they wanted to know. "You make a keeping-track line for a bushel of grain, but then you eat it. It's gone. What was the point of keeping track?"

"It prevents quarrels. You can store a fact in the clay. If two men fight about who owes money to whom, the clay proves who is right and who is wrong."

"Deciding who is right and who is wrong is the task of a king," said a princess I had liked until then. "Has Menelaus not even figured out what a king does? No wonder Helen left him for a better man."

"If there is a war, Callisto," said another princess, "you have proved that it will be over in a day. The warriors of

Troy against a man who worries about counting his pottery? It will be a joke."

"If you can call Menelaus a man. Couldn't keep Helen, could he?"

Andromache tried to change the subject. "I think Paris and Helen will have a son," she said. "Helen is carrying the baby very high; that always means a boy."

Nobody wanted it to be a girl. Girls are all right, in their place, but glory comes with sons, and Paris expected glory, Helen expected glory, King Priam and Queen Hecuba and every prince in Troy expected it.

But Helen already had a boy.

I checked on Pleis as often as I could. By night he slept in the tiny house of Paris and Helen. By day Kora, the pockmarked bear woman, carried him to the palace to abandon him among the royal children. I had bribed each of their nurses with the rest of my wasp-in-amber beads. They took the beads, but I did not know how much time they spent on the son of the enemy.

Rumor had reached us that Agamemnon and Menelaus were putting together a fleet. Battle fever rose and people were eager for the clash. The presence of Menelaus' little boy pleased no one.

"Helen is preparing the baby clothes," said Andromache. "She certainly can weave like a queen. Have you seen the pattern she is doing for the baby blankets?"

No, but I had seen the clothes Pleis wore. The same he had worn on the *Ophion*.

"Have you been in their sweet little house yet? Queen Hecuba let Helen pick anything she wanted from the treasury to furnish it. She said Helen must have the best of everything."

215

"Then why is that horrible old giantess Kora on Helen's staff?"

There was a chorus of groans. "Nobody wants Kora around."

"Nobody wants the little boy around either. A son of the enemy? They should have put him to death to start with."

Day after day, snow blurred the horizon and the passage of time. Yet the days leaped forward and winter was flung aside.

The salt marsh filled with flowers. The willows by the Scamander River were laced with yellow buds. The wind was soft and the sky was warm and we had the first real news of ships from a port across the sea.

They said there were a thousand ships.

A thousand sheep, yes. But a thousand boats? It was a foolish rumor.

Then we heard that not one of those thousand ships could sail against Troy. There was not a whisper of wind on the sea. Menelaus could not go to war.

How Troy laughed.

But there are ways to bring a god to your side. They are done through the king, and the king of kings was not Menelaus, but Agamemnon his brother.

I am sure Agamemnon expected to sacrifice a hundred black bulls. But no. The word of the gods was that he must make his own child holy. It is not hard to make things holy with a lamb. But to make war holy with your own daughter?

The army chose Iphigenia, the cousin who had spent a summer at Amyklai and been such fun for Hermione.

I remembered a shrine on Siphnos, clamped to the side of a cliff. Iphigenia must have died at such a place. I am sure she went bravely to the altar. I am sure she tried to make it easier for her father. I am sure she neither begged nor cried out.

But even on the orders of Zeus, how terrible to slit your own daughter's throat.

Had Agamemnon wanted to disobey the god?

Had he screamed at his assembled army—Let Paris keep Helen! Forget the treasure! Forget the insults! *Just let me have my daughter, my dear Iphigenia.*

But weakness does not make a king.

"A Jew lived here once," said Andromache.

"What is a Jew?"

"It's a people near Sidon, where Paris had such a brilliant victory and returned with such treasure."

Where civilized life vanished at a banquet table, I thought, and we were all pirates, and all the world our prey.

"The Jew had a king named Abraham. *His* god also required that he make things holy with the death of his son Isaac. But at the very last moment, his god rushed out of the sky and said Abraham didn't have to kill him after all."

"There must have been feasting in that household," I said.

Talk of war draws young men.

How they loved to prepare. To sharpen the knives and javelins. Practice with the sword. Feint left and shift right. Squint into the sun and make plans for glory.

Chariots were harnessed, drivers dashing toward the sea as if to meet an army, but in fact, just racing their friends and then gathering under the great oak at the Scaean Gate to talk of war.

But the young man I wanted to see was not drawn to war.

"I have not heard from Euneus," said Hector, all black beard and dark frown. "He will be one with Menelaus."

"He will be neutral," I said, although war talk did not concern me and I should not have spoken.

Hector looked at me. "When a friend needs you," he said, "there can be no such thing as neutral. He has not come to help us, therefore he is against us."

Friends of Paris gave parties.

Friends of Hector offered strategies, for he would be general over all.

Men from a dozen kingdoms came to prove their valor. When the war ended, they would gain wealth and splendor from the ruin of Menelaus and Agamemnon. Pelasgian sailors arrived. Thracians with their hair all in a tuft. Carians decked in gold. Horsemen from Phrygia and men with boars' tusk masks from Mysia and men with tattooed hands from Paphlagonia.

The tents of the allies stretched for miles on the grass. Now across the plain were a thousand campfires. A new sound filled the air: the din of ten thousand men talking.

And then came the ships of the allies of Menelaus, the greatest gathering Earth has ever seen.

All at once they came, swiftly, fiercely. There were so many that they closed the mouth of the bay, like the jaws of war.

Iphigenia had died well.

Helen knew the ships by their flags and stood on the ramparts with King Priam and Paris, calling out the kingdoms, while Hector, appalled, counted out the ships.

"That flag!" cried Helen. "That's Boeotia!"

"Fifty ships," whispered Hector.

"The Locrians!" she said gleefully.

Forty black ships.

Argos and Tiryns. Eighty black ships.

Twelve from Salamis, fifty from Athens, eighty from Crete.

When Paris and his thirty-three ships had pulled up on foreign land, Paris had faced his ships outward so he could flee. But these ships faced the shore. They were not leaving in haste.

"All these captains," asked Priam, "took oaths in the Blood of the Horse to defend you?"

"Yes," said Helen, glowing with joy.

No, I thought. Menelaus corrected you. They took oaths in the Blood of the Horse to defend *him*.

"Those are interesting ships," said Priam, pointing. He might have been admiring acrobats at a feast. "They are painted not just with eyes, but with red cheeks."

"The ships of Odysseus of Ithaca," said Helen. "A crafty man and dangerous."

And then came the ships of Menelaus himself. Sixty strong.

And the ships of Agamemnon. One hundred.

Every ship was its own procession to war.

As each vessel drew close, its sail was furled and stowed. Its anchor stone was tossed into the sea and its cables made fast. Its crew climbed out into the breaking surf, leading the sacrifice.

I was so proud of Menelaus. He would not pull up on strange soil without making it holy. I wondered where he had obtained so many white heifers, so many black bulls.

"He bought that stock from Euneus," said Hector.

"Euneus will be neutral," said King Priam cheerfully. "It's all right. If the war lasts more than a day or two, we might need to exchange prisoners or some such thing. Euneus will handle that."

Cassandra had said the war would last ten years. Nobody believed her. Only Hector seemed to believe it would be more than one battle.

"Already," said Hector gloomily, "based on counting the oars, there are five of them for every one of us."

"We can stay inside our walls," said Priam reassuringly. "We have more supplies than they could possibly bring by ship. They can't get at us and we don't need to fight."

"Of course we need to fight," said Hector. "They will slaughter our people, Father. In the city below. In fields and hills, in marsh and forest." Hector paced back and forth. He was huge. There was no room for anyone else on the battlements when he marched around. "Do you think they are civilized, these Greeks?" he demanded. "They are animals. Wild dogs in a fever. They will kill the innocent to force us into battle."

Menelaus would never kill the innocent! I wanted to shout. You Trojans are the ones who murder a host. We wouldn't do that.

Cassandra was suddenly next to me. "You are thinking of Paris," she said very softly. "Paris murders. Hector, never. He is just and fair, honoring at all times the best in his fellow man."

From what I had seen, war produced the worst in my fellow man, not the best.

"Cassandra," said her father the king, embracing her. Priam did not ask why she was not in her tower. He did not send her back.

Helen was furious.

Not only was Hector gloomy, but Cassandra and I were the two girls Helen least wanted to remember during her hour of triumph. With Cassandra literally under the king's arm, however, Helen could do nothing about that god-swept princess.

I was easier.

To Aethra, Helen snapped, "Shave her skull again tonight and bring her for me to look at. She is no princess. I know she has stolen a birthright." To me, she said, "The gods will punish you, girl."

"And the seven ships now sailing into the harbor, Helen dear?" asked Priam. He might have been asking about a variety of rose—whether the bloom was double or single, pink or yellow.

Helen forgot me and looked eagerly to see who else had come to fight over her. The hulls of the seven ships were black with pitch. Their sails were red. Their insignia was a twisted blue fish.

"From rugged Olizon. I do not know their captain. They are experts with the bow. They appear to have fifty rowers to a ship, so before you are three hundred fifty brilliant shots." Helen was trembling with joy. For this had men stood in the Blood of the Horse: *to die for her.*

But the men of the twisted fish would die for me.

XV

I WALKED AND AETHRA HOBBLED, holding my arm. We were no different. My heart was hobbled. I was so proud of the hair I now had. It had grown several inches and the curls were beautiful and tight. Andromache said that any woman who used a curling iron would be jealous; any warrior preparing for battle. Andromache thought I could go without the turban now. She said I was lovely and very feminine and would be the envy of all.

I did not risk explaining that my hair was short because I had offended Helen.

I loved my hair. I wanted Euneus to see it. I wanted him to smooth it down and wrap it around his fingers and . . . and if Aethra did not obey Helen, she would be punished.

We went to the house of Paris. It was empty. Every royal resident of Troy was on the battlements, entertained by the sight of the Greeks. The other residents of Troy were standing below the walls, getting a view wherever they could. Only Hector seemed to take the prospect of war seriously. Everybody else expected a party with some dead Greeks at the end of it.

The courtyard was lovely, though small; the inner room beautiful, with so much gold and amber that it glittered even without torches. The only other chamber was the bedroom of Paris and Helen. A tiny cradle awaited the new birth.

I felt sick and worried. "Where does Pleis sleep?"

Aethra pointed. Behind a jog in the wall, and up two steps, was a little closet, too small even for a slave to curl up. A fleece and a few toys filled the floor below a single window. The window opened into an alley so narrow that almost no light came in.

O my Pleis. "Where do you sleep?" I whispered.

"There is an attic. Very low ceilinged. You cannot stand upright. But then, my spine is so twisted I cannot stand upright anyhow. I am better off than the rest of the slaves."

"Does Kora sleep there?"

"Kora sleeps in the courtyard."

"Outside?" I said. "All winter?"

Aethra shrugged. "She is just another dog to Paris." Aethra found a sharp blade among the possessions of Paris, and we went out into the courtyard for the light and Aethra began to cut off my hair while I began to weep.

As every gleaming curl fell to the paving stones, I felt weaker and weaker, as if it were my blood falling there; as if this were my death. I had to sit on a stone bench and grasp the rim of a great jug full of flowers.

"Lovely," said Aethra sadly. "Like the petals of a rose. Your glory."

Everyone used the word "glory" now. Each soldier hoped for glory. No one seemed to understand that for one man to attain glory, another man must die. Cassandra too had mentioned glory. *The gods will take your greatest glory.*

"Aethra, what if my hair doesn't grow back?" I whispered. "Cassandra said the gods were laughing at me even now. That they would take my greatest glory just when I thought I was safe."

Aethra stared at my bald head. Then she rested her old wrinkled soft cheek against it. "Poor child. I am so sorry."

"It couldn't happen!" I cried. "The gods would not be that mean!"

"The gods are always mean," said Aethra. "Does the life I lead make you think of gentle loving gods? Does the body I live in look like one blessed by a kind god? When I missed my grandsons by two days, was this arranged by a generous god? And Nicander—when he angered the gods with that egg of lead, did the death of five infant sons come from a forgiving god?"

We are told to fear the gods. I had forgotten to be afraid.

On Siphnos, when I chose not to tell Menelaus the truth, I had known the gods would punish me. I had shrugged. It is never good to shrug when a god is there. "I didn't do anything so very bad," I whispered.

"What did you do?"

"I lied. Helen is right, Aethra. I am no princess. I stole the name and birthright of Callisto. I am just a hostage from a rocky isle without a name whose parents did not want me back. I had no value, so I took Callisto's value, that I might not be made a slave."

Gently the old queen kissed my naked head. "We all bargain with the gods, my dear. They, however, do not bargain with us."

The ships of the Greeks continued to arrive. Along came support and supply ships, bringing timber and tents and slaves, barrels and crates and sacks. There had not yet been a battle, but Troy no longer controlled the water: not the

224

Hellespont, not the far shore of the Hellespont, not the Aegean, and not the nearby islands in the Aegean.

King Priam was not concerned. "Our allies who had to come by sea are already here," he said. "The remaining allies will approach by land anyway. And no matter how much food and water they bring by ship, we will always have more food and water."

"No soldier signs on for free," said Hector. "Every one of those Greeks expects to be paid, and not from the treasury of Menelaus. They expect to be paid from *our* treasury, when they sack our city."

"Then they will die poor," said Priam, smiling.

As for the poor of Troy, they seemed no more worried than their king. They did not leave their huts below the citadel, their children still played ball in what would surely be the battlefield, while their tiny flocks of sheep and goats nibbled grass where the attack would begin. No mother packed the family goods; no father carried his children to the safety of the great walls; no girl stopped spinning.

The greatest worry of Troy was that Menelaus might want to fight Paris in single combat.

A duel would be proper and just and there would be no way to avoid it. Nobody had come all this way to watch two men jab at each other. Troy's allies fretted that they might not get to fight. Not to mention that Paris would lose. If Menelaus requested a duel, they would try to make him fight Hector, because Hector would win.

Luckily, Menelaus made no such offer and Troy was spared the humiliation of admitting that the prince who had started this was not prince enough to end it.

By day, the two armies would fling taunts, preparing for the hour in which they would fling spears.

"When we have broken down the walls of Troy," yelled the troops of Menelaus, "we will take the faithful wives of your dead. Every princess in Troy will pay for the deeds of Paris!"

It is the promise of the battlefield—the winner gets to rape the wives.

Since the Greeks had not brought any women, the Trojans could not make the same threat against them. Trojans had to be content with describing what would happen to the men they slaughtered. "Your bowels will spill into the sea for eels to devour! When we feast after our swift and easy victory, Trojan vultures will feast on your eyes."

"Shut the window," said Andromache. "I hate this. What if something happens to Hector?"

It will happen to you, I thought. You are the princess they refer to.

We spun. You can spin as you walk, as you sit on a donkey or lean on a wall. We spun in fear. I had done nothing but spin since Aethra had shaved my head again. I was terrified of Helen now, terrified of all gods and all punishments. Terrified even of Andromache, who one day would pluck off my turban to admire my red curls, my glory.

There would be a great feast this evening. It had been arranged that battle would take place in the morning. Priam wished to celebrate the coming victory.

"Menelaus and Agamemnon and their tens of thousands will also feast," said Andromache suddenly. "I look at their camp every night. Their fires are a fence of flame. Tonight, those soldiers will crouch in the shadows around Menelaus and Agamemnon, planning the death of Troy."

It was true.

"Planning the death of Hector!" cried Andromache.

This too was true. Hector would be a greater enemy in war than Paris.

"You love Menelaus," she accused me. "You want him to win!"

I remembered the kingly courtesy with which Menelaus rescued me from Siphnos; the warm smile when he'd bought me the magic jar. How he cuddled Pleis and teased Hermione and roughhoused with Aethiolas and Maraphius. It was a strange word—"love." The love I felt for Euneus, whom I had known only hours, had sustained me through the long winter. The love I felt for a puppy named Anthas, which I had snuggled only for minutes, still tugged on my heart. But the love I felt for Menelaus, whose careless kingship had brought us to this terrible pass, was sad and tired.

"I want to be neutral, Andromache. Like Euneus." I felt neutral. My hair was not growing back. My scalp was as smooth as the palm of my hand. I could hate neither the gods for their punishment nor myself for my lies. My heart was as flat as the plains around Troy. Even when I thought of Euneus, my heart did not leap. I had not even the strength to plan the demise of the men of the twisted fish. What would be, would be. Some would win, some would lose. I would just exist.

Neutral is a terrible thing to be.

"Hector says Euneus is a traitor." Andromache was weeping. "And you, too, Callisto, are a traitor. I, daughter of the king of Cilicia, have adopted Troy. Helen, daughter to one king of Sparta, wife of another king of Sparta, has adopted Troy. But you, daughter of Siphnos, have not. Yet Troy has been good to you. I have been your friend. Hector has been your friend. And you do not swear to be a daughter of Troy."

"I would never betray Troy, Andromache. I treasure your friendship. Deeply do I respect this city and her people."

We spun.

"Helen is right," said Andromache. "You should not be among us."

No, my princess. It is Helen who should not be among you.

But Andromache, my friend, waited for me to go.

"I thank you for this winter of friendship," I said to a real princess. "I too weep. I shall find a place in a distant hall and trouble you no more."

The future queen of Troy did not say goodbye. She did not call me back.

I was not so neutral, after all.

I wept.

Stumbling down dark halls, I rushed to the bedroom I could no longer share with Andromache and retrieved my Medusa and my fleece. I had never returned the mud-stained divided tunic of the squire nor the ugly cap. I took them, too. And my slingshot, just in case.

There was only one person in the world now who loved me.

I went to the palace nursery, where the toddlers and babies of the princes were being watched during the feast. Pleis was not there. "He's with Kora," said a maid, "in the house of Paris and Helen. No royal parents want the son of Menelaus playing around their children. You won't see him here again."

I left the palace, elbowing through packed streets, deafened by the curses being thrown at Menelaus. Time and again my fleece with its pathetic treasures was nearly jostled from my grasp. So many soldiers filled the city that I was invisible. I did not have to worry about being seen by a princess. No princess would go out in this wild drunken spear-swinging crowd.

But Kora would. There she stood, over a great trencher of roast lamb, dipping each piece in salt and rosemary.

Kora had left Pleis unattended.

I hastened to the house of Paris. The door opened easily and without sound. They do not bolt their doors in Troy, for they are all one family. The place was empty. Paris and Helen were undoubtedly on the battlements, and the slaves were in the street, eating greedily and well.

Pleis was in his little closet. His dinner had been set on the floor, as if he were a dog. He was playing with blocks and had not eaten much. I had not eaten much either and reached for the bread.

Between the bread and yogurt, something gleamed. It was wet, round at the edges. It did not look like food. I was puzzled.

"Silver," Pleis told me. "Pretty." He smacked it with spread fingers. The puddle split into silver raindrops. Pleis pushed them together with one clumsy finger until they became one again and he beamed at me, proud of his trick.

Quicksilver.

Poison.

Set before a child who still put most things into his mouth.

Even I could not believe this of Helen. Surely she did not know. But Paris knew.

Evil man, I thought. Paris wants you to die the day of your father's arrival, my Pleis. Perhaps he wants to deliver your little body to your father, Menelaus.

I wanted to burn the halls of Paris to the ground. Stab him with his own spear. Hold his corpse in the air for the vultures to pick over. I was as angry as any god. I was not neutral.

I slid the quicksilver onto the slab of bread and flung it out the window. When Kora returned, she would think Pleis had eaten it.

I did not want Pleis to be hungry anytime soon, so we went out into the city and joined the festive crowd. I fed him sweet cheese and thick dark bread with honey. I fed him plump raisins and made him drink cups of goat's milk. We got back to his little cell just as the servants began returning to the household. He was full and sleepy. "Night, night, Calli," he murmured.

I didn't ask Pleis to keep my visit secret. I doubted if anybody wasted time talking to him, and tonight of all nights, Helen would be thinking of other things.

I left by the window. Vaulting up to the sill made me think of the great high horse, and the rich scent of its sweat; of Euneus, and the warm clasp of his arm.

I slept in the alley. I was not alone. Hundreds of infantry slept in the streets also.

When the sun rose, I found an inch of space on ramparts jammed with spectators, that I too might watch the mighty conflict.

Paris had had his hair done. All the warriors had, of course, for none dared ask the blessing of the gods and then not be at his best.

No kingdom resembled another in the modeling of hair. Some warriors wore braids, some achieved curls with hot irons. Some brushed their long flowing locks or divided their hair into topknots. Paris was partial to an arrangement of gold wires, knotted with great skill so his head was tasseled like a robe.

I was jealous of every one of them.

I hoped anger would sustain me all the days of my life, because certainly beauty would not.

Two squires helped Paris arm. How fine were the buckles and straps that held his gleaming breastplate, how tall the plumes of his helmet. He carried two spears, his reflex bow on his back and his battle sword at his hip.

From the camps of the allies came ten thousand. Cavalry and infantry, bowmen and spearmen, darters and slingers. Hundreds of generals. Hundreds of horses.

From their ships came the Greeks. Even though we had counted ships, and knew how many rowers per ship, we trembled. They were ants pouring from a hole in the ground, and like ants were without number. Like ants, could they be stepped upon?

I did not think so.

Nor did the Trojans. Every man stroked his weapon, testing the sharpness tested only minutes before. Whereas in the night I had heard ten thousand murmuring voices, now I could almost hear ten thousand pounding hearts.

From the ramparts high above his fifty well-armed sons, King Priam prayed.

His voice was old and shaky, so his heralds, standing at the corners of the vast walls, repeated after him, shouting the prayer phrase by phrase over city and fields.

Father Zeus . . .

   Father Zeus . . .

      Father Zeus . . .

231

Ruling over us all . . .

us all . . .

us all . . .

"Send me a bird of omen!" cried the king to the gods. "Let me see the eyes of your eagle! Prove that your power flies over Troy."

But no eagle came.

No hawk.

No falcon.

Not even a sparrow.

The wind blew. The grass leaned down. And the sky was empty.

Without warning, clouds covered the blue sky and the sky swelled yellow like pus in a blister. As a turtle pulls in its head, so did two armies hunch down, uncertain of the plans of Zeus.

But Hector ignored the terrible omens. "Open the gates!" he roared, and the gate with the snarling horse was pulled to the side and an equal roar came from the throat of every ally.

Paris was pale. "Hector, we have to postpone the battle. The signs are against it."

"Bird signs," Hector said in contempt. "The only omen is whether you fight for your country." In a huge voice, he shouted, "My soldiers! Beat these invaders into the sea!" Hector charged like a boar.

Paris, hundreds of armed and eager men at his back, left the gate more rapidly than he had planned. If he had planned to leave at all.

The horse's head gazed after him.

———

As flood seizes the river in spring, overflowing its banks, tearing away the soil and turning the clear water to mud, so came the armies.

They met in a whirl of blood. Far down the battlements from where I stood, Andromache screamed and covered her eyes, while Helen slammed her fists down on the battlements and, like a soldier too long in the trenches, swore with joy.

Shield hit shield with a crash as of cymbals. Stones hit faces, darts punctured lungs, spears found bellies. Men screamed in rage and pain. Horses shrieked like men. When a soldier fell, the hordes leaped upon him to rip off his armor.

The Trojan habit is for brothers to handle a chariot. But the enemy knew how to meet a charge of chariots. The brother who drove would get an arrow through the eye and with the terrified horses out of control, the brother who held the spear was spilled to the earth and swiftly killed. Trojans died two brothers at a time.

Hector fought like ten men. He forced himself through a wall of shields, bringing so many Greeks to the ground that around his feet was a quivering mass of plumes.

But the Trojans pushed nobody into the sea.

The Greeks were stronger. Relentlessly, they pushed the Trojans toward the walls on which we stood.

Helen was as god-pierced as Cassandra, swaying to the rhythm of war. Above the clangor and death, above the terror and pain, her voice rose. "I am Helen of Troy! This is my battle! Fight for me, you men. Suffer and bleed for me. *Die for me.*"

They were afraid of Helen on the ramparts and edged away from her, shivering as one does at the beginning of fever. But they were slow to be afraid of the battle. Slow to grasp that Troy was losing.

The peasants who had not abandoned their outlying huts had no time to correct their error. Whole families met the springing tip of the spear, their fallen bodies crushed by plunging horses as if they'd been grains of wheat on the threshing floor.

Trojan hearts sank. Trojan hopes were dashed.

"Menelaus is murdering our children!" shouted Paris, from a rather safe spot near the gates. I had not been aware that Paris cared about the safety of children. "Menelaus tramples our children in his path!" he shouted, arousing the men to greater fighting. "Menelaus stabs to death the helpless infant!"

Who were the Trojans to claim they protected the weak? If Paris or Priam, if Hector or Aeneas had cared about mothers and babes, they would have ordered every peasant into the city and closed the gates behind them.

But as a rallying cry, it had no equal.

It had never really mattered what had happened between Menelaus and Helen. Never really mattered whether Paris had robbed a temple. But children mattered.

"Swear to the deathless gods," roared the heralds from the towers, "that Menelaus will die!"

Troy surged back, heart renewed and resolve quickened.

The Greeks lost ground. The men of Sparta closed ranks to keep Menelaus safe. He would receive the protection of thousands.

But the son of Menelaus had no shield.

XVI

THE BATTLE DID NOT go to the strongest.

The battle went to sunset.

No one can fight in the dark. It is not possible to tell friend from foe. The sky turned purple, the Greeks crossed back over the Scamander River, and a truce was arranged for the next morning so the bodies might be gathered.

The wounded were carried into the city and laid out in rows, filling the main avenue. No one considered using the great space of the Palladium. A man would rather die than lie there.

The city of Troy was in shock. They had believed Paris, that war would be a dance, a party; that the only dead would be the enemy. All night the people wailed in grief and the wounded moaned in pain.

A boy in a dirty wool cap and a barbarian's divided tunic is good for carrying. All night I brought buckets of water from the city well for washing the blood off the wounded.

When dawn came at last, each side buried its own. Warriors put down their weapons. Work parties lifted corpses and closed the eyes of the dead. Horses pulled body carts instead of chariots. Trojan mourners streamed toward Mount Ida, for the holiest burials would be on her slopes.

Hector and the princes and their generals gathered just

outside the Scaean Gate to plan the strategy for the next battle. Only Hector had understood that there would be a next battle. It was late in the morning before Helen was back on the battlements. No doubt it had taken her that long to fix her hair.

I left my bucket by the well and went to the house of Paris, but Kora stood in the door.

I went in by the window instead.

Pleis was alone in his tiny room. I held my finger to my lips so he would stay silent, but he was overjoyed to have company. "Calli!" he shouted happily. "Sto!"

I lifted him onto the sill, boosted myself up and dropped us both down. A few quick turns in back alleys and we found a stream of mourners to join.

I was just another slave boy in a short tunic and close-fitting cap. Boys, however, care for sheep, not babies. I told myself that the eyes of mourners were too filled with tears to wonder about Pleis and me.

The son of Menelaus sat comfortably on my hip and chatted in the way of tiny children proud of new words. "Bunny bunny bunny," he told me. "Long ears. Long, long, long."

He was right about that. I wanted no long ears in Troy to hear us. "Shhh," I whispered. "Be silent as a bunny. Wiggle your nose, not your tongue."

Pleis loved having his nose tickled. His high silly giggle blended into the keening wails of the mourners. They left by the Dardan Gate, which led to Mount Ida. We walked among them for a quarter mile and then I slid into a thicket and clambered down the steep grassy hill.

I found the path Andromache and I had taken to the horses. The horses had been herded to safer more distant pasture, but the fences remained, thick with thorns and flowers.

Since I had watched the battle from the ramparts, I knew that anyone up there could see us perfectly. I could only hope they thought nothing of it.

We waded through long grass. My heart was racing so fast I was out of breath. My hands felt slippery.

"Down, Calli," said Pleis, wiggling. "I get down. Down down down."

"Not yet. Be my good bunny rabbit."

The grass ended. I was on the battlefield. The earth was churned and torn. We were utterly exposed. I was a boy with a child in my arms, crossing a field of corpses.

The day was hot and dusty, the sky a thick hazy exhausted blue.

We crossed a hundred feet, and then another hundred.

We skirted a party of Trojans lifting the much-stabbed body of a friend onto a cart.

We passed a soldier turning over an unknown corpse and discovering that it was a friend. To the music of his weeping, we took another hundred steps. Here and there, a shrub or patch of reeds had survived the feet of war. I aimed for each tiny thicket. The ships seemed no closer.

I prayed to my goddess but felt no presence.

I prayed to Apollo and to Athena, but they had never been my gods.

O, Nicander, my king, with your grave in the sand. Petra, my queen, your fate surely hard. Callisto, my princess, burned alive. Give me grace to save this boy, as I was not able to save you.

We were reaching the end of the battlefield. After this final work party, we would be in a no-man's-land. Still a quarter mile before we reached the ford in the river.

Now there were only six or eight Trojans between me and my goal.

Thousands of Greeks. To reach Menelaus we would have to pass hundreds of beached ships. How would I prove our identity to those captains? They were not men to waste time on questions. Truce or not, they would pick up the nearest spear and dispose of a spy in an excellent disguise— childhood.

Pleis shifted on my hip and looked back at the city. "Mama," he said, astonished and happy. "Look, Calli. Onna wall. Mama."

He had learned a new skill. He had learned to wave. "Mama," he called, waving.

I caught his hand. "Shhh, Pleis, be a bunny rabbit, don't make a sound."

The Trojan party were laboriously shifting a dead horse to reach the body it had crushed.

Pleis was too little to connect his mother with the loneliness of his little cell. He loved her. He pulled his hand free and waved again and called much more loudly, "Mama!"

On their knees around the dead horse, the Trojan men looked up. One was Zanthus. He knew me right away. "Callisto?" he said, puzzled. "Pleisthenes?"

But the Trojan next to him closed rough hands around my wrists. "The little Greek princess," he said, spitting in my face. "A spy for Menelaus, are you? Taking his vermin child with you?"

King Priam heard my case as if it were any other; as if it were a dispute over a bad debt or the location of a fence. Some of his princes were there. Paris. Deiphobus. Hector. His queen was there, and Helen, of course.

They had taken Pleis from me. I would not get him back. Menelaus would not get him back either.

I remembered saying to Bia at Amyklai, *Helen will kill me.* *Yes,* Bia answered. *Delay that as long as possible.* I could postpone my death no longer. There was but one thing I might still accomplish. I could take down the men of the twisted fish.

"As I crossed the plain to bring his son to Menelaus, I overheard a plot, my king," I told Priam. "There are seven ships from Olizon. Their men plan to sneak into the city where the wall is weakest, by the fig tree. During the night they will break into the sacred temple of Athena and steal the Palladium. Thus would Troy be defeated."

People paused. All Troy knew that the city would fall without the Palladium.

"No," said Paris. "That is *your* plot, girl. *You* were going to organize that expedition. *You* would betray Troy."

"I would not betray this city!" I cried. "Troy has been kind to me. With your women have I spun. With your princess have I shared a joyful winter. I too worshiped at the Palladium and dedicated myself to the goddess. I tell you this to save the Palladium. You must kill the men of Olizon."

King Priam, in his sweet elderly way, seemed actually to consider my words.

"You lie!" said Helen, flinging words as she would have liked to fling a knife. She turned to Priam. "The girl was traitor to me, my dear father. Me—whom she claims to serve. She snatched my sweet son from his crib."

I knelt before Helen. "I do not plead for my own life, O queen," I said, "but for the life and safety of Pleisthenes. Your sweet son is in grave danger. He—"

Helen whirled upon me. I thought she would slap me, as she had Cassandra, but she took hold of the woolly cap and yanked hard. There was a collective gasp from the court. I knew how my naked skull must gleam. Shame joined terror in my heart.

"Daughter!" exclaimed Priam, getting to his feet. His sons sprang up to steady him and he bustled forward. He took my hand and raised me up. He laid a hand on my smooth scalp. He kissed my cheek.

I do not know who was more amazed—Helen or me.

"Thea!" called Priam.

It is a name meaning "divine" and, in Troy, is given to the head priestess of the Palladium. This Thea was large and dignified, in robes woven of scratchy coarse thread. She too laid a hand on my head and kissed my cheek. "Welcome, child. You said you had dedicated yourself to the goddess, and so you have. You have surrendered your hair, your greatest glory. Thus does a maiden display her love for the goddess."

Thea placed her thumb on my forehead to bless me, exactly where Petra had done it all those years before. "You will serve the Palladium all the days of your life, daughter. You will experience poverty, because along with hair, you will lose all earthly things. You will not see daylight again," said Thea dreamily. "Beneath our temple are long dark tunnels, which lead to cisterns of water and great stores of treasure. There will you serve, in the bowels of the earth."

Truly, the gods had spit upon my prayers.

But Helen of Troy was smiling. A life of poverty and a bald skull were certainly a punishment to her taste. "I shall walk those temple steps, girl," said Helen, "and know that you are under my feet. Toiling in the dark. Forever my slave."

———

240

The sacred temple had been cut into bedrock. Narrow steps laddered down and down and down. Water dripped from walls and oozed out of cracks. Moss grew, and fungus, and slime. The hem of my novice's robe was wet. I curled it up and over my arm to keep it dry and Thea said, "No. The water is a gift from the goddess. The rest of your life, your feet will be chilled by that sacred water."

My head ached from the cold. I asked for a kerchief or a veil.

"No," said Thea. "The goddess must always have your shining head in sight. Every day you must prove again that for her sake you have given up your beauty and set aside your hopes for a husband and a family."

O Euneus. I did hope for a husband and a family. All winter I pretended and I hoped. But all I will have of you is memory and all you will have of me is one bead that wasn't even mine; it was Hermione's.

I thought of the puppy I had held for one afternoon. Anthas. Flower. I would never see a flower or a puppy again.

Down we went into the treasury of Troy. Wet rooms gleamed in Thea's torchlight as a courtyard gleams after rain. There sat the tribute taken from generations of ships passing through the Hellespont.

"Here," said Thea, "do we keep bronze and tin, iron and gold, silver and copper. It must not turn dim and dull. Every day you will circle, polishing the possessions of the Palladium."

I did not bother to address my goddess of yesterday. She does not dwell in the underworld and does not care about metals precious to kings.

If I am fortunate, I thought, and die at fifty as most

women do, I will pass thirty-seven years rubbing the sides of ingots. "I am a fine needlewoman," I said brightly. "In the goddess's honor—"

"No," said Thea. "The daughters of King Priam embroider for the Palladium. Your service is like your head, bare and humble." She stroked my scalp. "This is most unusual, my child. Your head is as smooth as a baby's bottom. No stubble. Did you use some special herb upon it?"

"The gods took my hair. It will never grow back."

"You are doubly blessed," said Thea. She led me down a tunnel whose ceiling got lower and lower until she was bent double, barely able to hold her torch in front of her. I crept behind. I could not bring myself to ask where I would sleep. Every surface was hard, wet and cold. I was beginning to realize that I would not be given a torch. I imagined myself in this dark slimy world. Eventually I would have to lie down.

At a swollen place in the tunnel, Thea paused and straightened a little. The tunnel continued, too narrow for a woman the size of the priestess. Sitting on a low pedestal before us was an idol, flecked with gray and streaked with black. The idol had neither face nor body. *It was another Palladium.*

For a long time, Thea and I knelt. When she backed away, I was too full of prayer to mind. I prayed for the real Callisto in death and for my Pleis in life. I prayed Hector would survive the war and Andromache would have the child she wanted to name after the Scamander River.

Without the torch of Thea, I could not even see the Palladium before me. I ran my fingers over its scarred and terrible surface and I bargained with the goddess. "O Ancient One, I shall serve you all the days of my life. You serve Pleis. He is a prince. Let him live."

242

There was nothing around me but cold and silence. There would not be light again. Not unless Thea returned to rescue me. Not unless I disobeyed and crept back up the tunnel, desperate for light and company.

I heard whimpering and knew it was mine.

I reached inside my ugly robe for my Medusa, to whom I had clung through every trial and sorrow. She was warm from my flesh.

After a long time, I sang to my goddess.

O goddess of yesterday . . . who guided me over the hazy sea . . . who held me safe in strange fortresses and slept with me by night . . . O goddess, be with me now.

Fragrance filled the cavern.

It was soft, like mint or early morn.

Come, it said.

I tucked my Medusa into my sash and crawled away from the idol, and on down the dwindling hole of the rest of the tunnel. My gown tore under my knees. The passage grew so narrow that I would have to back up to return. Wet rocks scraped my back. I crawled through an inch of icy flowing water. With my fingers I explored the floor ahead of me and always there was more tunnel.

And still the fragrance called.

The floor began to slope sharply down. I crawled with my hands far below my knees, pitching forward, but without room to fall.

The fragrance filled my nose. I felt the soft touch of leaves.

"O goddess of yesterday," I whispered.

I was out of the tunnel, and I was out of Troy, a thousand feet from the citadel and far below it. Hundreds of torches lit the great walls. It was more magnificent than the sky.

I did not fully emerge from my hole but peered through grass as a rabbit peeks from the clover. The sweet scent I had followed was hay; the first cutting of the season. By moonlight I could see it drying in heaps.

There were many gods to thank. Many bargains to be struck. When I had finished praying, I turned myself around, rooting like a rabbit, and crawled back up the tunnel, my knees bleeding and my hands raw, up and up the slippery dark. When the tunnel was high enough that I could get off my knees, I felt the walls until my fingers found the idol.

"Let me pass, Ancient One. I am in the safekeeping of another god. I will bring you flowers on my return. You have not seen flowers before. I know, because at your feet there are no wilted petals, no dry blooms, no trace of honor. I will honor you."

I crawled on.

And then I could stand and then there was light.

XVII

FROM THE PALLADIUM STEPS, I watched priests and priest-esses still circling funeral pyres. They had been honoring the dead all through the day and all through the night, and still there were more dead to be celebrated.

Hundreds of Trojan soldiers were awake, standing on the battlements, staring at the distant campfires of Menelaus. I hoped they were thinking of the soldiers from rugged Olizon and planning to kill them. At least Nicander would be avenged.

Never had a city been so well lit. Every door had its torch. Every corner, every wall, every stair, every tower. The blessed safety of dark did not exist. Nor was Troy asleep. Grief and fear were too acute for rest.

If I was caught I would be twice killed: once for leaving the temple precincts and once because I was the Greek princess.

My novice's tunic was harsh cloth, badly spun brown goat hair. It smelled barny and was partly rotted from drag-ging for years on wet floors. I tore several inches off the bot-tom for a scarf to cover my head, which must have gleamed like marble in the torchlight. My knees showed, cut and bruised from crawling. Perhaps I would look like a squire, wounded with my master in the battle.

Since I could not creep and could not hide, I marched firmly down the temple steps, crossed the square and threaded around a row of wounded men. Down the steps that clung to the walls of Hector's palace I went, down the steps fastened to the side of Priam's palace, and into the alley that led to the house of Paris.

I studied the door. It would be open, but I could not risk using it. I hoped I was strong in the magic tonight. I picked all the flowers in the front-door jugs. Then I circled the house, went to the window and boosted myself up onto the sill. I had just swung my legs over when I heard murmuring voices.

Paris and Kora.

I dropped back into the alley and crouched.

"It still hasn't worked," muttered Kora. I looked up. She was so big that her shoulders and head were above the sill. One glance out the window and she'd see me.

"We don't need the quicksilver anymore," whispered Paris. "Just leave the boy among the wounded."

"What if he walks away or cries out?" said Kora.

"That will be good. I want him noticed."

Kora grunted in confusion.

"Kora, he's the son of Menelaus. All I need is one raging widow, one vengeful son, one grief-crazed brother. Then the boy will die by the sword."

It was a good plan. It should work well and quickly. Any of the Trojan wounded and any of the Trojan nurses would recognize Pleis.

"Won't Helen want to know how the child got out of the house?" whispered Kora. "She'll hate me. I'll be killed for not keeping an eye on him."

"I'll explain that away," said Paris.

No, you won't, I thought. You'll let Helen do anything she wants to Kora. You don't care what happens to a slave. You want to be rid of Pleis. Drowning didn't work, playing with your sword didn't work, poison didn't work. Another man's sword will work. How like you, Paris, to arrange for another warrior to fight even the smallest battle.

Kora was suspicious. "How will you explain it to Helen?"

"I will say I sent you on an errand," said Paris irritably, "and we expected the child would stay asleep. He must have wakened on his own and toddled out into the street. These things happen."

These things didn't happen, actually. Pleis was not strong enough to pull open the front door and if he wakened on his own, he would try to find his mother.

Sandals clip-clopped softly. One of them was leaving. Was it Paris, returning to bed?

It would take Kora a few minutes to waken Pleis. She wouldn't want him sobbing; Helen might hear. As soon as Kora's head was no longer framed in the window, I would run to where the wounded lay. When she set Pleis down, I would get to him first. But there were no dark corners tonight in which to lurk. And if I hung about the streets, I would be sent on an errand. And what if Kora set him down earlier? And what if Pleis was recognized and attacked before I could get to him?

I heard the little snuffling sounds Pleis made when he was half-awake. "There, there," said Kora. "Stay asleep, little Greek."

I would have to do something far worse than tell a lie.

I vaulted onto the sill. Kora had gotten Pleis to his feet.

She was holding his little hand as he rubbed his eyes with the other.

I launched my entire body at Kora, slamming my Medusa into her head. It cracked her skull. There was nothing magic about it. Stone is stronger than bone.

When we came to the swollen part of the tunnel, I felt the wall in the dark until I found the idol and there we knelt.

"You have given us passage, Ancient One. I will not betray you or Troy. Here are the flowers. As soon as I am able, I will make a good sacrifice in your honor."

Fragrance spilled out of the tunnel.

Down the long wet slant we went. I had to push Pleis in front of me, because if he were to stop, I would not be able to reach back to get him.

He was very slow. He was very scared. He was only two. "Calli," he said anxiously, "sto."

"It's all right," I told him. "We are strong in the magic."

It would be daylight when we reached the end of the tunnel. Kora's body would have been found. Pleis' absence known. But Paris would raise no alarm. Such would be suspicious. It was the priestess Thea who would raise the alarm. Did Thea know where this tunnel came out, even if she herself could never have used it? When we reached the end, would there be soldiers crouched around the opening?

I wished Pleis did not have to go first. Whatever happened, it should happen to me first. But it was not to be.

"Pretty!" said Pleis in amazement. "Pretty, pretty." And he was gone.

I put my nose into the fresh air and looked around. Pleis was halfway out of the flowers and into the field. I caught him by the ankle and he giggled and fell.

I was trembling with exhaustion. So little sleep, so much fear and one terrible deed.

It is war, I told myself. It is the battle I fight. The equation of life is very equal. For one to survive, another must die. Pleis will survive, Kora had to die.

Nobody liked Kora, I told myself. She was planning to kill a child. Her death is proper and just.

But even as Nicander had been stabbed in the back, I had killed Kora from behind.

There was no glory in it. It was just an ugly truth from which I could never escape.

We were enveloped in noise: an army in the morning, the waking voices of ten thousand men. I looked across the hay field where I had thought to go. Paphlagonians and Lycians and Dardanians were camped there. Carians and Mycians and Phrygians. Sharpening their spears for another battle. Finding their horses, leading them to the chariots.

From the windy walls of Troy came Hector's great roar, instructing his troops.

Pleis and I were trapped. Caught between two armies soon to clash. "Goddess of yesterday," I breathed. "O be with us now and all the days to come."

A flock of sheep wandered near. They seemed to have no shepherd. Perhaps he had died in yesterday's battle. The sheep needed him and were calling. A lamb has a sweet little bleat, but sheep moan and groan like wounded men. The flock milled around, bumping one another and complaining.

"Hold my hand, Pleis," I said. "No matter what happens, do not let go my hand."

"Calli, carry me," he said, holding up his arms. He was tired and confused and he had been so good. But I could not carry him because then from the battlements of Troy they would see exactly what they had seen the day before: the same girl pretending to be a boy; the same child on her hip; the same ridiculous attempt to escape.

They would have us back in moments.

I stepped among the sheep, dragging Pleis and singing, making of my voice a pipe. The sheep were glad to see a shepherd and came quickly to butt me in the side, and all of us together went into the fields of hay. Pleis didn't like the great dirty sheep pressing up against him and began to sob. The sheep bleated louder.

I am a silly shepherd boy, I told myself. I've forgotten that there's a war. I see nice long grass over by the river, perfect for my flock.

I herded them forward, pushing against their heavy sides, and they were slow and annoying in the way of sheep. I rammed forward and some hurried to stay with me and some lost interest and some ran ahead.

We were in the no-man's-land.

Beyond the river, the Greeks were massing for battle. Behind me, the Trojan allies gathered.

From the tangled thickets and long fields we had just left came the shrill whistle of two fingers in the mouth. The call of the real shepherd. My sheep muddled nervously. "Don't leave me," I sang to them.

The flock left, bolting back the way we had come.

A girl as thin as a twig and a boy no higher than a flower walked alone at the edge of a marsh.

The wind that batters Troy flung my tattered gown around my knees and tore my makeshift scarf from my head. I snatched at it, but the wind—ally of Troy—was too quick. My naked head gleamed in the morning sun.

From the high thin tower came a high thin cry. *"Stop them!"*

I had forgotten Cassandra, who knew everything. Who knew me.

"Child of the island!" screamed Cassandra. "Son of Menelaus!"

I was sobbing as I stumbled over the ruts of war. Weeping as I ran, I dragged Pleis roughly. I would be tearing his poor little arm from its socket. "I *am* a friend to Menelaus, Cassandra," I admitted to the princess on the tower. I did not raise my voice. She who knew everything would surely hear me. "But I will not betray Troy, O princess. I have lied about many things. I am not lying about that. I owe Zanthus and you, I owe Andromache and Hector. I owe Troy. My task is to give a little boy back to his father. Betraying Troy, Cassandra, will go to Helen."

"Stop the shepherd!" screamed Cassandra. "That shepherd is friend to Menelaus."

I stiffened my back to armor myself against the spears to come. I hoped that Pleis and I would tumble together into death and that I could hold his hand against fear.

But nothing happened.

I could not help myself. I looked back.

Cassandra was framed against the drenched-in-gods blue of a Trojan sky. The wind threw her dark hair in her face like a veil. The troops continued to gather. Hector continued to give orders. Only Cassandra was looking at us.

She touched her fingers to her lips and cast a kiss in our direction, as an acolyte casts flowers before the altar or the king casts wine upon the sea. Blessing us.

She had saved our lives. For she *did* know the truth: I

would not betray Troy. Nor had she accused me of it. The moment she said who we were, nobody believed it.

"Little princess," said Menelaus, kissing each cheek as if I were lovely and desirable. "What courage! To walk away from those mighty walls. To march right out the Scaean gate, carrying my son between the poised spears of princes. Truly you are strong in the magic."

No, I thought. I'm just a very good liar. Even to you. Even now.

The lord of lords, Agamemnon, and his generals stared at me. Menelaus' captains came to look. His infantry and cavalry, spearmen and archers gaped at the ragged, bruised, scabbed and bald creature before them.

There had not been a battle that morning after all. Menelaus said it was victory enough to have his son back. In vain did the Trojan armies assemble.

Pleis had fallen asleep with his little head against his father's cheek, his hair wet from his father's warm tears. Some time passed before Menelaus could set him down and think of other things. "Anything you wish is yours, my princess," he told me.

It was a promise Menelaus could fulfill. He could give me anything.

But the thing I craved most was not land or gold, not power or princes.

"I wish to be forgiven for a lie. A lie that is a crime before god and king. I am not Callisto, daughter of Petra and Nicander of Siphnos. That princess died at the hands of the pirates. I was a hostage whose parents did not want her back. I stole a royal birthright, that I might not be abandoned or enslaved. In truth I am Anaxandra, daughter of Chrysaor and Iris, from an island without a name, just a rocky place in the sea."

The king stood at the edge of a sea white with foam.

I stood at the edge of my life.

I was as tired as Pleis. There were no soft beds or warm baths in a war camp. What will happen to me now? I thought dully. I cannot bear to sit in the tents of Menelaus as Troy is brought down.

I had thought that Menelaus would answer softly, my future quiet between us, but his voice was as a trumpet, for all his men might hear. "Anaxandra!" said the king. "You are mistaken. You are noble of spirit and royal of heart. You have always been a princess."

I looked at Menelaus for a long time and then I looked back at the ramparts of Troy.

O Cassandra. I—even I—did not believe you. You told me it was no lie to call myself princess.

Menelaus placed his thumb in the middle of my forehead, where I had felt the force of many blessings before him. "I give you your name," said the king. "Anaxandra. You have brought honor to that name. And I give to you Siphnos, which you have earned twice over."

A thousand men cheered, for I had given them their first victory: I had snatched their little prince from beneath the sharp spears of an entire army.

"Soon," said Menelaus cheerfully, sounding like the loving father of Hermione, the one who had wrestled with his older sons and snuggled his littlest boy, "your red hair will grow out and once again be your glory."

"O my king," I said sadly, "the gods are punishing me for stealing the name and the heritage of a princess. They have taken my glory. I will never have hair again."

Menelaus looked at me oddly. Then he stooped so his great red beard nearly brushed my face and his eyes were only inches from my eyes. "I misspoke," he said. "For hair is only an adornment. It is not a glory. The glory of life is the heritage and the parents with which you are born. The gods took your parents from you forever and that is punishment all the days of your life. But your lovely hair, my princess, is growing in." Gently, he ran his palm back and forth over stubble on my head.

I put my hand to my head. Hair.

A queen can be fathered by a swan, and a horse sired by the wind. A princess on a tower can know all things. And an angry god can take back his wrath.

"But long before that," said Menelaus, straightening up and grinning at the windy walls of Troy, "this war will be over, and we will be safely home."

The war will not be over, my king. And I do not know if you will ever be safely home. I did not ask Cassandra.

I thanked my goddess that I was not Cassandra, forced to know the future.

"You cannot stay in my war camp, little princess," said Menelaus. "I have no women here to care for you. But we are not far from an island whose king is neutral and will help us. Kinados," he said to his captain, "how far is Lemnos?"

"Half a day's sail. I could get her there by nightfall."

Truly, I have been lucky in my kings. Nicander. Menelaus. Priam.

Euneus.

O my king.

AFTERWORD

Archaeologists have found the real city of Troy, but was there actually a Trojan War? Was there a Helen or a Paris or a Menelaus? Scholars argue about this, but the ancient world was sure the Trojan War had been a real event.

The most important ancient writer about Troy is Homer, who lived around 800 B.C. He composed *The Iliad* and *The Odyssey*. I had not read these books since high school, and when I reread them, I was entranced and had to research Homer, and the Trojan War, and the mythology associated with very ancient Greece. When I wrote this book, I was thinking of Homer, but many other ancient writers, like Hesiod, Apollodorus, Virgil, Ovid, Thucydides and Herodotus, also wrote about the Trojan War, and many famous ancient playwrights like Euripides used its characters in their tragedies.

If there was a Trojan War, it happened during the Bronze Age, about 1250 B.C.

Here are the "true" parts of my story—but in this case, "true" means what ancient authors tell us. Perhaps it isn't true; perhaps it's all myth. Ancient writers don't agree with one another; there are different versions of each event.

Agamemnon rules Mycenae. Homer calls him "lord of the far-flung kingdoms." His younger brother Menelaus, described by Homer as "the red-haired king of Sparta," marries Helen, daughter of Zeus, conceived while he was disguised as a swan. There is an oath over the dead horse in which Helen's suitors promise to defend the man of her choice. Helen's brothers are the twins Castor and Pollux (the Gemini sign in the zodiac), and her sister Clytemnestra does marry Agamemnon.

Menelaus goes to Troy to ask the gods to end a plague in his city. This prayer is granted. After he has gone, the king of Troy, Priam, sends his son Paris to Sparta. The figurehead on Paris' flagship is the goddess Aphrodite, and he is escorted by his cousin Aeneas, son of Aphrodite. Aeneas will be one of the few Trojan survivors of the war and will sail west to become a founder of Rome; his story is in Virgil's *Aeneid.*

The rescue of Priam's sister Hesione may be a reason for sending Paris to Sparta, but Paris has three other reasons.

First, he is a pirate. Piracy is an honorable profession in *The Iliad* and *The Odyssey.* Odysseus (the pirate for whom *The Odyssey* is named) is always called "sacker of cities," which is fair, since he destroys more than twenty, while Achilles, the most famous Greek fighter and the main character in *The Iliad,* proudly lists a dozen.

Second, Paris has killed a little boy and will purify himself at the temple of Apollo in Sparta.

Third, in a story that I skip, three goddesses—Hera, Athena and Aphrodite—have quarreled over which one is loveliest. Paris is the beauty contest judge. Aphrodite says that if Paris announces *she's* the loveliest goddess in heaven, Aphrodite in return will give him the loveliest woman on earth. That's Helen. So Paris picks Aphrodite and therefore

Paris gets Helen. It doesn't seem to matter that Helen's already married.

In the midst of Paris' visit, Menelaus leaves for his grandfather's funeral in Crete. Kinados is the name of his captain.

Most sources agree that Helen goes eagerly with Paris; some say she is kidnapped.

Helen and Menelaus have a nine-year-old daughter, Hermione, left behind when Helen goes with Paris. Some sources mention three sons—Aethiolas, Maraphius and Pleisthenes. Helen takes only baby Pleisthenes to Troy. She and Paris also take the palace gold and temple treasure. Getting this treasure back is a major reason for the war. (In Greek, the word "treasure" means "something that can be laid away." Everybody keeps treasure, whether it's gold, bed linens or spears.)

Helen takes five maids with her, including the former queen Aethra. Aethra's background is complex. She is the mother of a very famous hero, Theseus. Theseus himself kidnapped Helen when she was a small child! Helen was rescued by Castor and Pollux, who then took Aethra as a slave. But Theseus cannot rescue his mother, because he is shortly murdered by a king who throws him off a cliff.

Helen and Paris have their honeymoon on an islet off Gythion, port of Sparta, and then sail for Troy. They're blown far off course. At Sidon, Paris murders and robs the king in his own banquet hall and loses two ships.

Meanwhile, Menelaus goes to Troy to demand his wife's return; he takes along the grandsons of Aethra. (I was not able to find a story that explains why these grandsons hadn't rescued their grandmother from slavery in the first place; perhaps they were too young.)

King Priam hasn't heard from Paris, doesn't know what has happened and cannot deliver Helen or the stolen treasure. He sends Menelaus away, though many Trojans think it would be better to kill Menelaus.

Paris and Helen arrive in Troy.

Agamemnon and Menelaus gather armies but cannot sail, because there is no wind. (Sailing distances for ancient ships are known: with a favorable wind, 200 miles or two days from Mycenae to Crete; 350 miles or three or four days from Crete to Egypt.) Iphigenia, daughter of Agamemnon and Clytemnestra, is sacrificed. (Clytemnestra will never forgive Agamemnon for killing their daughter; many ancient Greek playwrights will write tragedies about what happens to that family next.)

War begins. It will last ten years. Although Homer says the Greeks never go home in all this time, it seems unlikely; the distances are short, there is loot to carry back from all the pillaging, and the Greeks never actually beseige Troy in the sense of closing it up and starving it out.

Even though they fight ten years to get her back, the Greeks do not love Helen. Achilles, who is on the Greek side, calls her "that blood-chilling horror." Euripides, who lives about four hundred years after Homer, says Helen is "loathed of God." In his play *The Trojan Women* he writes that Helen "has drawn her breath from many fathers: Madness, Hate, red Death and every rotting poison of the sky."

But Troy adores Helen. King Priam never holds her responsible for the ten years of war and the ruin of his city.

What does Helen look like? Homer does not say. One of the most famous phrases about her—"the face that launched a thousand ships"—is not by Homer but by Christopher Marlowe, a sixteenth-century English dramatist.

Homer does not use the word "Greece" or "Greeks"; these words come later in history. The fighters on Menelaus' side are called Argives, Danaans or Lacaedemonians. Each separate tribe is also referred to by its own name, so Achilles' men, for example, are Myrmidons. This is too many labels, so I do use the word "Greek."

What language do these people speak? In *The Iliad,* everybody can talk to everybody, though Homer does say that the allies of Troy speak many languages. I have everybody speaking at least some Greek.

Ancient Troy is not literate. The Trojans have no alphabet and no writing.

Parts of Greece, especially Mycenae, Agamemnon's capital, use a script we now call Linear B. The keeping-track lines I describe are among those deciphered. There is no personal writing—no letters, no diaries. Writing seems to be exclusively for lists and records.

Horses are highly regarded, but not much used, since saddle and stirrups are not yet invented. There is no "horsepower" yet either, because no one has come up with a yoke for a horse.

Priam has fifty sons and twelve daughters. All but one son will die in the course of the war. (His name, confusingly, is Helenus.) Cassandra is a daughter with the gift of prophecy, her sad doom that nobody ever believes her. She is considered mad and is usually locked up. She is alive at the end of the war and taken home as concubine by King Agamemnon. Cassandra and Agamemnon are murdered by his wife, Clytemnestra, as they walk in the door of his palace. (His son Orestes and his other daughter Electra later murder Clytemnestra to avenge their father's death.)

The Palladium may have been a primitive wooden statue

of Athena, or it may have been a meteorite. Stealing it, which Aeneas does at the very end of the Trojan War, results in the collapse of the city.

Hector is called "tamer of horses," and his horses do have the names I used. Hector does say that Paris should have been stoned to death.

Andromache is the daughter of the king of Cilicia. Later on, Achilles will pirate in Cilicia and kill her father and all seven of her brothers. By the end of the war, she and Hector are married and have a little son whom they name for the Scamander River but who is also called Astyanax. One of the loveliest passages in *The Iliad* is when Andromache and Hector hug their little boy before Hector goes to die in battle.

Euneus is the king of Lemnos, and he does stay neutral and sell supplies to both sides. Early in the war, when things are not so bloodthirsty, the Greeks take many prisoners and ship them to Lemnos, where they are either enslaved or ransomed home. Euneus' father is the very famous Jason, captain of the Argonauts, who a generation earlier sailed across the Black Sea to find the Golden Fleece.

Homer does say, "It is a shivery thing to kill a prince of royal blood."

Hector does yell, "Bird signs! Fight for your country. That is the best, the only omen."

Anaxandra's prayer is actually uttered by Telemachus in *The Odyssey,* who says, "O God of yesterday, listen and be near me."

My description of Anaxandra's hair is actually the description of Odysseus: "curls like petals of wild hyacinth but all red-golden."

Aristophanes, another ancient Greek playwright, says that rain is Zeus pissing through a sieve.

The scrap of poem I quote (*Seven ways of terror in a forest all of pine. The empty.*) is actually by a poet named Sappho, who lives two hundred years after Homer.

Medusa is a Gorgon. Her sisters are goddesses, but she is mortal. She has snakes for hair, and her eyes can transform people into stone. When she dies, she gives birth to the winged horse Pegasus.

Most people just want to know about the wooden horse. This story is not in *The Iliad*. It is referred to in *The Odyssey* (Book 4) and *The Aeneid* (Book 2).

Nicander, Petra and Callisto are fictional. Iris and Chrysaor are fictional. Anaxandra is fictional. The rocky isle without a name is fictional.

One name is intentionally spelled incorrectly. Herakles is the famous Greek hero, but we usually call him Hercules, so I too use the Latin spelling.

There is an island of Siphnos. One fateful year, its king does send a leaden egg to Delphi instead of gold, and as a result his gold mines are flooded.

When Troy is finally sacked, a Greek fighter from Lokris named Ajax defiles the Palladium. His descendents must make up for this sacrilege. For many generations, the Lokrians send daughters to serve the goddess. These girls are conducted in secrecy and darkness to the temple, forced to shave their heads and live in grim poverty. If they are seen in public, they are killed. In A.D. 100—more than a thousand years after Troy falls—this is still happening!

There are many translations of Homer. Even Lawrence of Arabia did one.

You can read *The Iliad* and *The Odyssey* as poetry, translated by Lattimore, Fitzgerald or Fagles and others, or as prose, by Rouse and others. The best young people's versions of Homer are by Rosemary Sutcliffe and illustrated by Alan Lee: *Black Ships Before Troy* and *The Wanderings of Odysseus.*

But since Homer himself sang the work and did not write it down, I think listening to *The Iliad* on tape is the best way.

What is *The Iliad*?

The word "Ilium" is just another name for Troy, so "Iliad" means "story of Troy." But *The Iliad* is not the story of Troy. It is the story of the Greek warrior Achilles and his manic behavior. Menelaus and Helen are minor characters. In the final year of the war, Agamemnon has taken away a girl Achilles loves. Agamemnon orders Achilles to submit cheerfully to this insult because Agamemnon is king and much more important. Achilles is outraged. To prove which of them is more important, he refuses to continue the fight against Troy. Fine, he says to Agamemnon. Do it without me.

But they can't. The Greeks may lose the war after all.

The gods and goddesses are very involved in the action. Apollo loves Troy; Athena supports the Greeks. Since there is an important temple to Athena in Troy, you would expect her to support the Trojans. She hates them because Paris didn't choose her to win the loveliest goddess contest. There is an enormous amount of slaughter in *The Iliad*—very detailed descriptions of how men die in hand-to-hand combat. When *The Iliad* ends, Hector is dead, but the war is not over.

In *The Odyssey,* ten years have passed since the end of the Trojan War. Once again, Helen and Menelaus are minor characters. Paris is dead and they're home again, an oddly dull husband and wife who can barely remember all that unpleasantness. Helen is now claiming that the war was all Aphrodite's fault and nobody should blame her for anything.

Odysseus has been struggling to get home for a decade, and supposedly *The Odyssey* is the story of his travels. But the book is really about his son, Telemachus. This now twenty-year-old boy has never had a father because Odysseus left when he was a baby. A terrible situation has arisen at home; the boy cannot cope and has no solution. *The Odyssey* feels contemporary: a boy with an absent father, weak mother and uninvolved grandfather. Telemachus is constantly dreaming of his father, whose return would make everything perfect.

Not told by Homer are the final stories of the Trojans. The son of Hector and Andromache is killed when the Greeks toss the little boy off the walls of Troy. Andromache is made a slave to a son of Achilles called Neoptolemus, one of the men who hid in the wooden horse. Neoptolemus marries Hermione, the daughter Helen left behind.

The only son of Priam not to die in the war is Helenus, Cassandra's twin and also a prophet. Helenus is spared and goes to live in Epirus. Neoptolemus gives him Andromache to marry, so at least one good thing happens to Andromache in the end. After Neoptolemus is killed, Hermione marries her cousin Orestes (the one who killed his mother to avenge his father).

Ancient Greek is not pronounced the way it looks. If it were English, for example, Hermione would be pronounced *HER mee own*. But the Greek is *her MY oh nee*. Menelaus is not *MENNUH luss* but *menna LAY us*. Andromache is *an DROM uh kee*.

For more information about Troy, the Bronze Age and the historicity of Homer (that is, how much is fiction and how much is fact), read Michael Wood's *In Search of the Trojan War*.

CAROLINE B. COONEY is the author of many young adult novels. They include *The Ransom of Mercy Carter; Tune In Anytime; Burning Up; The Face on the Milk Carton* (an IRA-CBC Children's Choice Book) and its companions, *Whatever Happened to Janie?* and *The Voice on the Radio* (each of them an ALA Best Book for Young Adults), as well as *What Janie Found; What Child Is This?* (an ALA Best Book for Young Adults); *Driver's Ed* (an ALA Best Book for Young Adults and a *Booklist* Editors' Choice); *Among Friends; Twenty Pageants Later;* and the Time Travel Quartet: *Both Sides of Time, Out of Time, Prisoner of Time* and *For All Time.* Caroline B. Cooney lives in Westbrook, Connecticut.